Dick Sigler
 # 2

CRUISING

Book Two of the
Men in Motion Series

G.A. HAUSER

D1608130

CRUISING

Book 2 of the Men in Motion Series

Copyright © G.A. HAUSER, 2010
Cover art by Stephanie Vaughan
Book layout/typesetting by jimandzetta.com

ISBN 978-1449-5928-0-6

Second printing The GA Hauser Collection
June 2010

This is a work of fiction and any resemblance to persons, living or dead, or business establishments, events or locales is coincidental.

All Rights Are Reserved. No part of this may be used or reproduced in any manner whatsoever without written permission, except in the case of brief quotations embodied in critical articles and reviews.

WARNING
This book contains material that maybe offensive to some: graphic language, homosexual relations, adult situations. Please store your books carefully where they cannot be accessed by underage readers.

Chapter One

"What do you mean you have something to do? The boat is going to leave in a few minutes." Brodie Duncan stood near a mound of luggage at the port in Seattle. "Melanie, what on earth do you need to take care of that we can't do once we're onboard?"

"I don't know, Brodie. Just something, okay? Do you have to know everything I need to do?"

"No. I don't. But I may need to know what you have to do five minutes before this fricken cruise boat leaves." Brodie knew she would freak out. The whole drive from Bellevue she had been quiet, evasive. Throwing up his hands, he asked, "Do you want to go with me on this cruise or not?"

"Yes!"

"Fine. Then grab your bag and let's go."

She was twirling her hair. He hated when she did that. It made her look like the definition of a dumb blonde. It didn't matter that she was pretty. Somehow it paled when coupled with the personality flaws Brodie had to tolerate. The amount of whining he endured to book this cruise, the expense, taking time off from work when it was busy, well...for what? To see the spoiled Miss Melanie Hughley making a face in disgust at the idea of spending seven days with him on a boat. Life with her never made any sense.

"Come on." He nudged her, heaving the heavy luggage to hand off to a porter. The bags were tagged and he walked up the gangplank with the so-called love of his life scuffing her high heels behind him.

Standing at the check-in desk, Brodie tried to get his temper under control as he handed the clerk his paperwork and identification. Turning around he asked, "Where's your driver's license?"

Melanie rolled her eyes, opened her designer purse, handing it to him. The clerk verified the ID, returning it quickly.

About to explode at her constant attitude of irritation, Brodie bit his lip, finished signing some paperwork, which included a copy of his credit card, handed back the pen, and moved aside for the next person in line. "Right. I need a drink."

Melanie announced, "I'm going to the ladies' room."

"Fine. I'll wait here."

As she walked off in what appeared a huff, Brodie couldn't figure out what he had done. She begged for a holiday on a boat. Well? Here they were on a damn cruise ship heading to Glacier Bay. Hadn't he fulfilled his obligation?

"Excuse me."

Brodie woke out of his dark thoughts to move aside for a man who was trying to pass by in the crowded lobby. Lord only knew how many human beings a ship this size could hold. Brodie checked his watch, growing impatient. How long does it take for a damn pee?

Noticing an open bench seat against the wall of the lobby, he dropped down on it wearily. The ship's horn blasted loudly. Right after it had subsided, an announcement commenced that all those who were going ashore must disembark now.

Brodie rubbed his eyes and yawned. He was already exhausted, envisioning a nap before anything else. "Christ, Melanie? How long does it take to check your fucking make-up?"

Finally growing upset, he decided to actually find the ladies' room entrance and wait outside. Down a long, narrow corridor, he located the door, leaning against the wall just outside it, arms crossed, trying to keep his demeanor calm instead of screaming at Melanie the minute she showed her face.

Another loud, basso horn blast sounded as well as a second announcement. They were about to set sail. Brodie wanted to stand on the outer promenade when they did. That was the idea, wasn't it? Wave to the people left on shore, throw some confetti?

"This is unbelievable." He stopped a woman as she stepped out of the ladies' lounge. "Excuse me, miss? I was wondering, could you just tell me if my girlfriend is all right? It seems like she's been inside there for a long while."

"What does she look like?"

"Blonde, shoulder length hair, blue eyes, ah, I think she's wearing a black blazer with a short skirt and high heels. Her name is Melanie."

"Okay, I'll call out her name."

"Thanks. That'd be great." Brodie smiled at her sweet gesture. A slight jerking and rumbling sensation passed over his body. He imagined the ship was being towed by a tug out of the port. "Man, I don't want to miss that." A few more seconds passed and the nice woman stepped out of the bathroom. "There doesn't seem to be a Melanie in there."

Brodie felt slightly disoriented and wondered if seasickness could kick in that quickly. "You sure?"

"As I can be. I called out her name, looked under the stalls, no one with blonde hair answered to that name."

"I must have the wrong bathroom. Thanks anyway." He hurried back to the lobby. Standing in the midst of a mound of tagged luggage all being transported to the cabins by a very efficient crew, Brodie spun around like a top, trying to remember which direction Melanie had taken. Growing frustrated, he removed his cell phone from his pocket, stepped outside for better service, and dialed her phone number about to scream in fury at her disappearing act.

The boat was indeed pushing back from the dock. A crowd of people waved goodbye from the shore. "Hello, Melanie? Where the hell are you? Which bathroom did you use?"

"I'm sorry, Brodie."

"Sorry about what?"

"I couldn't do it."

A sensation of dizziness followed the comment. "Couldn't do what?"

"Go. I couldn't go on the cruise with you."

"What?" He rushed to the edge to look for her on the dock. "Are you telling me you're not on this goddamn boat?"

"No. I can see you standing at the rail."

Squinting, trying to discern her from the rest of the crowd, he finally noticed a blonde wearing a black blazer. "Why? Why did you do this to me? I don't get it. You begged me for this trip. I took time off. Melanie, what the hell is going on?"

"I just don't love you anymore."

"You tell me that now?" he shouted, noticed someone near him looking at him strangely, and lowered his voice. "I'm standing on a cruise ship, Melanie, by myself, leaving on a holiday that was supposed to be ours."

"I know. Sorry, Brodie."

"Sorry? Sorry?" He was raising his voice again.

"I have to go. I just flagged down a cab. Enjoy the vacation, Brodie, you need it. Did anyone ever tell you that even though you're good looking, you're very high strung?"

Before he could roar his retort, she disconnected. There was the leggy blonde running on her spiked heels, waving at a yellow cab.

Watching in utter amazement, Brodie felt like a bride being left at the altar, utterly humiliated. "How did I not see this coming?" Shoving the phone into his pocket, he suddenly realized he could not get off the ship and was literally stuck on this floating island with thousands of strangers. "I need a goddamn drink."

Taking the room key out of his pocket, he read the number of his state room, wondering where the hell it was. Numb, wandering against the flow of happy couples and squealing children, Brodie hoped the bars would be serving. Navigating the hallways as the boat seemed to rock side to side, Brodie mumbled, "My luck I'll get seasick." Passing a dark casino, café, and dance club, Brodie found that everything was closed off at the moment. "Great."

Brodie headed to an elevator, taking his paperwork out of his pocket to find a map of the place. "Right, main floor. Where the hell's that?" Seeing it was three floors below the lobby area, he disregarded the crowded elevator and opted for the staircase. Down three floors was no problem, but walking the length of two football fields to his room amazed him. It was as if someone had laid the Empire State Building on its side and he was moving from base to tip. The sheer size of the cruise ship was astounding. He had no idea they were so enormous. Stopping at a door, he read his key, the room number, and slipped the credit card like object into a slot. The light turned green and he pushed back the door. A tiny cabin, two single beds, a table and chair, closet, and bathroom came into view. No porthole. Those rooms were a fortune. Besides, he thought, how much time would they spend in the room anyway? Melanie had stopped fucking him as well. Who needed a view to fall asleep?

Tossing the keycard on the table, his bags already efficiently placed near the bed, Brodie noticed Melanie's beside his. "Great." Lifting it to shove aside, he shook it and heard something rattle. Out of curiosity he rested it on one of the beds and unzipped it. "Holy shit." The bag was filled with newspapers. "You bitch! You had me lug a sack of crap all over the damn place for you?" Dropping down on the bed, Brodie realized that Melanie never meant to go on this trip with him even as he waited at her apartment door when she handed him the bag. "Why the hell didn't you just tell me then?" He was completely confused. Taking out his mobile phone, he noticed there was no signal in the bowels of the boat. He threw it on the bed, flopped down next to it, stared at the ceiling, and now, more than ever, felt the boat listing side to side. "I don't believe this is happening. What the hell did I do to deserve this?"

Chapter Two

He hadn't realized he'd dozed. Opening his eyes, checking his watch, Brodie felt his stomach grumble. Maybe now that they'd been at sea for more than an hour, everything would be manned and available. The gentle swaying of the boat was messing up his balance. "I hope I can get used to this."

Standing, checking his wallet for cash, he entered the small, clean, well equipped bathroom to pee and wash his face. Holding the wall to make sure he didn't miss the toilet as the boat listed, Brodie shook his head in frustration. "A whole week of this shit. Not peeing straight. And I haven't even had a goddamn drink yet!" Brodie managed to finish without splashing the floor and flushed the commode, washing his hands and face at the sink. Checking his reflection in the mirror, seeing his hair slightly disheveled from his nap, he wet his hands and ran his fingers through his thick brown mane, trying to tame it. He needed a shave. Having woken up early to get them to the port on time, he figured he'd do it once on board. Melanie constantly whined if his face wasn't closely shaven. "You're scratchy. Don't, it hurts."

Shivering at the recollection of that horrible beast who had left him on a cruise ship and ran off like a coward, Brodie stood tall, filling the tiny space and told himself. "Just because you're not here, Mel, doesn't mean I'm not going to get laid."

Shutting off the light, he picked up his key and surveyed the map of the boat. There were bars on four of the levels. He couldn't miss. Walking away from his cabin, back towards the lobby check-in desk, Brodie noticed signs directing him to the lounges and casino. Passing the silent, unoccupied roulette tables and one-armed bandits, he continued on his way, trying to walk straight down the hall with the constant movement of the ship under his feet. A crowded bar came into view. "Bingo." He gave the interior a quick survey, noticing one section of gray-haired people, and another of very young twenty-somethings. Knowing he fell slightly above the latter and way below the former, he had no idea where to go. And being single sucked. A lone stool stood vacant at the bar. He sat down, wondering how long it would take for the rest of the passengers to figure out he was the lonesome loser on the trip.

"What can I get for you, sir?"

"Yes, uh, a glass of scotch please, make it a double."

"On the rocks?'

"Straight up."

"Your room number, sir?"

"Oh." He pulled out his key. "Here."

The man nodded, wrote out a receipt, had Brodie sign it, and handed him a copy. Brodie shoved it into his shirt pocket. Sipping the strong alcohol, he imagined running up quite the bar tab for this little venture, but at least he wouldn't be buying duty-free perfume and cosmetics for the spoiled brat.

Since he was nearer to the outside of the ship than he had been in his room, Brodie took out his mobile phone from his pocket. He did get a signal. Dialing, standing up and moving to the entrance of the club where he could talk privately, he waited for it to connect.

"Brodie?"

"Hey, Paden."

"What's going on? I thought you were supposed to be going on vacation."

"She left me. I'm on the stinkin' boat and she ditched me." When silence followed, Brodie took another sip of the strong liquid. "You there, Paden?"

"I knew it."

"You knew it? What the hell do you mean, you knew it?"

"Brodie, she's horrible. I have no idea what you saw in that woman."

"Now you tell me? You're my best fucking friend and now you tell me?" Brodie lowered his voice again. It was too crowded for anything that resembled real privacy. "Couldn't you have mentioned that before I got stuck on this ship?"

"You wouldn't have listened. I'm telling you, Brodie, women are trouble. Especially the trophy bimbo types you end up with."

"My gay friend is telling me about the trouble with women." Brodie finished the scotch in another gulp, shivering at the burn.

"You'd be better off with men."

"I would be. I'm starting to believe that, Paden. Maybe you should have come with me instead."

"Uh, I don't think Tim would understand."

"He wouldn't mind. I would just borrow you. To experiment with." Brodie had a quick look around the area.

"Mr. Duncan, don't you go getting bi-curious on me."

"Why the hell not? A lot of good being heterosexual's got me. I'm standing in a damn bar, getting drunk on my lonesome, on my way to fucking Ketchikan!" Tipping the glass so the last drop hit his tongue, Brodie licked at it, then sighed, "I'm a sad fucking bastard, Paden. A sad bastard."

"Shut up. Go find a single woman and screw her brains out. You'll never see those people again."

"I should find a fucking man. I swear, you never seem to have any problems with your relationship, Paden. Just me."

"A man? What the hell are you talking about? You're a womanizer, Brodie! But the women you choose suck."

Brodie heard some static on the line. "You're fading out on me."

"Just have fun! You needed a vacation. Go a little crazy."

"I will."

"I want a full report."

"Goodbye, Paden. I can barely hear you." Disconnecting the phone, Brodie looked at the display. "No signal" showed on the LCD panel. He turned it off, stuffed it back in his pocket, scanning the dim bar. "He's right. I have the wrong taste in women. I'm sure as hell sick of prima donna pussy."

Requesting a second double, shooting it down, Brodie felt the alcohol go to his head due to his empty stomach. Adding to the fuzziness of his brain was the constant movement of the boat under his feet. Setting the empty glass on the bar, Brodie headed to the outside deck to get some fresh air. Up one flight, out a heavy metal door, he stood at the rail as the mega ocean liner cut through the water towards the coast of Canada and Vancouver like a schooner. The wind blew cold, being the first week of May, and he soon became too chilly to stand there without a coat. As he walked along the promenade, couples were everywhere, holding hands, kissing, playing with small children. He felt as if he stood out from the rest, simply by his lack of someone attached to his elbow. *I'll bet the only solo men on this boat are the crew.* He should do it. Find a man to play with. Did he want to screw an employee?

"Oh, just face it, Brodie, you're on your own. Deal with it." He found his way back to his room, ordered a club sandwich, and ate it alone.

Lying back on the narrow single bed to sulk, he moaned, "Life really sucks at the moment." He rubbed his eyes, trying not to well up emotionally. Two double scotches in his veins weren't helping matters. But as he revisited the entire chain of events that led to him being single on a cruise, he felt his chest tighten. How many failed relationships did this make? He'd lost count. Paden was wrong, he wasn't a womanizer. He didn't cheat on them. He just couldn't relate to them on a deep level. But Paden was right in one aspect, his choice in women sucked. But that was where he ended up all the time. Trophy types. Why?

Brodie crushed the pillow under his head, staring at the walls of the tiny cabin, hearing the hum of the ship's enormous engines. He imagined Paden and Tim having sex. They were both very good looking men. It wasn't the first time he'd thought about those two kissing or sucking each other. Thinking of men having sex was the only way he could get himself off. Wasn't that a clue?

He didn't know many straight men who were close friends with gay men. And most certainly didn't have a best friend who was gay. "Oh, Brodie," he sighed, rubbing his rough jaw. "Just do it. Stop fighting it because you're afraid of what everyone will think of you."

But thinking about doing it, and actually finding the kind of man he wanted to touch, that was a different story. It wasn't going to just be any man. It had to be a particular type. *Well, shit, if I'm going to do it, I'm going to do it with someone I am turned on by.*

Imagining finding some stud in a white sailor suit, sucking his dick in a dark hallway, Brodie got an erection. Opening his zipper, taking out his cock, he closed his eyes and fantasized the events leading up to a sexual encounter. A smile, a wink, flirting, a quick signal to rendezvous. A touch of a crotch, tight pants shoved down muscular legs, a cock in his mouth, sperm on his tongue...

Brodie tensed up, shooting come onto his stomach, slowing down his hand as he caught his breath. "Who am I kidding?" he laughed sadly. "I never think of women when I do it to myself. What the hell am I so afraid of?" But he was. The labeling, the exile from his family, the reaction at his job. He'd built up such a macho image of himself for the world to see, he knew no one would believe it. He wasn't sure he did himself. Oh, no. He knew. Deep inside, he knew exactly what he wanted and what turned him on. Now he had the opportunity for an onboard fling with no strings attached. Was he going to spend the week jerking off? Or...

~

His first test of nerves at flying solo came that evening after they left the port in Vancouver and began their sea excursion. A piece of paper was stuffed under his cabin door. He and his partner were invited to sit at the captain's table for dinner. Staring at the note in confusion, he had no idea why he had been selected. Since he was curious and nervous at the same time, Brodie called the hotel desk. "Yes, uh, I just got an invitation for dinner at the captain's table."

"Oh, very good, sir."

"Uh, any reason why?"

"It's done at random. There's no meaning to the selection. It's just a chance for a few of the passengers to get to sit and chat with the captain and his crew."

"Oh."

"Is it all right, sir? Would you rather not?"

"No, it's fine. I just wondered...uh, I'm alone. My," he swallowed down the bitterness, "my partner didn't come on board."

"Don't worry. You are welcome to join the captain on your own."

"Sure, whatever." Brodie thanked the man, hanging up, looking at the invitation. "Now I feel like I'm on the damn Love Boat about to meet Captain Stubing."

Showering, shaving, Brodie dressed in a dark suit and knotted his tie under his jaw in the bathroom mirror. Waves of rage kept washing over him at the idea of facing a room full of strangers without a girlfriend on his arm. He was humiliated. People didn't take cruises on their own unless it was a singles' cruise. And this ship hardly met *that* criteria, it was couples as far as the eye could see.

Craving more hard liquor to stop the fluttering of fear in his mid-section, Brodie chided himself on his cowardliness and snarled at the mirror, "Just because you're on your own doesn't mean you're any less a man, Brodie Duncan. So, shape up or ship out!" Musing over the pun, he added, "Literally!"

Grabbing the room key, for that was all he required since buying alcohol was just a signature on a paper, he locked his room up, walking down the enormous hallway behind a gray-haired couple holding hands, dressed in a tuxedo and sparkling sequined gown. Looking down at his business suit, he hadn't imagined he'd need a damn tuxedo. Since the couple seemed to know where they were going, Brodie followed behind them silently. The elevator took them to the promenade deck. A huge number of people were there, milling around, drinks in their hands. Squeezing behind the mob, Brodie searched for the location of that open bar. Over the heads of the passengers he had a look inside the main dining area. It was lit by chandeliers and sparkling with gold and silver like a five star hotel. The size of the room intimidated him on sight. Huge round tables allowing ten people to sit together were arranged in rows leading all the way to the stern.

"Jesus," he muttered in terror.

Ordering a shooter of tequila, Brodie bolted it down, leaving the glass on the bar. Escaping the thick mob, he returned to the hall, leaning back against a window that overlooked a dark never-ending sea.

A man caught his attention. Brodie assessed him for fuckability. Tall, dark, thick hair, chiseled jaw, high cheekbones, he had light eyes but Brodie couldn't tell the color from where he stood. Broad shoulders, muscular, tight ass. "Oh yes. Perfect." Strangely enough, the expression on the handsome man appeared pinched. As Brodie stared, unobserved, he soon guessed the reason why. A sharp-faced, icy brunette seemed to be henpecking that handsome man, her expression contorted in anger.

"Oh, you poor schmuck. I know what you're going through." Brodie could almost imagine the argument. *Everyone is in a tuxedo! I told you to rent a tux! Why didn't you listen to me! Blah, blah, blah.* Poor bastard.

When the man's gaze caught Brodie's, Brodie felt his insides ignite and his cock twitch. The man's glance moved away just as quickly and Brodie took a moment to catch his breath. "Holy shit." He hadn't expected his body to react quite like that.

Finally the crowd moved as a group inside the bejeweled dining room. Feeling completely self-conscious, Brodie took the folded invitation out of his jacket pocket and showed it to a uniformed waiter. "Can you point me in the right direction?"

Nodding his head graciously, the waiter brought Brodie to the head table where a small card rested in front of his place setting with his name on it. "Thanks." Brodie sat down, noticed a card next to him that read Melanie Hughley, and frowned in annoyance.

Instantly his private waiter approached him. "Would you like me to pour some wine, sir?"

"Yes. Please."

"Red or white?"

"Red." Brodie shifted in his chair nervously. *Keep going, more, more...*

The man filled his glass and moved to do the same to the next couple that had sat down. Brodie gulped the strong, dry wine, dying to get this dinner over with and get drunk.

Hearing an angry, high-pitched woman's voice, Brodie tilted to his right. Sitting at a nearby table was that gorgeous man and his badgering wife or girlfriend. "She's still at it?" He shook his head sadly. "Give it a rest!"

"Sorry?" the elderly gentleman sitting next to Melanie's empty seat asked.

"Nothing. Talking to myself." Brodie tried to smile.

"It's exciting, sitting with the captain."

"Huh? Yeah. Exciting." Brodie wished he shared the old man's enthusiasm. The room was packed with sequined gowns, black tuxedos and sports jackets, jeweled throats and earrings, it was as if dinner was some grand ball. Brodie didn't expect such extravagance. Ironically, he thought Melanie would have eaten it up.

That man caught his eye.

Brodie froze, the wine glass hovering in his hand, empty and needing refilling. The gaze lasted seconds, but to Brodie it felt long and filled with some strange expectation. The old man next to him was talking but Brodie didn't hear anything but some unintelligible syllables. The ice queen nudged the handsome man to get back his attention. When the connection broke, Brodie had to catch his breath. His cock was hard as a rock under his dress slacks and throbbing. "Jesus Christ, what the hell was that all about?"

"Sorry?"

Brodie shook his head. "Nothing." The old man must be hard of hearing. A waiter tilted the bottle over Brodie's glass. Impressed with the service, he sat back, watching the red elixir fill the bell of the stemware. "Thank you."

"My pleasure, sir."

An older, distinguished gentleman in a white uniform approached his table. Two other men in white were behind him. Brodie figured it was the captain and two crew members. What was he supposed to do? Stand? Clap?

Seeing the old man rise up politely, Brodie hoped his erection had gone down enough not to be noticed. In paranoia, he only stood halfway, waiting for them to sit down, quickly covering his lap with his napkin, just in case. Safely concealed under the table, Brodie introduced himself as the captain and crew did the same.

"Are we still waiting for someone?" The captain gestured to the empty chair next to Brodie.

His face blushing in humiliation, Brodie replied, "No. Uh, my girlfriend got sick last minute. She insisted I shouldn't miss out."

"Oh. Sorry to hear that. Well, we hope she's better soon. We have a doctor on board if she needs one."

Brodie just smiled, finishing his second glass of wine.

When the food began to appear on the table, Brodie was floored at the quality of the meals and the number of courses. Gobbling the delicacies down, he didn't realizing how hungry he was. Buzzed on the wine and the tequila shot, he allowed the conversation to become a hum in his ear, not really listening until he was addressed directly. When dessert arrived, Brodie was already stuffed. He sat back and stared at the chocolate, cannonball-shaped ice cream as if it were torture. "Damn, you know how many hours of running I have to do to burn something like that off?"

The captain dabbed his lip, offering, "There's a running track on the sports deck."

"Is there?"

"Yes. Just go all the way to the top. One floor down from the sky deck."

"Oh. Great." Brodie stared at the chocolate orb. "One taste."

"We could wrap it up and you can give it to your sick friend."

"Uh, no. That's all right. She's allergic to chocolate." Brodie wondered why he was lying. Was it that horrible to admit you were ditched? *Yes!*

Savoring the chocolate that melted on his tongue, Brodie blinked his eyes wide as that man, that handsome man, and his shrew stood up from their table. Sitting upright in his seat as they made their way past him, Brodie swept his eyes from the man's spectacular face down his broad chest to his crotch. The chills that coursed over his skin made him shiver. Trying not to linger on the man's bulging zipper, Brodie immediately connected with the man's eyes as he drew nearer. The charge of excitement at the contact of those light irises nearly knocked him off his chair. Unable to prevent it, Brodie's lips curled at the corners into a wicked smile. It was instantly reflected back. When the man moved away, Brodie caught a scent of the man's cologne in the gentle gust of air that brushed his face. Once again he was dealing with a hard-on that pushed against the fabric of his wool pants. "Holy shit."

The captain leaned near. "Everything all right?"

"Yes. Fine." Brodie reached for his glass of water, sucking it down. Once he had softened enough to not embarrass himself completely, he stood, shook hands with the captain and crew, and left the dining room.

His heart was still beating hard in his chest, but at least his cock had calmed down. Brodie read so much into that gaze, he envisioned midnight rendezvous and afternoon delights. Slowly relaxing his pulse, Brodie made a reality check. The man was with a female. Hello? Forget the connection. It was just a look. Nothing more.

Chapter Three

Waking early the next morning, Brodie dressed in his gym shorts and t-shirt. Tying his laces as he sat on his unmade bed, he made sure he was ready, stuffing the keycard into the front of his briefs for lack of a pocket. Walking down the long corridor, he used the elevator and hit the button for the sports deck.

Feeling the wind the instant the doors opened, Brodie shivered, pushing against it as he began jogging laps around the boat. Several other hardcore fitness fans were doing the same, as were some seniors in sweat outfits, walking briskly. After an easy pace for his first lap, he increased his speed, which warmed him up and helped him feel as if he were actually burning calories. Catching up to a few runners quickly, he noticed another male in tight, red shorts, running at an impressive pace. Always competitive, Brodie imagined passing him by, keeping his smirk to himself. As he approached he admired the fit man's muscular arms and shoulders revealed in his skimpy outfit. Moving to his side, about to overtake him, Brodie glanced sideways at the man's profile, choking in surprise at seeing the handsome man he had admired at dinner.

The moment Brodie came into the man's peripheral view, he turned to look. "Hey."

"Hey!" Brodie answered enthusiastically, running side by side instead of passing like he had planned.

"Trying to keep up the workout, you know." The man panted between his words.

"Exactly. Christ, the food is rich, isn't it?" Brodie gazed down at the man's long legs and elongated stride.

"Too rich. It's killing me."

"Uh, I'm Brodie, Brodie Duncan."

"Julian Richards. Nice to meet you, Brodie."

"Yeah, you too." Brodie kept pace with Julian easily but wondered if Julian would rather run alone. "Am I bugging you?"

"No, not at all. It's nice to have a running partner."

"Yes. It is." Brodie smiled to himself, thinking *Christ, what a fucking bod!* If he didn't stop that train of thought, he'd be running with a hard on. "How many laps have you already done?"

"Just started. I assume it's a quarter mile lap."

"I have no idea." Brodie felt the first blast of his own heat as he began warming up. He wasn't feeling cold any longer.

"What do you do normally? I do about three miles."

"Sounds good. We are on vacation, after all."

Julian let out a sarcastic snort at the comment which intrigued Brodie.

"Not going well?" Brodie asked.

"Never mind. You don't want to hear it."

Oh, you are so wrong! Brodie tried not to smile. "It's okay. If you want to talk about something, I'm here."

Another lap passed and they said nothing. As if Julian had enough time to consider the option, he sighed, "Damn girlfriend is driving me nuts."

"Oh?" Brodie wiped at the drops of sweat running down his temple.

"What a fucking bitch. I can't do anything right."

"Ah. Know the kind." Brodie smiled.

"Never mind. You don't want to hear it."

No! I do! Brodie lost count of their laps imagining licking the sweat off of Julian's square jaw. "You been dating her long?"

"No. Only a few months. I met her at work and now I'm sunk. If we have a bad break up, I have to look at her nasty face every day."

"Work, that's a no-no." Brodie inhaled the ocean air deeply as he began laboring with the fast pace.

"I know. Broke my own damn rules."

"What do you do?"

"Investment banking. You know, stock portfolios. She's a teller."

"Where? I mean, where do you live?"

"Seattle. You?"

"Bellevue." Brodie's insides were jumping. They lived twenty minutes away from each other.

"Really? Microsoft man?"

"Geez, how did you guess?"

"Doesn't everyone who lives in Bellevue work there?" he laughed.

"Yes, probably."

After twenty minutes of running at almost a sprint pace. Julian stopped, looking down at his watch.

Tripping to halt his stride, Brodie leaned over his legs to catch his breath, his hands on his knees. "Three miles?"

"Should be." Julian gasped for air, standing up taller and inhaling deeply.

Slowly recovering from the exertion, Brodie snuck a peek at Julian's crotch. His t-shirt was drenched and sticking to his chest. Running his tongue over his salty lips, Brodie wanted to taste the sweat of Julian's body so badly he had an image flash of rushing the man and licking him on the neck.

"So?" Julian wiped at his face with the tail of his shirt, showing off perfectly cut abs. "You here with your wife or something?"

"Wife?" Brodie cringed involuntarily. "I'm not married."

"I noticed an empty seat next to you at the captain's table. Are you here alone?"

Humiliation quickly replaced the lust he was feeling as he ogled those well cut external oblique muscles. *Oh fuck it.* "Yes. I'm here alone."

Julian took some time before he said anything as if studying Brodie's expression. "Why am I getting the feeling that wasn't the game plan?"

"I'm starting to freeze out here." Brodie gestured to the door. Julian nodded, following him inside the corridor. Once they were out of the wind, Brodie whispered, "It's pathetic. My girlfriend picked our first cruise to dump me." *Okay, I said it. Yes, I'm a loser.* As he waited for the sympathy to appear on Julian's fine face, something else emerged. Gazing at those blue eyes, Brodie wondered if his own light blue eyes had the same effect. Instantly his crotch lit on fire. Utterly mortified by it, especially when

Julian's glance swept downward, Brodie knew his tight shorts concealed nothing.

"What on earth is her problem?"

"Huh?" Brodie nonchalantly covered his hard dick with his hand. "Whose problem?"

"Nothing. Ya wanna catch a sauna or sit in the Jacuzzi?"

"Sure." Brodie had no idea where those amenities were, so he tilted his head for Julian to lead the way. As he walked behind him, his cock rubbed against his sweaty thighs. He was dying to reach inside his shorts to adjust it, but too many people were coming and going in the narrow hall. Walking down the stairs to the lido deck, Brodie was surprised at all the goodies he hadn't been aware of. A salon, bar, two pools, a weight room, and small kiosks of deli, pizza, and grilled food appeared.

Julian pushed open a door, holding it for Brodie. The scent of chlorine instantly wafted up his nostrils. A showerhead protruded from a tiled wall. As Brodie stood by, Julian took off his t-shirt, tossing it aside, rinsing the sweat off his body. The twitching in Brodie's cock was growing intolerable. Remembering the room key, he reached inside his shorts, peeling it off his moist skin. As he did, Julian's eyes caught the act. Holding the card as if to show him it wasn't a lewd act, just one of practicality, Brodie knew damn well his shorts weren't concealing his admiration of this stud. As the water soaked Julian's tight red shorts, Brodie noticed the silhouette of a large erection. *Son of a bitch.* Julian walked to the whirlpool, settling into the heat.

Swallowing his shock at realizing Julian's physical reaction mirrored his, Brodie pulled the damp shirt over his head, tossing it near Julian's, standing under the warm spray. Rinsing his hair and face, Brodie spun around to wash off his back and noticed Julian's gaze was connected to his crotch. *Oh, this can't be real.*

Shutting off the water, paranoid the other spa patrons could tell what was going on, Brodie placed his key on top of his shirt. With Julian's eyes lingering low on his body, Brodie eased into the churning water, thankful for the cover of bubbles. The noise of the jets echoed in the steamy room. A very young couple had joined them, playing and flirting overtly in front of them.

Brodie slid over to where Julian relaxed, moving his butt across the tiled ledge under the hot water. Once he was close enough to communicate, Brodie smiled sweetly at him. Julian returned the grin.

"Have you ever been on a cruise before?"

Brodie shook his head. "No. First time."

"Me too. I didn't know what to expect. I mean, although it's a big boat, I'm getting a little claustrophobic."

Brodie scooted back, as if the comment meant he should give Julian more space.

"I didn't mean that." Julian chuckled.

They both looked over at the couple as the woman sat on her boyfriend's lap. Brodie said, before he thought about it, "Bet he's got one hell of a hard on."

At the lack of a reply, Brodie turned to look at Julian's face. The intensity of his expression made Brodie's skin prickle. "Sorry. Was that crass?"

"No. I don't offend easily."

"Good. I can be slightly crude on occasion. I think that's one of the things that turned Melanie off."

"Women." Julian shrugged, as if nothing more had to be said.

"Yeah, women." Brodie looked back at the young woman again. She wasn't attractive in his opinion, but neither was her boyfriend. A good match.

"So," Julian cleared his throat, "you're doing this whole venture solo?"

"What choice have I got? She ditched me a second before the damn boat took off."

"That's harsh."

"Tell me about it." An elderly man joined them in the hot tub, distracting Brodie. "But to be honest, I think I might have a better time without her."

"Oh?" Julian leaned closer to hear.

"Yeah. Well, she nagged me a lot about drinking too much. And I know that would only have been the beginning."

Julian rolled his eyes. "I've already been chewed out because I didn't bring a tux. Who wants to wear a damn monkey suit to eat dinner?"

Brodie smiled at his accurate appraisal. "I thought you were getting an earful at dinner last night."

"I was. Oh, are you assigned to the captain's table?"

"No. I think they pick people out at random. I actually have a different table assignment. I don't remember the table number."

"Too bad you can't sit with me. I mean, us."

A flush of boiling heat washed over Brodie. "Is this thing getting hotter?" He gestured to the water.

"Maybe. I'm ready to get out." Nodding his head, Julian stood, stepping out of the whirlpool onto the tiled floor.

After hopping out of the boiling pool, Brodie turned the shower on again, trying to rinse off the chlorine. When he spun around, Julian was staring at him. Instantly Brodie's hard-on returned. Moving out of the spray, Brodie picked up his t-shirt and key, holding the damp material in front of his crotch. Julian stepped under the showerhead. To Brodie's horror, Julian stared directly at him while he smoothed his hands over his bare chest. Unable to tear his eyes away, Brodie knew this was a come on. No one did that without wanting something.

His eyes traveling down that perfect physique, he saw the outline of a large engorged penis. Brodie imagined getting on his knees pulling down those wet red shorts and sucking him deeply into his throat.

"There you are!"

At the woman's voice, Brodie felt as if he'd been smacked in the face.

Julian shut off the water spray, using his t-shirt as a crotch-shield as well. "Amelia, hey. I was just having a soak before I came back to the room to shower."

"You took forever, Julian. Jesus. I've already had breakfast. I don't understand why you need to exercise on our vacation. Can't you take ten stupid days off?"

As Julian was ushered out of the spa, he turned back to look over his shoulder. Brodie couldn't believe the expression of longing on the man's face. Biting his lip in frustration, Brodie walked slowly out of the room, dripping wet, down the long corridor to the elevator. All the way to his cabin, the haunted look on Julian's face drove him insane.

Chapter Four

A lunch buffet was set out on the promenade level. Brodie couldn't believe the amount of food that the cruise line presented. It was obscene. Filling his plate with fruits and vegetables, leery of his waistline and the amount of running he would need every day to burn off the fattening meals, he carried his healthy choices to a table with a view of the water.

The rocking of the ship hadn't stopped, but he had gotten used to it. He didn't notice it much until he was horizontal on one of the twin beds in his cabin at night, which was when the swaying became more pronounced.

Opening up his napkin and picking up a fork, Brodie stuffed a piece of watermelon into his mouth, and spit out the seeds into his hand. Passengers came and went, some standing on line for the buffet, others passing through to eat poolside or at the restaurants. He hadn't fully explored the boat yet. The thing was so big, he was sure there were shops, bars, clubs, and pools he had yet to discover. Maybe today. They were still at sea and nearing the Inside Passage. He knew which inside passage he'd rather be sliding through.

A piece of sweet pineapple on his tongue, Brodie froze as he caught sight of Julian and Amelia, plates in hand, moving up the long row of delicacies. Chewing the fruit and swallowing, Brodie admired Julian's skin-tight, beige chinos and white short-sleeved shirt. His dark brown hair was slightly longer than Brodie's own, brushing the back of his neck and covering the tops of his ears. Amelia was, in Brodie's opinion, that trophy selection of woman he'd so many times succumbed to. Either he had to adjust his taste in women or his gender selection. And Julian could use the same advice. Hello? Two wicked hard-ons? What the hell else could it mean other than they turned each other on, big time.

But knowing the denial he had lived with for twenty-eight years, he imagined Julian in the same boat. Smiling at the pun, Brodie said, "We are on the same boat. Duh."

As he shook his head at his own humor, he opened his mouth to stuff in a strawberry. Before he ate it, Julian spotted him.

Pausing, the red ripe strawberry hovering near his lips, Brodie's breath caught in his chest and instantly his cock rose to the occasion. Julian's expression mirrored his. They simply stared at each other in awe. Just to see his reaction, Brodie opened his mouth wider, pushing the strawberry in, licking his lips as he chewed. Julian's face paled slightly. *Man, ditch the witch!* Brodie knew they wanted to touch each other. This was absurd. Amelia seemed to be babbling incessantly, oblivious to the leering her boyfriend was bestowing on another man. When Brodie began to peel his banana, Julian appeared ready to pass out.

Brodie gave the banana some head, loving teasing this gorgeous man. Julian's trance broke when Amelia nudged him. Brodie chewed a bite of the banana, his eyes never leaving the mismatched couple. But he'd been there, lived the nightmare, and wondered if Julian was trapped so deeply in denial that even a onetime taboo kiss was out of the question.

With his plate now full, Julian followed where his woman led. As he passed Brodie, Julian made sure Amelia was oblivious first, giving Brodie a very dirty smirk. Brodie returned it with interest. A lot of interest.

As they moved out of sight, to the opposite side of the boat, Brodie moaned in agony, rubbing his hand over his hard cock discretely, yearning for a once in a lifetime fling with another man. Of course it would be once. Just to satisfy his curiosity. He wasn't gay.

Opening his eyes from his fantasy life, he found two older women standing next to his table for four. "You mind if we join you?"

Seeing there were no other unoccupied tables in the room, Brodie nodded, sitting up in his chair and moving his plate closer to his body to give them space.

The two average looking, middle-aged women introduced

themselves, blushing shyly. Brodie didn't catch their names, nodding, not sure if they were on the prowl or not. Trapped in a mundane conversation about glaciers, Brodie finished his plate of rabbit food, politely excusing himself so as not to insult anyone. They giggled and batted their lashes coquettishly, but it was lost on him.

Brodie searched the overcrowded room for a last gape at the object of his desire. Every table, every chair was occupied. The noise of chatting, forks hitting china, and the hum of the engine noise in the background made it feel chaotic. Finding him finally, Brodie paused, wondering if he could send out some kind of silent signal. It must have worked because Julian glanced up from his plate of crab legs and shrimp. Feeling bold and daring, especially since Amelia's back was facing him, Brodie very quickly touched his zipper. The expression on Julian's face told him he must have sent a zinging shock through the man. It seemed Amelia noticed it as well. Like a harpy she spun around to see what had caused the reaction. Brodie turned on his heels and walked out of the room.

~

"What are you looking at?" Amelia asked.

"Huh? Nothing." Julian went back to cracking the crab legs.

"You seem very distracted, Julian. I don't like it."

"You don't like anything, Amelia. I even get the impression you don't like me." He slurped the meat out of the shell, wiping his hands on a cloth napkin.

"You're okay. I like you."

"Oh, that just makes me warm and fuzzy all over," Julian replied sarcastically. "This trip was your idea. Don't brood."

"I thought it would bring us closer."

"Has it?" Julian squeezed a lemon wedge over his shrimp.

"No. You're annoying me."

"Am I?" Julian wasn't amused, though he pretended he was.

"Yes."

"What exactly am I doing that's so annoying?"

"I don't know. You don't want to do anything I do."

"Like what?" Julian ate another shrimp, looking over Amelia's shoulder in case Brodie made another appearance.

"I want to go to the shops."

"Okay." He shrugged.

"And you disappeared in the morning."

"I told you I was going to keep up the workout routine. Come on, Amelia, it's all of an hour."

"And I told you to bring a tuxedo."

"Not that again. There are plenty of guys in business suits, lady. Please stop throwing that in my face." Julian finished his food, using the napkin to wipe up his sticky hands.

"I'm not having fun."

Seeing her pronounced pout and tightly knotted arms, Julian laid his napkin on the table. "What do you want to do?"

"There's nothing to do on this damn boat."

"First of all, that's not true. Do you want to gamble?"

"No."

"Swim?"

"No."

"Have a sauna and Jacuzzi?"

"No!"

"Right. There's a movie theater, a salon…"

"A salon?"

"Yes." He thanked the busboy as he removed the dirty plates.

"Like in hair and nails?" Amelia held her hands up for inspection.

"I assume so. I think they even offer massage."

"I could go for that."

"Good." Julian sipped his glass of water, meeting her expression of annoyance. "What?"

"But that's just for today. What will I do tomorrow?" she whined.

"I think tomorrow we arrive at Juneau. We can book an excursion."

"What the hell is there to see in Juneau?" She crinkled her nose.

Julian sat back and gazed at her in disbelief. "You did know this was a cruise to Alaska, right?"

"We should have gone to the Bahamas. It's so cold on deck."

"Why didn't you ask me to book that instead?"

"I thought you wanted to see Alaska."

"I told you I didn't care either way."

"Well, you screwed up then. I wanted to go to the Bahamas." Julian rubbed his face in agony.

"I'm going to get my hair and nails done before dinner tonight." As she collected her purse, he nodded. "Good."

"See ya."

"See ya." He sat there, trying not to feel exhausted and angry. "I must be fucking insane." Gazing out at the choppy water, Julian daydreamed. And when he did, those images included Brodie. Christ, the guy was hot. Insta-wood. And he knew damn well the feeling was mutual. But—and it was a very large but—was he interested in a gay fling? A touch of forbidden flesh?

A sensation of fire scalded his skin and his dick grew hard. *Well, that answers that question.* He laughed sadly. Why was it so difficult to admit? Why didn't he just give it a try? Twenty-seven years old, constantly imagining a gay conquest yet never acting on it. Was he insane? He lived in Seattle for cryin' out loud. You could be gay there. It didn't matter to anyone. But did it matter to him? Maybe. Imagining telling his mother and father he was gay made his skin crawl.

Scanning the room, seeing the crowd finally dispersing after they had consumed an ungodly amount of food, Julian wished Brodie would wander back through, standing there rubbing his dick again. How amazing was that? How bold. But their obvious attraction for each other spoke loudly after the run. Two huge hard-ons. What better proof did he need that he was hungry for a taste of male flesh? There it was. An invitation. And how perfect was the situation? Amelia aside, it was an onboard tryst. No strings attached. Okay, he lived in Bellevue, but it wasn't as if they would actually cross paths again. They could experiment and then off they would go to their private lives. No one the wiser.

"You must have a private room, Brodie. Your insignificant other ditched you. Where are you now?" Checking his watch, Julian realized Amelia would be tied up for hours getting her hair and nails done.

Jumping to his feet, he stopped at a men's room to wash the

sticky seafood off his hands, checking his hair and face in the mirror quickly, intent on the hunt.

~

Brodie stood at a roulette wheel. He never gambled. But what was twenty bucks? A fresh glass of scotch in his hand, he put down a chip and watched the ball spin around the wheel. Lost again.

Last chip. He moved it onto a number.

"I'd try number nine."

Pivoting to look over his shoulder, Brodie found Julian almost pressed against his back. The shock of chills that raced over Brodie almost made his spill his drink.

The wheel spun, the ball settled in number nine.

"Told ya." Julian shook his head.

"If you were my Lady Luck, you arrived twenty dollars too late." Brodie tried to turn around to face him, but that meant he would have to brush Julian's body to do so. He had to finish his scotch to build up that kind of courage.

"I don't gamble." Julian stepped back.

Sighing in relief, able to face him without rubbing against him and possibly alerting Julian how hard he had become, Brodie replied, "Me neither. Just bored."

"That sounds familiar." Julian rolled his eyes.

"Oh?" Brodie stood in front of a slot machine, slipping a quarter into it, pushing the button, watching the icons spin.

"Never mind."

Julian's body was almost pressing against his again. The heat transfer was driving him mad. Brodie watched as two cherries and a bell clicked into the machine. "Lost. I can't win." Closing his eyes, imagining pushing back, rubbing his bottom against Julian's crotch, Brodie had to inhale a deep breath to control himself.

"Want to take a walk out on the promenade? Get some fresh air?"

"Sure." Brodie finished the last drop of scotch, setting his glass aside. As he followed that tight set of ass cheeks covered by thin beige fabric, he imagined telling Julian to head to his room instead but chickened out. Even though the guy appeared interested, he didn't know if any of this would go anywhere.

Pushing through two heavy metal doors, they were instantly smacked with the cool breeze. Julian led them to the back of the boat where the wind was blocked and didn't freeze them. Brodie gestured to two open chairs. They sat down, facing the choppy water and glimpse of coastline that was far out in the distance.

"Where's your girlfriend?"

"Getting pampered." Julian's eyes narrowed in the bright light.

"You two close?"

"No. I think she wishes she did what your girlfriend did. She's done nothing but complain since we've been onboard. I don't know what the hell to do."

"Been there. Wrote the book." Brodie watched as happy couple after happy couple strolled by, hand in hand. "I sometimes feel like there's something wrong with me. I can't seem to find what I'm looking for." Brodie felt Julian's gaze. He turned towards him, seeing the crisp color of blue reflected in his eyes from the ocean.

"I hear ya," Julian replied.

"You think it's just some unreachable level of expectation on our part?"

"I don't know. I only know I have lousy taste in women. I meet the shallowest bimbos on the planet."

Brodie started laughing.

"What?"

"You sound like me. Maybe we're both in need of something different."

Julian's straddle widened until his leg touched Brodie's. Brodie met those blue eyes again. He opened his mouth to ask him if these little overt signs meant Julian wanted to connect, or if they were just playful and meant to go nowhere. Nothing came out of his mouth.

"Something different?" Julian asked. "Anything in particular?"

Say it! Say it! Tell him you are bi-curious! Say it! "No, nothing specific. Just not what we're used to." Oh, he wasn't making any sense at all.

"Like?"

Brodie rubbed his rough jaw and gazed out at the expanse of water. He didn't answer. He had no idea what to say.

Julian cleared his throat. "You...uh, you ever see that movie...uh, *Brokeback Mountain*?"

Whipping his head around at the comment, Brodie found apprehension in Julian's eyes. As if Julian expected to be punched out for such a brazen statement. "I have."

"You..." Julian cleared his throat, adding as a disclaimer, "I'm not gay, I just thought it was a decent movie."

I'm not gay? Brodie was confused. *Okay, I'll play.* "I'm not gay either, but those sex scenes were hot."

"Yeah. Really hot."

Great, now he was hard again. Brodie laced his fingers together and covered over it casually. Julian's leg moved, rubbing against his. Brodie was about to combust. The twitching in his cock was making him crazy. Taking a quick glance, he noticed Julian's chinos were bulging. Rubbing his eyes in agony, Brodie wished one of them had the damn guts to say something. Something that meant, "Christ, let me suck the damn thing!"

"Is the dinner tonight formal?"

Brodie couldn't care less about the damn dinner. "I have no idea."

"I hope not. I don't want to hear about the fucking tux again."

They grew silent. More family groups and couples passed. As they did Brodie wondered if they assumed he and Julian were a gay couple. Did they look like they were? *Two pretty boys? Hm?* He smiled at the thought.

"You going on an excursion when we hit Juneau?"

Brodie emerged out of his fantasy life to answer. "I don't know. Are you?"

"I'd like to. I mean, I assumed we took the cruise up this way to see Alaska. At least I did."

"Are you going with, uh, Amelia, is it?"

Julian's face soured.

"If she's not interested, I'll go with you." Brodie hoped the witch got a case of food poisoning.

"Oh. Cool. I'd appreciate that. She didn't seem receptive when I mentioned it. She just moaned about the weather and wished we were in the Bahamas."

"Christ, she's Melanie's twin."

"Melanie?"

"The girlfriend who ditched me."

"Oh, right." Julian pushed down on his crotch casually.

Brodie knew damn well why. *Think! Think!* He felt like pounding his head with the heel of his palm. There must be someplace to go on this boat to pin Julian to a wall and kiss his fucking lips. Knowing his cabin was always available, Brodie tried to come up with a ruse to get him there. There just was no plausible excuse. *Brokeback Mountain?* Jesus!

~

Julian was going completely insane. He couldn't even look at the man anymore. Peering down at his own lap, seeing a slight, damp stain appear on the beige material, Julian rolled his eyes in humiliation. He was so fricken hard he was about to die. Making the mistake of touching himself had squeezed a juicy drop of pre-come out of his dick. How absolutely mortifying was that?

Just tell Brodie you want to see his cabin. Make something up!

Two women walked by, giggling flirtatiously as they passed. Just as Julian averted their eyes, Brodie muttered, "We should just hold hands so these idiots think we're taken."

Whipping his head towards Brodie, Julian visualized grabbing Brodie's hand and bringing it to his lips. When Brodie's blue-eyed gaze contacted his, Brodie whispered in apology, "Sorry. Dumb idea."

"You..." Julian's throat closed up, but he pushed through it. "You have a window in your cabin?"

Brodie's face lit up. "No. Want to see it?"

"Uh, sure."

~

Yes! Yes! Brodie hopped off the deck chair, almost asking Julian to race him to it. *Tag, you're it!* Trying not to sprint to show how anxious he was to be in a room alone with Julian, Brodie stuffed his hands into his pockets, strolling along, whistling, anything to appear nonchalant and not overeager. Besides, what if Julian was just interested in the cabin? That was always a possibility. Maybe he'd paid for one with a view. Idle curiosity. If that was the fact, how would Julian react to a pass? Brodie had been punched before. He wasn't afraid of a belt in the jaw.

Nearing the central staircase, Brodie informed Julian as they descended, "I'm down on the main floor, at the bottom of the ship. You know. Cheap room."

Nodding, Julian replied, "So are we."

"Oh." Almost saying, "then our rooms are most likely the same," Brodie bit his lip at utter the stupidity of that line and kept moving.

His keycard in hand, Brodie opened the door, took a quick gander around the hall, slipping inside as if they were indeed sneaking.

The moment that cabin door shut tight, Brodie's nerves kicked in. Tossing the key on the desk, he said, "Well, here it is. Two twin beds and a head."

"Yup. Same as ours. Only ours are pushed together."

"Lucky guy," Brodie sneered.

"Is that her luggage?" Julian pointed to a pink floral bag. "I sure as shit hope it isn't yours."

"Funny. Yes, but check this out." Brodie opened it, setting it on a bed. "Newspapers. You believe her?"

"Oh man, that's cruel. Why don't you toss that nasty thing overboard?"

"I wish I could toss a nasty thing called Melanie overboard." Brodie zipped it up, throwing it down on the floor.

"I'm sorry, Brodie. It must have been horrible being dumped like that."

"I don't really want to talk about it." Well, since they were alone and no one was making a move, Brodie asked, "You ready for a drink?" Waiting for a reply, Brodie was about to pick up his key when he noticed Julian's hand moving to his crotch. A small stain was visible alongside the flap of the zipper though Julian attempted to conceal it. Slowly absorbing the implications of that damp spot, Brodie caught those blue eyes appearing terrified at being found out.

"Maybe we can call room service." Brodie was going completely insane. They both wanted it, yet neither of them were willing to make that first move. Maybe if they were drunk they could blame it on the booze. No harm, no foul.

Trying to function with all the blood in his body racing to his dick, Brodie picked up the phone. "What the hell's the number for room service again?"

"Brodie."

The breathy sound of Julian's voice made the hairs rise on Brodie's body. He set the telephone back in its cradle and slowly turned around.

Julian was trembling visibly. But through that fear, he opened up his hands, palms forward, in what appeared to Brodie as an invitation.

Swallowing hard as his mouth watered at the opportunity, Brodie didn't know what to do. He knew what he wanted, but he still felt as if something needed to be clarified. "Julian, what…what exactly?"

"I don't know." Julian shook his head. "All I know is I'm fucking hard as a rock."

Instantly Brodie's gaze dropped. That stain appeared to be growing. If it weren't for his jeans, he was certain his crotch would look the same. As if pleading, waiting for Brodie to make the first move, Julian hissed his name again, boldly opening the top button of his slacks.

"Oh God." *Can I do this?* It was one thing to pretend, to fantasize, but could he actually touch another man?

"No? No way?" Julian shook his head, as if asking, trying to read Brodie's expression.

Even in the tiny room, Brodie had to take a step closer to Julian to be able to make contact with him. He took that step, thinking it was a giant leap for mankind. Where should he begin? What were they expecting from each other?

Since Brodie was bold enough to close the gap separating them, Julian made the next tentative move, touching Brodie's arm. At the light caress, Brodie melted. And this man hadn't even gone near his cock yet. Closing his eyes, Brodie let out a hiss of air at the yearning that was unbearably strong, stronger than any impulse he'd ever felt before. *Julian is willing! Do something!*

Julian's hand slid down Brodie's forearm to his wrist. Brodie felt his body go into meltdown. His hand was clasped just as he imagined it would have been on the deck a moment earlier. He gripped Julian's palm tightly, petrified of doing anything that may have consequences down the road. *If I do this? Am I gay? Can I go back to not being gay? Is this permanent? Like a tattoo announcing what I really want and feel?*

"Brodie," Julian whispered again, as if pleading, meeting his eyes.

The chills ran up Brodie's spine when Julian repeated his name. It made him want to get on his knees and suck him. Hard. "Are...are you sure, Julian?" *Why was he asking such a stupid question?*

"I'm not sure of anything, Brodie."

The reply was too predictable. It made Brodie feel like an idiot. Julian's hand clenched his in a vice hold.

Brodie forced himself to look deeply into Julian's blue eyes. The man was outstanding. Absolutely amazing. With his right hand, Brodie touched Julian's cheek, cupping it softly.

Another visible tremor passed over Julian's body. Brodie wanted to kiss him. *Should I? Should I just lean in and try it? Kiss a guy? Kiss Julian Richards on his first maiden voyage into what, gay Alaska?*

He was leaning that way. Closer, the scent of Julian's cologne, his body, everything was turning Brodie on so much, if anything even brushed his cock he'd come. Making a feeble attempt, Brodie used the hand cupping Julian's face to raise his jaw up. Closing his eyes, Brodie allowed his lips to brush Julian's. The zing of pleasure raced right to the tip of his cock. Julian moaned as if he were in pain. Straddling Julian's legs for better balance, since even a feather could topple him over at this point, Brodie pressed his lips more assertively against Julian's mouth. It was so hot, their lips touching that way, Brodie felt a swoon washing over him, making his knees shiver. Pausing, parting from him, Brodie asked, "Okay?"

"*Yes,*" Julian whimpered, his hand giving Brodie's another clenched squeeze.

Brodie went for another kiss. At least it was a starting point. This time he licked his first, wetting them. Pressing against Julian's mouth again, Julian's lips parted. Brodie's cock throbbed like mad. He wanted to release it. The feeling of it being trapped was maddening. When their tongues touched, Brodie thought he'd lose consciousness. Parting from the kiss, panting, he met Julian's horrified expression.

"What's wrong?" Julian gasped.

"I have to sit down." Brodie dragged Julian with him onto the single bed. His knees were shaking. He couldn't stand on this rocking ship and have his knees quivering. He'd fall over.

Okay, where were we? Facing Julian full on, Brodie closed his eyes and went back to that mouth. This time it was already open and eager. Slowly the timid tongue touching seemed to grow more relaxed. The essence of testosterone was overwhelming Brodie's senses. The roughness of Julian's jaw, his scent, the strength of Julian's mouth and tongue, the masculine moaning and sighing was making Brodie's head spin, and not just the one on his shoulders. Crazy thoughts passed through his mind. *How long do we have to do this? Could we kiss like this all night? Would anyone miss us? Amelia? Does Julian even care?*

Snapping back to reality and the mouth he was attached to, a man's mouth, mind you, Brodie found they had fallen into a pattern of tongue swirling. Imagining that tongue on his cock, and vice versa, was making Brodie's head hurt. *You are gay you asshole! Did you ever kiss a woman like this? Was your cock ever this fucking hard?*

But even as his internal dialogue accused him, Brodie felt terrified of the truth.

They parted. Panting, catching their breaths.

"Holy shit," Julian whispered.

"No kidding!" Brodie's chest was rising and falling like he'd run laps on the top deck.

"I swear, Brodie, I never kissed a man before."

"Me neither, Julian. Christ, I am so fucking hard."

~

Julian knew what he wanted to do, but some little voice in his head was scaring him to death, calling him names. And there was Amelia to consider. Once he and Brodie passed the point of no return, which in Julian's opinion they already had by swapping spit, where did this leave him? *Gay? Am I now a gay man? Gay lifestyle? Buying gay magazines? Going to gay clubs? What the fuck am I now?*

Brodie was shifting on the bed. Julian knew they were both dealing with unbearable hard-ons. If any more moisture seeped through his chinos, he'd have to change them.

"What now?'

"How the hell should I know?" Brodie panted, unable to catch his breath.

Feeling as if he may have already crossed some imaginary line, Julian rested his hand on Brodie's thigh. The moment he did, Brodie's body tensed up and his breathing went into overdrive.

"If you touch me I'll cream," Brodie warned.

Lowering his eyes to Brodie's tight jeans, Julian could see his cock pressing hard against the fabric. Smoothing up that long muscular leg, Julian stopped before actually cupping Brodie's cock. Using the side of his hand, he pushed against it, moving it.

"My God," Brodie moaned. "What the hell are we doing? Are we insane?"

"Obviously." Julian nudged the huge mound again, watching it shift to the side and return again.

"Does this mean we're fucking gay?"

"Probably." Julian knocked his knuckles into that amazing bulge again.

"Christ. I can't be a fag. I swear I'll never hear the end of it."

"But who will know?" Julian asked, wanting to grab that big dick and squeeze. "Just you and me. That's it. So what if we mess around a little? Most people do things that are out of the ordinary on trips like this. You know, that attitude of I'll never see these people again."

"We live twenty minutes away from each other."

"So? I'm never in Bellevue. We never have to see each other again."

Brodie appeared to be considering it.

"Well?"

"Well what? What do you want to do?"

Julian knew damn well he wanted to suck Brodie dry. He just didn't know what Brodie's reaction would be if he actually vocalized it.

~

Brodie looked down at his lap as that large, masculine hand kept nudging his dick. Knowing someone had to do something or they'd be hard for hours, Brodie dropped back on the mattress, his feet still planted on the floor, and opened his jeans up, releasing his bent cock. Once again his body going completely haywire, Brodie couldn't contain his breathing.

~

The shock of seeing that enormous penis sticking out of Brodie's jeans was like a punch in the gut. It was the first man's penis he had seen in person since showering in baseball practice as a teen, and most certainly the first erect one. It was long and blushing with color. A glistening drop hung at the tip. The urge to shove it down his throat was making Julian writhe where he sat staring at it. Glancing briefly at Brodie's expression, seeing him looking directly back, Julian assumed it was now up to him to actually do something. After all, Brodie had initiated the kiss, and now he was the first to expose himself. As if he were about to touch a live wire, Julian prepared himself. Lying on his side, he gave Brodie's posture and sex appeal another good once over as his hand hovered near that enormous dick. Timidly he wrapped his hand around the shaft. Brodie's hips elevated off the bed, pushing into Julian's palm. Swallowing his anxiety, Julian tried to erase all the negative thoughts out of his head and pretend this was just some frolic into the unknown. He'd experimented with women, why couldn't he experiment with a man? No one needed to know. No one.

Making another sweep of Brodie's amazing body and face, Julian pumped Brodie's cock a few times. More drops appeared at the head.

~

Brodie was going insane. Every fiber in his body screamed out for an orgasm. And that shy hand wasn't moving fast enough to give him one. It was torture. Arching his back, pushing up into that hot palm, Brodie didn't know what else he could do to beg for more friction, other than vocalizing it, which would be embarrassing. But having this male hand around his dick was the most amazing experience he had ever had. Beautiful Julian Richards was lying next to him on a bed, jerking him off. How many times did he fantasize a man touching him? Sneak peeks at Paden and Tim when they kissed hello and goodbye? Too many.

Julian's thumb rubbed through the sticky drops on the tip of his dick, massaging the slit and making Brodie squirm in ecstasy. Brodie felt his balls tighten. He was so close, so damn close.

~

Julian licked his lips. He wanted to taste that drop. See what it would feel like on his tongue. Biting his lip, imagining sucking the juice out of that hard cock, Julian felt his own longing growing out of control. *Oh, fuck it!* He went down on Brodie, pushing that mushroom shaped head into his mouth. He lapped at that salty drop and felt Brodie's attempt at getting in, deep and fast. Resisting at first, Julian finally relaxed his jaw, allowing Brodie the penetration he must be craving. Knowing damn well a shot of come was looming in the near future, Julian kept asking himself if he should back off, let it drop onto Brodie's belly. By the time he decided, *yes, suck it, swallow*, Brodie warned, "I'm coming."

As if waiting for the recoil of a gun, Julian sucked harder, faster, and Brodie's cock went into an explosion of pulsating and throbbing.

~

Brodie was astounded. "You sucked it," he panted, "You sucked it." *OhmyGod! I'm gonna die! That was the most amazing fucking thing I have ever experienced*!

Julian's cheeks blushed as if he were ashamed. Brodie sat up, grabbed his face and kissed him, lapping at the flavor of his own come from Julian's mouth. Julian grunted in shock as Brodie tugged him down on the bed. Brodie rolled on top, pinning him to the mattress, rubbing his exposed dick on Julian's beige bulge. "Oh Christ, Julian, it was unbelievable."

Julian blinked up at him in awe at his reaction.

Biting his top lip, Brodie sat up, slid back on Julian's thighs, opening those slacks up and yanking down the zipper. Feeling as if the moment had come that he had been waiting for for twenty-eight years, Brodie dove down on Julian's erection and sucked it to the base.

"Ah!" Julian shouted in surprise. "Holy shit!"

Closing his eyes in euphoria, Brodie knew it would be fantastic. Knew it. That scent of testosterone, male sex, cologne, sweat, it was an aphrodisiac and it was making his head swim. Gripping that long cock at the base, Brodie sucked it to the tip, then down to his hands again. It didn't feel odd, it didn't make him want to choke, it just felt right. Absolutely right. And the thrill it was sending to his re-hardened cock reinforced his thoughts. *Yes! I knew it! Yes! Come for me! Come for me you beautiful god!*

~

Julian had never expected such a vigorous blowjob. Having his cock sucked by a man, someone who knew how it felt, where all the spots of pleasure were, well, who knew it would rock him to the core? *Okay, Julian, you're gay. Okay? No more deciding. Sex like this? Every night? I'm gay!* He felt like shouting out his epiphany, but before he did, he shot out come like a fountain. And that sexy mother-fucker was draining every last drop from him as if he needed more to satisfy him. And Julian knew if Brodie kept it up, he'd have more to give.

Feeling his heart pounding through his hand as it rested on his chest, Julian closed his eyes as Brodie's hot tongue continued to lap at him gently. "Oh man…" he sighed, "that was unbelievable, Brodie."

"Julian, you taste so fucking good."

Chuckling, never hearing Amelia exclaim that in any of their sexual play, Julian actually couldn't remember Amelia ever sucking it at all.

~

Brodie didn't want to stop. Was he supposed to stop? Finally giving Julian's cock a rest, Brodie stared at Julian's dark pubic hair and the line of hair that led to his belly button. As Julian recuperated, his breathing still heavy, Brodie pushed Julian's white shirt up his chest, wanting a better look at the whole package. As he exposed Julian's torso, Brodie sat up so he could get a better view.

"Jesus, Julian. You're fucking amazing."

Julian reached out his hand, touching Brodie's arm gently. It brought Brodie's attention back to his eyes. Stretching across the narrow mattress, Brodie leaned over Julian's chest, kissing him. As Julian opened his mouth wide to suck on Brodie's tongue, Brodie maneuvered himself so he was resting on top of Julian's body. Their two dicks lay side by side between them. Rock hard.

Brodie wanted to do this all week. Forget the stupid dinners, the corny night club acts, just let them fuck for a week, order the food delivered, stay naked, and never leave the cabin.

His hips began to move again as his hunger became insatiable. "You any idea how long I've waited to do this to a man?"

"Really?"

Brodie blinked, "Did I just say that out loud?"

"Yes," Julian laughed.

"I'm such a dork."

"You're not a dork." Julian brushed Brodie's hair back from his forehead. "It's fantastic, Brodie. I suppose I should say the same thing. I'm just petrified of the label that goes with it."

"Don't talk about it." Brodie frowned. "Let's pretend it's normal." He pumped his hips against the ones under him. "Jesus, I need to come again."

"I suppose it is a 'normal' lifestyle for some men."

Brodie thought about Paden and Tim. "Forget that." He rolled to his side and played with Julian's dick again.

"What time is it?" Julian checked his watch. "Crap."

Brodie felt a pang of jealousy.

"Amelia should be out of the salon by now."

"So?"

"Brodie, please. You know I've come onboard with a woman."

"Yeah, a woman who irritates you."

"Nonetheless, I am stuck with her for the duration of the trip."

Feeling betrayed, Brodie leaned back. "Oh? Nice one, Julian. Make me feel used why don't you?"

"Brodie!" Julian protested when Brodie stood up angrily.

"I get it!" Brodie fastened his jeans. "Just an experiment. No problem. Same to you, pal."

Julian sat up on the bed. "Cut it out, Brodie. There's no need for this."

"No need? No? So you go on your merry way playing Mr. Straight with the ditzy Amelia while I sit alone in this fucking cabin wishing you were here?" Brodie bit his lip. What was he saying? It sounded like he was attached or something. "Never mind. I'm just tired. I get it. Go."

Slowly Julian stood. After fastening his pants, tucking in his shirt, he held Brodie's shoulders, unable to catch his eyes. "I'll do what I can. But I have to be fair. Amelia and I are on this trip together. And I can't crush her. Think about what Melanie did to you. And it would be worse. She can't leave."

Nodding, Brodie knew he'd overstepped his boundaries. "Yes. I know. I don't know why I got so possessive."

Julian held Brodie's jaw and kissed him. When he parted he replied, "Because there's something here, Brodie."

"Is there?" Brodie laughed nervously.

"Yes."

Shrugging pretending it didn't really mean anything, Brodie followed Julian to the door.

"Christ, I should shower, I probably smell like you." Julian laughed.

"She won't know."

"We'll meet up. I'll manage something."

"Okay, whatever."

Julian kissed him once more, vanishing out the door. As Brodie closed it, he rubbed his face tiredly. "I knew this was a bad idea."

Chapter Five

It took every ounce of courage he possessed. Brodie dressed in a casual pair of black slacks and a long sleeve cotton shirt. It wasn't another gala event. Just informal tonight, but jeans weren't allowed. Looking in the mirror on the dresser in his tiny cabin, Brodie imagined a quick bite, then perhaps a stroll around the promenade to walk off dinner, followed by shoving some coins into a slot machine and several glasses of hard liquor.

"So? Do you look like a queer now, Brodie?" he asked his reflection. "Sucked cock. So? What does that make you?" A nasty sneer curled his lip. "A cock-sucker." The thought made him laugh. "Yeah, so what."

Pocketing the key, taking a quick look at the state of the room, he tried not to recall the gorgeous stud that had been lying on his bed a few hours ago. Brodie shut off the light and left the cabin.

On his way to the dining room, as usual, couples abounded. Snuggling, kissy-kissy, romantic pairs of men and women all two by two like Noah's fricken ark. It made him sick to his stomach. Split in half over what he had done with Julian, Brodie wondered why he never fit into that mold. There really was no reason for it. He was brought up like a normal guy. His dad threw a ball to him in the park. They loved sports, sat through many a Seahawk and Mariners game. He drank heartily, loved fitness and activities involving hard working bouts of sweat, grew facial hair. *I'm a man. Yes, I am.* He hummed the Chicago tune in his head. Pausing before entering the intimidating space of the massive dining hall, Brodie took out the tiny card that indicated his table number. *Twenty-two. Where the fuck is twenty-two?*

"Can I help you?"

Sighing with relief at the same kind waiter that had assisted him the night before, Brodie showed him his card. "Any idea where that is?"

"Follow me, sir."

Moving passed the table he knew was reserved for Julian and Amelia, Brodie hoped he was clear on the other side of the room so he didn't have to see them together. At first it hadn't mattered. It sure as shit did now. If they kissed he'd go ballistic.

"Here you go, sir."

Not far enough away. Shit. "Thanks." Brodie tried to be polite and smile at the two senior citizen couples already sipping wine. "Hi." He made a slight wave, sitting down, knowing his state of being on his own would be the topic of discussion. He couldn't very well say his chick was sick all week.

They introduced themselves as if he would remember their names a minute later. Nodding, mumbling his name, having to repeat it for them as they tilted their hearing aids his way, Brodie enunciated it clearly, "Brodie. Brodie Duncan," while placing the napkin on his lap, trying not to grow annoyed. He wasn't angry at them, he was angry at the world.

"Oh. We thought no one was sitting in those seats," one of the old ladies said. "No one was there last night."

"I was invited to sit with the captain." Brodie almost kissed the waiter as he poured him a glass of red wine. "Thank you."

"My pleasure, sir."

Immediately sucking down half of the glass from the anxiety he was enduring over this flying solo fiasco, Brodie felt the eyes of four senior citizens scrutinizing him.

"The captain's table. That's nice."

"Yes. It was nice. It wasn't any special deal. They just choose people at random."

"Are you on this trip alone?"

Brodie figured that was coming next. "Uh. Yeah." He didn't have to explain anything to them. What were they? His goddamn grandparents?

"Well, there are a couple of nice women at our table," one of the ladies informed him, which he took as a warning not as the promise of companionship she intended. "Glenda and Marlene. There's also

45

a young couple here on their honeymoon, Sandy and Bob. Very nice people."

Goodie. Brodie finished his wine.

As the room filled and the noise level cranked up, he kept his eye on the door for Julian. They were two large round tables apart, but ironically facing each other as they sat. A small commotion of greetings brought him back to reality. Glenda and Marlene descended on their group. Both were chubby, mid-forties, with short hair and light make-up. Brodie assumed they were a gay couple but was quickly proven wrong when the flirting began.

"Brodie did you say? That's a nice name." Marlene pointed to the empty chair that separated her from him. "Is your girlfriend coming?"

One of the old ladies butted in, "No dear, he's here on his own. A nice eligible bachelor."

Oh God, shoot me. Brodie reached for the wine bottle but the waiter beat him to it and poured for him. "I'll give you a fiver if you keep this thing filled all night." The waiter smiled knowingly.

"What do you do, Brodie?" Glenda leaned across her friend to speak to him.

"Computers. Nothing exciting." He gulped the wine trying to rush the effects of a good high.

"Do you live in Canada?"

"No. Washington."

"Oh, we're from Oregon." Glenda smiled sweetly. "Where in Washington are you from?"

About to scream at what was beginning to feel like a job interview, Brodie didn't know if he could take this every night for an hour or two. But it went against his grain to be rude. "Near Seattle."

"Oh." Just as Glenda geared up for another question, Brodie noticed the last two occupants of their table of ten arrive. The couple that were smooching in the whirlpool. Could life get any better?

An arm reached across him, pouring more wine. Brodie blinked in surprise. "Keep that up and I'll give you more than a damn five!"

The waiter laughed shyly.

At his joke, Brodie found everyone staring at him. "I was kidding." He shook his head, avoiding their curious gazes.

Sandy and Bob were introduced to him, as if he cared.

"We're on our honeymoon," Sandy crooned, her hand tightly clasped to her pudgy, short-haired hubby.

Nodding, Brodie figured that explained the pawing they were doing in public. "Congratulations." He smiled at them. Then he noticed Julian making his way to his table, Amelia beside him. The sharp ache in his gut made his amiable expression change. The moment Julian sat down, he immediately scanned the area. They caught eyes.

"Are you here alone?" Sandy asked.

Brodie was lost on a set of blue eyes gazing at him in longing.

"Yes, he is," Glenda whispered to her.

"That's cool, I guess. I would never have the guts to come on a ship on my own."

Bob nudged her to be quiet. Sandy pouted at the rebuking. "What?"

Brodie ignored them, pretending he didn't hear.

Salads appeared in front of them quickly as the waiters began the long process of feeding the massive crowd.

Watching Amelia touching Julian was making Brodie lose more than his appetite, his humor was leaving he room as well.

"Brodie lives in Seattle and works with computers," one of the old women informed the newlyweds.

"Oh." Bob nodded, eating his food with large mouthfuls.

His third glass of wine consumed, Brodie was finally feeling something he craved, being drunk. There wasn't any other way to handle this mess. His new lover was over there, smiling and being charming while that woman touched him, and this table of strangers no doubt wondered what the hell was wrong with him that he couldn't find a friend to take with him on a cruise.

Brodie thanked the waiter sweetly after the man filled his fourth glass of wine.

Glenda whispered, "I take it you're enjoying the wine…What about the food?" she added.

That comment he caught. Giving her a scolding look, he replied,

"Yes, I am enjoying the wine. I assume that's all right with you."

The table went cold.

"Yes!" Glenda waved her hands in a frantic gesture. "I didn't mean anything by it."

He shook his head, *Great, now I have my mother at the damn table.*

Slowly conversations between the other occupants seated with him erupted to low murmuring around him. Drunk. Yes. He was now drunk. The food was incredible, but he couldn't eat it. Two bites and he set his fork down, draining his glass. Those damn blue eyes kept finding his. Brodie was about to scream in anger. *Stop looking at me! Okay? You're sitting with your fucking whore! I bet you fuck her tonight!*

"Are you going to the cabaret show later?" Marlene inquired.

"Huh?" He was barely there, wishing he could cry into his pillows. "Show?"

"There's a cabaret event later in the Atlantic room. I love those shows. I think they said it was the best of Broadway, or something."

"Sounds great." Brodie couldn't stand it any longer. Before his dessert arrived, he pushed out his chair. "See you all. I'm heading out."

They waved, forcing smiles at him. He knew they knew he was stewed. They'd have a nice long chat about him after he left. Did they feel sorry for him? He didn't know, or care.

Imagining falling on his face, Brodie did his best to walk in a straight line on a shifting boat. It was in fact not a straight path and actually curved around other circular tables and happened to pass a certain person.

As he approached, Julian had an expression of fear that Brodie interpreted as "Don't come over here and say anything!" *Don't worry, I won't.* But they caught eyes, so much so, Brodie almost walked into someone seated in their chair dining contentedly. Moving aside at the last minute so as not to collide with the oblivious man, Brodie wanted to pause as he stumbled on his way, but the look in Julian's eyes told him to keep moving, which he did.

As he passed, he heard Amelia's tittering laughter. He cringed, managing to get out of the dining room without tripping.

Muttering profanity under his breath, Brodie cursed everything in the world that wasn't fair. The halls were almost vacant as everyone was dining leisurely. It was nearing seven. Twilight loomed above the horizon. Pausing at a window, Brodie gazed out at the black sea and their destination beyond. Alaska, the last of the wild frontier. Maybe he should stay there. Jump ship. Become a lumberjack.

A warm sensation seeped through his inebriated mind. Heat. Heat on his back. His focus moving from beyond the glass to the reflection in it, Brodie found another body silhouetted behind his. He spun around in surprise.

Julian whispered, "I only have a minute. She thinks I'm in the men's room."

"What do you want?" Brodie knew he was slurring his words, but he tried to pretend he was sober.

"You. I want you."

"And? You want me but you're sitting there with, what-the-fuck-her-name-is giggling and flirting. Gonna get laid tonight, Julian?"

"Shut up."

"Shut up?" Brodie laughed, looking around the hall.

"You stupid asshole." Julian peered over his shoulder in paranoia. "You think I can get you out of my fucking mind now?"

"I'm too drunk for this." Brodie rubbed his face. "I swear if you stay there I'm going to suck either your mouth or your cock."

Julian grinned. "You are so toasted."

"I know." Brodie shrugged, as if he were helpless.

"How about a quick smooch in the men's room?"

"You kidding me?" He felt his blood pump.

"Hurry."

Knowing he couldn't move his wobbly legs fast enough, Brodie followed that tight set of buns to the men's lounge. A few passengers where inside, washing their hands or standing at the urinals.

~

Julian knew if they went into a toilet stall together it would be spied. Did he care? He didn't know the answer to that question. Moving to the last one, Julian entered it, waiting. Brodie managed to get in it with him, struggling to close the door behind them. Julian had to move around the gaping toilet to give them room. The moment that door closed, Julian went for Brodie's lips. Tasting the red wine, having had had plenty of his own, Julian sucked on Brodie's tongue and teeth, missing him even though it had only been a few hours since they were together. When Brodie let out a long, deep moan, Julian shushed him, laughing at the insanity.

"Sorry. You just feel so good." Brodie ran his hands down to Julian's slacks, rubbing his erection.

"You're not interested in those women at your table, are you?" Julian asked between nibbles of Brodie's ear, his neck.

"Hm?" Brodie shoved his hand inside Julian's dress slacks, groping him hungrily.

"I mean, you won't go with one of them, right?"

"Right." Brodie paused, meeting his eyes. "What did you ask me?"

"Never mind." Julian wrapped around him again for another kiss. As he mashed tongues with Brodie, Julian felt his zipper open. A shiver rushed through him.

Brodie parted from Julian's mouth, kneeling down in front of him. When Brodie's lips surrounded his penis, Julian had to bite back his groan of ecstasy. Peering down, he realized that Brodie has his own cock out, jerking it as he sucked.

"Holy shit." Julian felt his anxiety being edged out by the thrill. Coming, his balls tensing up and his cock pulsating, Julian forced his eyes open to see Brodie ejaculating onto the tiled floor. Gasping for air, Julian couldn't prevent a sound of satisfaction from passing his lips. It seemed to echo in the tight space.

Brodie grinned up at him wickedly.

"Unreal," Julian whispered.

Standing, fastening his own zipper, Brodie hissed, "You better tell her you have a fucking headache."

Tucking his spent cock back into his briefs, Julian met those demonic, drunken eyes. "I will. Don't worry. Besides, that's what she always tells me constantly. Turnabout is fair play."

"You taste so fucking good." Brodie leaned against him heavily.

"I have to get back. I know how she gets."

"One more kiss."

Julian leaned forward, lavishing in the tongue swirling. It made him hard once again. Parting reluctantly, Julian whispered, "Let me get back. We'll meet in the morning, for our run."

"Eight?"

"Yes."

"Okay." Brodie opened the door of the stall, stepping out.

Julian held his breath wondering how many people would see them. As he exited, too many did. Grinding his jaw painfully at the obvious act of two men leaving the same damn toilet, Julian hurried out, avoiding eye contact at all cost.

~

Brodie paused as Julian gave him a last, loving smile before he reentered the dining hall. Okay, it wasn't perfect, but it was better than he expected. Sobering up slightly, Brodie decided it was time to explore all the nooks and crannies of this behemoth ship. One never knew what one could find. Anything was possible. He knew that better than most.

~

Julian sat back down at the table. Amelia was tipsy and laughing loudly.

"Julian, honey, Joe just made the funniest joke while you were in the men's room."

"Oh?" Julian wondered if the scent of Brodie's cologne was mingling with his. He could certainly smell it.

"Yes. What was it again? Something about Eskimos?"

Julian shook his head. "It's all right, Amelia. I don't have to hear it."

"There's a cabaret act tonight," she informed him. "Broadway musicals. I'd like to go."

Julian checked his watch. "I was hoping to go to bed early."

The amused expression on her face dropped to fury in two seconds flat. Julian knew Amelia didn't care who heard their disagreements, she'd certainly shouted at him in public more than once.

"I knew it." She guzzled more wine. "I told you you don't want to do anything I do. And you never even commented on my hair."

Hair? He paused setting back to see it. It was set in strange rings on top of her head, sprayed stiff with something resembling plastic coating. "Looks nice. Amelia, I'll go to the cabaret, I'm just a little tired."

Her expression softened. When she touched his leg he had wanted to shove it away. As if she didn't have the rights to it any longer. It took everything he had to resist getting her red painted fingernails off his body.

"You're always tired. You work out too hard. I told you not to run while we're here on the cruise." Facing the other couples at the table, she replied, "He thinks he has to run every day. I don't get it."

As several comments about the virtues of exercise versus the pain in the ass of working out began to ping-pong around the table, Julian dazed off and imagined crawling in bed with his new lover.

~

The cabaret was so cheesy Julian couldn't tolerate it. As the evening wore on and wore him out, he kept checking his watch hoping the stupid show would end. By eleven he was completely drained as Amelia clapped, her eyes lit up like two candles in a cave. "Babe," he whispered, "I'm dying here. I have to go lie down."

"But the show's not over."

"I know. Please. I'm completely wiped out. Can I just call it a night? You can stay. Hang out with Jenny and Paul." Julian pointed to a couple they had befriended that had been assigned to their dinner table.

"Go. I don't give a shit, Julian." She flicked her hand at him.

"Amelia, I'm trying. But my head's pounding and I'm about to drop dead."

"Bye."

He tried to sit there for another few minutes but his body and head were screaming for him to get horizontal. "See ya back at the room." He pecked her cheek.

She didn't react, just sat still with her eyes glued to the show.

Once he'd left the noisy auditorium, he felt even wearier. Rubbing his temples, craving a painkiller, Julian scuffed his feet to the cabin. After what had felt like a mile of walking the length of the ship, he opened the door to their stateroom, kicked off his shoes, and immediately searched for an aspirin. Swallowing two down, he undressed, looked over at the twin beds pushed together, and imagined separating them. No doubt when she finally made it to the room, she'd be noisy, flip on lights, anything to show him how annoyed she was. In just his briefs, he dropped down on the bed, falling fast asleep.

Chapter Six

Rising to his wake-up call, Brodie felt slightly hung-over, but he'd been worse. Lacing his running shoes, standing up and looking down at the tiny pair of white running shorts he had brought, he sighed tiredly. He never imagined the dilemma of hiding an erection in them. "What the fuck. He already knows I'm hot for him." Stuffing the key down the front of his briefs, Brodie left the cabin, on his way to the sports deck. On the climb up the staircase he overheard an older couple discussing the docking of the ship in Juneau. Frowning despite himself, Brodie imagined bypassing the tour in case Julian and Amelia were going as a couple.

Stepping out onto the breezy deck, Brodie rubbed his hands together for warmth and looked around. It was an enormous boat and there were several doors leading to the outer deck. Unfortunately he and Julian hadn't narrowed down the location. Too cold to stand and wait, Brodie began an easy warm up lap, hoping to find Julian as he did.

After completing a loop, Brodie began to get annoyed. He checked his watch. It was after eight. "Nice one." He assumed Julian was going to be a no show, and ground his jaw as he sped up to his normal running pace.

~

Moaning in agony after hardly getting any sleep, Julian rubbed his eyes. He remembered Amelia coming in at one in the morning, drunk, staggering, turning on all the lights in the room, and making enough noise to rouse him out of a very deep slumber. Checking his watch, seeing it was after eight, he cursed under his breath, jumped out of bed and pulled on his running gear.

Amelia was out cold on her side of the bed, her make-up smeared, her sticky ringlets crushed. Grabbing the room key, Julian jogged the length of the corridor, taking the stairs two by two.

~

Finishing his third lap, Brodie came upon Julian just as he was coming through a heavy metal door to the deck. Imagining running by him, making Julian sprint to catch up, Brodie reconsidered and stopped short. "Hey."

"Sorry. Go, don't stop." Julian began jogging.

Brodie caught up, trying to talk and breathe at the same time. "Overslept?"

"Yes. Sorry. Had a bad night."

"Did you?"

"You don't want to hear it."

"Wanna bet?" Brodie could tell Julian was laboring with the pace, so he slowed slightly.

"It's just crap, Brodie."

"If it's about you and Amelia I want to know. Are you all right?"

"Slept like shit."

"You want to stop?"

"No. Just go easy."

Brodie pulled back to a lazy jog.

"Sorry."

"No. It's all right."

"Anyway, we went to that stupid show last night."

"And?"

"Well, it sucked as far as I was concerned. I just wanted to hit the sack. I was exhausted. Amelia is a night owl. She gets off on dancing and partying all night."

"Let me guess…" Brodie smiled wryly, "twenty-one?"

"Ha ha. No. She's twenty-five, but she's still a party animal. I never was. I have no idea how she does it, but she can keep going until the wee hours of the morning."

"So? You were dancing all night?"

"No." Julian wiped at his dripping face. "I went to bed around eleven. I left her at the cabaret. She was furious. She had some other people there with her. There's a couple that sit at our table that are decent."

Brodie wanted to move faster. He hated the slow pace, feeling as if he wasn't getting a proper work out.

"Anyway, I went to bed, and when she clamored in at about one, she woke me up. I had a hard time getting back to sleep. I forgot to arrange a wake-up call. I'm surprised I managed to get up in time to run at all."

"Can we pick up the pace?"

"Sorry." Julian sped up.

"So? Where's the infamous Amelia now?"

"Still in bed. I figure she'll be out for hours."

"You sign up for that excursion?"

"Not yet."

"Want to go?"

After a pause in the conversation, Julian said, "She most likely won't be up for it."

"I'm not talking about her." Brodie almost shouted at him, but bit his lip.

"Oh."

They made another quick lap around the deck, passing everyone else in the process. Brodie was feeling pretty good. He's slept almost ten hours last night, and the slight woozy feeling from the booze had worn off, sweated out of his pores.

"Well?" Brodie wanted an answer.

"When I get back to the room, if she's still asleep, I'll leave her a note and we'll go."

"Okay." Brodie knew it was going to be a challenge getting to spend time with Julian. He was desperately trying to understand. He knew if Melanie had stayed on board, this connection never would have occurred, and he'd be catering to Melanie's every whim.

Running in silence, Brodie could hear Julian laboring, but it was up to Julian to slow on his own or stop. Brodie tried to be sympathetic. And he would have been if the reasons hadn't involved the dreaded girlfriend.

Twenty minutes later, Brodie halted, catching his breath, leaning over, hands on his knees. Julian looked to be in agony, dropping down on the floor of the ship, lying on his back, his knees bent and the sweat pouring from his skin.

Brodie recovered quickly, using his shirt to wipe his face.

"Come on, old man." He reached down to Julian.

Julian clasped his hand and was hauled to his feet. "I hate it when I feel this way. I love the run and this one sucked."

"Too tired for the Jacuzzi?"

Julian checked his watch. "That excursion leaves at ten."

"Okay. Let's head to the lobby and see if we can still sign up." Brodie held open the door for him. As Julian passed through, Brodie caught a whiff of his sweat. "Damn, you smell good."

Julian gave a breathy laugh as he tried to recover from the exertion.

Walking behind him, Brodie salivated over Julian's tight ass, sweat soaked shorts, and shirt. Unable to resist, he went for a light squeeze of his bottom.

Julian choked in surprise and spun around. "Bad boy!"

"You have no idea." Brodie grinned, falling in beside Julian as they hurried down the endless corridor to the stairs.

~

Standing in line at the reception desk, Julian wiped at the tiny droplets that continued to run down his face. "Yes, uh, we were wondering if we could join the tour."

"It's completely full. Sorry."

Julian made a sour face at Brodie.

"But," the clerk said, "you can explore the town on your own. Just be back on board by four pm."

Julian checked Brodie's expression. He shrugged. They stepped away from the desk to allow the next person in line to approach. Julian whispered, "I'd rather do that. I mean, do you really want to be on a bus with a bunch of senior citizens?"

"You want to check on your other half before we make any type of plan?"

"Yes. Go shower. I'll meet you back here at the lobby."

"What if she's with you?"

"She won't be. I'll get out either way to let you know."

Brodie checked his watch. "An hour?"

"Okay."

Brodie winked at him as they walked to the staircase descending to the main level where their rooms were located. When it appeared

Brodie was going to lean over for a peck goodbye, Julian shook his head, smiling. "You really are something."

"Hey, just a quick one on the cheek." Brodie checked the vacant halls.

Julian did as well. Feeling sure they weren't being spied, he kissed Brodie on the lips.

"Damn!" Brodie exaggerated a shiver. "Instant hard-on."

Julian spied Brodie's hand as it cupped his crotch.

"Stop or we'll never get out of here."

"Come to my room. Shower with me."

"Are you kidding?" Julian laughed sadly.

"No. Go see if she's still sleeping. If she is, grab your shit and come to my cabin."

Julian wanted to. Very badly. "What if she wakes up?"

"I'll give you ten minutes. If you're not here, I'll go clean up and meet you in an hour upstairs."

"Okay." Catching Brodie's excited smile, Julian prayed Amelia was in a coma-like sleep. He hurried to his room and silently opened the door. It was dark in the interior since there was no porthole. As quietly as he could, Julian turned on a light in the bathroom, keeping the door partly closed so no light hit Amelia's bed. She was still out, her breathing deep and loud.

Tiptoeing to the closet, Julian held his breath as he removed clean clothing from it. Hearing Amelia stir, he froze. She shifted and rolled over, but didn't wake. Setting his handful of things by the door, Julian wrote a quick note to her on the ship's stationary.

"Didn't want to disturb you. Went to Juneau for a look around. See you at dinner."

He knew she'd be furious, but she'd be even more upset if he woke her up. Biting his lip, grabbing the key, shutting off the bathroom light, Julian crept back to the door and opened it. Pausing at the click of the latch, he waited. She didn't move. Once he was out in the hall, he gathered up his clothing better so nothing dropped out his hands, and was about to race to Brodie's cabin when he found him standing in the hall.

"Go," Julian whispered, gesturing for him to move.

Brodie jumped up in glee, removing his key from his shorts and rushing to his door. As if they were thieves, they slipped into Brodie's cabin, shutting it tight behind them.

The moment they were alone, Brodie pinned Julian to the door, cupping his jaw in both hands and kissing him. Julian's body covered in chills. Dropping the items of clothing he had been clutching to his chest, he gripped Brodie's hips and began grinding against them.

~

Loving the feel of Julian's coarse, unshaven jaw in his palms, the heat from Julian's body as it pressed tightly to his, Brodie knew he could go completely wild on this man. It was rough, aggressive, and so exciting he was already gasping for breath and his heart was pounding under his ribs.

Moving his hips side to side, he felt his cock riding over Julian's and back again. The friction was making him delirious. And Julian's tongue spun in dizzying circles around his, giving his tongue head and sending zinging sensations to the tip of his penis.

Needing to breathe deeply, Brodie parted from the kiss to groan, "Julian, I just can't get enough of you."

"I know. It's crazy." Julian held onto Brodie's bottom, a hand on each cheek, and humped him hard.

Seeing Julian's eyes seal shut, his teeth clench, Brodie started dragging Julian's shirt over his head. Julian raised his arms high, assisting Brodie in taking it off. Brodie took the opportunity to trap Julian's extended wrists in his left hand, smoothing his right all over Julian's bare chest. Julian vocalized his enjoyment in the most exquisite little whimpering moans Brodie had ever heard.

Brodie went for his right nipple, licking it, followed by a playful nip. Julian's groans grew louder, his weight shifted from side to side. Brodie released his wrists, digging his fingers into Julian's gym shorts. Julian dropped his shirt to the floor, held Brodie's face, and kissed him again. Deep sucking kisses that screamed for more taste, scent, and satisfaction.

With both hands Brodie grabbed Julian's cock straightening it from where it had been bent down the leg of his shorts. Gripping the base tightly with one hand, moving between Julian's legs with his other, Brodie felt Julian's balls tighten at his touch and the delicious sweaty heat between Julian's legs. As Julian widened his stance, his lips went slack. Brodie backed off from their kiss to see his expression. Watching Julian's handsome features morph into one of ecstasy, Brodie pumped Julian's cock in his fist and massaged Julian's balls. All the while he played with Julian's body, his own was going berserk trying to deal with the yearning for penetration and satisfaction.

Craving Julian's taste, Brodie dropped to his knees, taking the tight shorts down Julian's thighs to his ankles. Once Julian was exposed, Brodie lapped at the tip and that glistening drop that shimmered out. The salty sweat, the masculine scent, made Brodie moan. When he did he felt the vibrations shudder through Julian's cock.

"Holy fuck," Julian whimpered.

Sucking him as deep as he could, almost to the base, Brodie wiggled his tongue underneath it, feeling the engorged vein, all the way to the head, where he tickled and circled the tip of his tongue wildly. Julian's cock pulsed, hardening to rock.

Brodie dug under his balls to his ass, pressing against it. Instantly Julian ejaculated, his body tensing up, his knees giving out.

~

Unable to function for a few moments, Julian's palms were flat against the door, holding him upright. Forcing his eyes to open, Julian gazed down at Brodie. His eyes were closed as he lapped at Julian's cock gently, holding it now in both hands.

Julian had never experienced a climax that intense. Never. It made his heart pound harder than their run. Swallowing down a dry throat, licking his lips and tasting the salt from both of their sweaty faces, Julian watched Brodie finally open his blue eyes, staring up at him. As if something in that handsome face flipped a switch, Julian shoved him back onto the carpet roughly. Gasping at the surprise of the movement, Brodie fell back, reaching out his arms to brace his fall. Julian wrenched the damp gym shorts down Brodie's body as he raised his hips to assist. Once they were off, tossed aside on the floor, Julian got a good eyeful of that large, engorged cock. Before he went down on it, he sucked his index finger, wetting it as

Brodie's chest rose and fell in anticipation. Julian had no idea what Brodie would do, but he knew damn well he wanted to penetrate him, get inside. *Christ, don't gay men butt fuck? There has to be something to it.* And the pressure of Brodie's finger on his own ass had been enough to make him spurt. A come button. Press it and presto, ejaculation. What was that all about? He needed to find out.

As Brodie reclined, his knees bent and straddled, his arms planted on the floor in apprehension, Julian first held the base of Brodie's cock, running his palm up and down its length. As their eyes locked gazes, Julian found that opening. Pushing passed the tight ring of muscles, he pressed against Brodie's scrotum, massaging it.

Brodie's eyes rolled back in his head. His lips parted, his eyes sealed shut, and his hips elevated off the floor. Julian smiled. *Yes, I knew it.*

"Faster," Brodie hissed, pumping his cock through Julian's hand.

Julian knew he could do even better than that. He crouched down, opening his lips, allowing Brodie to fuck his mouth. Fingering Brodie's ass, sucking hard on his dick, Julian instantly tasted come. Closing his eyes in satisfaction, Julian drained him, loving to please him, and loving more than that as well.

~

Brodie was in shock. Nothing had ever been stuck up his ass before. Never. *Holy shit. What was that all about?* Blinking, seeing Julian's wry smile, Brodie tried to swallow down a parched throat. "Next time, I want that to be your dick."

"Yeah?"

"Yes! Julian! Jesus Christ!"

"I had a feeling."

"So did I! A feeling I can't describe."

"Let's shower, babe. It's getting late." Julian stood, reaching down for Brodie.

Brodie took off the rest of his workout clothing. "Julian, I…"

Julian paused after he turned on the water in the shower.

Stopping short at those adorable baby-blues, Brodie closed his mouth.

61

After climbing into the stall, Julian wet down under the spray. "What were you going to say?"

"Never mind." Brodie found a bottle of shampoo and squeezed some into his palm.

Swapping places, they scrubbed clean and kept silent. Brodie kept losing himself on Julian's chest, abs, rounded shoulders, long runner's legs. His cock began bobbing in response.

He wanted to stick his dick so deep inside Julian, his balls would slap Julian's ass. Just the thought of getting inside that handsome man's body sent him into heat.

Julian rinsed his face, wiping the water from his eyes. He looked down, smiling. "Are we insatiable or what?"

At the comment, Brodie found his erection mirrored on Julian. He started to laugh, soon roaring with it. Joining him in the hilarity, Julian rested his hands on Brodie's shoulders, trying to contain his own laughter.

The moment they touched, Brodie embraced him connecting them under the water all the way to their knees. Closing his eyes as the elation turned to passion, Brodie suddenly felt afraid, as if he was growing too fond of this man. As a shiver of anxiety washed over him, like the cascading shower, Brodie felt his cock being handled. Peeking down between them, he found Julian had both of their cocks in his grip. The sight of their two protruding penises rubbing together in Julian's large hands sent a shiver down his back. Brodie began moving his hips in time with Julian's stroking, as Julian did the same. Holding onto Julian's biceps for balance, Brodie couldn't get enough of that sensation, their cocks rubbing together in the tight grip of Julian's palms. Thrusting aggressively upwards, Brodie soon began to rise once more. "Come with me...come."

"I'm there, I'm there," Julian gasped.

Brodie let go, sending his sperm against Julian's tight abdomen as he felt Julian's hot come hitting him. Once again, struggling to gasp for breath, Brodie felt emotion catch in his throat. Impulsively he embraced Julian, rocking him side to side. He wanted him. He wanted him very, very badly.

~

Dressed in jeans, a long sleeve t-shirt, and a leather jacket, Julian descended the gangplank to the cement barrier and dry land. Brodie right behind him, Julian paused as he stood on terra firma, turning over his shoulder to laugh, "Christ, my legs are wobbling."

"How bizarre." Brodie stood still.

"Sea legs?" Julian asked.

"I don't know. It's just weird."

"Well? Where should we start?"

"Look at that." Brodie pointed. "There's a fucking Starbucks."

Julian searched the tiny main street and did indeed see the familiar logo. "Cool. Coffee?"

"Excellent."

As they strolled together to the center of town, Julian wanted to hold Brodie's hand. It just seemed right. Seeing several passengers from their boat lingering around in every corner of the tiny village, Julian had to be content just to brush Brodie's shoulder gently. He opened the door for Brodie and was hit with the pungent aroma of strong ground coffee. Finding a place in line, Julian felt his stomach rumble hungrily since they had played with each other through breakfast and missed their chance to eat.

As they approached the counter, Julian eyed the croissants hungrily. "Yes, I'd like a double latte and one of those ham and cheese croissants." He tilted back to Brodie. "I got it, order what you'd like."

"Thanks. I'll take the same."

The woman behind the counter nodded. "You want it heated up?"

The men exchanged looks, shaking their heads. "Nah," Julian replied, too hungry to wait.

Stepping aside, they watched as their food was set on plates and their coffee was made with a hissing of the espresso machine.

"I feel like I'm back in Seattle," Brodie whispered.

"I know. It does feel like that."

Taking their order to a table, Julian sat down, opened the lid of his coffee, sprinkling a packet of sugar in it.

Brodie devoured the sandwich quickly with big, macho bites.

Since he was just as famished, Julian wasn't shy either. The food down to flaky crumbs in seconds, Julian stirred his steaming cup, waiting for the coffee to cool off enough to sip.

"Where should we go after this?" Brodie blew the rising mist off his own cup.

"I don't know. I suppose just a stroll around town. Do you want to see anything else? I guess we could get a cab or something."

"Nah. Not really. I agree, just a stroll around the shops."

Nodding contentedly, Julian noticed Jenny and Paul enter the coffee house. "Crap."

"What?" Brodie twisted to look over his shoulder.

"Just spotted one of the couples from our dinner table walk in."

"And?"

"I don't know. Nothing." Julian had left Amelia a note saying he was coming into town. He shouldn't feel paranoid at being seen with Brodie. Another woman, yes. Not another man.

"Julian!" Jenny gushed when she noticed him.

Julian tried to smile. "Hi, Jenny. Paul."

Jenny looked around the small interior. "Where's Amelia?"

"She was still in bed. Late night."

"No! Did she stay at the dance club all night? Paul and I left a midnight. I can't believe she kept going."

Grinning tightly, Julian replied, "Yes, she's a regular dancing queen." Seeing Paul and Jenny staring at Brodie, Julian cleared his throat, "Uh, this is Brodie. He's on the cruise too."

"Hello, Brodie." Jenny reached out to shake his hand. "I'm Jenny and this is my husband, Paul."

"Nice to meet you." Brodie shook both their hands.

"I take it your significant other is out like a light still as well."

Julian winced slightly. In some place in his mind he wished Brodie would lie, but that may lead to complications down the road.

To Julian's amazement, Brodie didn't reply at all. Instead he changed the topic. "Anything worth seeing here in Juneau?"

Paul spoke up. "I was just going to get a Starbucks t-shirt that says Juneau on it. I don't think anyone I know would believe there's one out here in the boonies."

"I figured as much." Brodie sipped his coffee. "There's nothing to see except mountains and grizzlies."

"Yipes!" Jenny made a face in fear. "No thanks!"

"See ya later," Julian waved, smiling, wanting them to leave. He stood, gathering up their trash to toss out.

The couple smiled back, walking to the long line at the counter.

"Let's go." Julian picked up his cup, swigging the remainder of his coffee.

Brodie did the same, stuffing the empty into a trashcan. As Julian left he found the couple staring at them. He gave a friendly wave and followed Brodie outside.

"I had a feeling if we stayed in there they'd sit with us." Julian zipped up his jacket.

"Even if they tell Amelia you were out here with me, I can't imagine her getting suspicious." Brodie paused, adding, "Unless you have gay tendencies she's aware of."

Julian studied Brodie's expression to see if he was serious. He certainly appeared serious. "Are you trying to piss me off?"

"No!" Brodie nudged him and they began walking down the road checking out the touristy stores that lined either side.

"Gay tendencies? What the hell is that supposed to mean?"

"I don't know. Like looking at naked men in the ads for cologne? Renting *Brokeback Mountain*?" Brodie teased.

"Shut up," Julian laughed.

"Why the hell did you ask me if I liked that movie? Man, you really amaze me. If I wasn't interested, I would most likely have hit you."

Julian shrugged. "I suppose it was a chance worth taking. And I wasn't wrong. Your dick was so hard I knew you had to be interested."

"Damn thing always gives me away. It's got a mind of its own."

"Yeah? What's it thinking now?" Julian grinned wickedly, brushing up against Brodie's arm.

"It wants to screw you. Hard."

"Mm! Nice."

"I have rubbers."

"So do I." Julian's smile stayed on his lips.

"We need lube."

Stopping short, Julian met Brodie's light eyes. "Shit."

"We have to get some."

"Oh God, no way." Julian shivered in exaggeration. "I can't. You get it."

"Come on, grow up."

"Grow up? Are you joking? Can you imagine Paul and Jenny seeing us together, buying lube?"

"No one will know."

"I'll let you do it."

Brodie postured right there in the street, puffing out his chest. "Look, Julian, I'm not going to be the one. It's not fair."

"It's better a guy buying it alone, than two guys buying it together!" he gasped, looking around in paranoia.

"Get lost. I'll fucking do it." Brodie looked up and down the strip for a drugstore.

"Hey, you don't have a crazy woman to deal with if someone sees you. Can you imagine what Amelia would do to me if she heard I bought lube? Give me a break, Brodie."

"I said I would do it. Now shut up. Where's the fucking store?"

"No clue. Let's keep walking."

~

Brodie noticed a corner shop and pointed it out. "How about in there."

"I have no idea. Go take a look."

"You're not even coming inside the store?"

"Are you kidding?"

"Jesus, Julian, I didn't have you pegged for such a chicken shit."

"Really?" Julian challenged, "And if the shoe were on the other foot and Melanie was here somewhere? And word got back to her that you bought a tube of lubrication—"

Brodie held up his hand. "I get it. Wait here."

Pushing back the swinging door, Brodie's eyes adjusted to the interior. The store had a 1950s feel to it, and had most likely been built in that era. A wall with shelves was stocked with animal feed, farm tools, flashlights, and batteries. Brodie kept looking. Down another aisle he noticed shampoo and baby diapers. Slowing down, taking a closer look, there was baby powder, cotton swabs, toothpaste... *Condoms, condoms, it has to be near the damn condoms.*

"Can I help you find something?"

At the man's voice, Brodie felt his gut freeze. "Uh..." Then he found them. The condoms were behind the man at the counter, along with cigarettes. *Shit.* Brodie approached the man slowly as if he were about to be executed. *Why is this so fucking hard? Does lube instantly mean gay? Don't straight couples ever use it?* He was clueless. He'd never bought a tube before in his life. In a moment of bravado, he told himself he made women wet. So, no need for lube.

Seeing a few other people were in the shop, but not standing near him, Brodie pretended he was still undecided until he spotted the familiar logo on a box. *There it is. Now ask for it.*

The man looked at him strangely. Obviously a local, he was big, burly, wearing plaid flannel, sporting a dark beard with wiry white hairs standing out of the brown shade, and deep creases in his forehead. This was no girly-man. He was the kind that killed girly-men for sport.

"Uh, how about a package of that chewing tobacco," Brodie pointed to a disgusting box of the tar. "Uh, those condoms, the Trojans, you know the one's with the ribs to please the ladies." He grinned as if he meant it. "Oh, and how about a tube of that KY shit?"

The man set the items on the counter. "That it?"

"Yeah." Brodie's heart pounded in his chest.

"Nineteen dollars and fifty nine cents."

Brodie handed him a twenty.

"Hiya, Brodie!"

Jerking around to see Glenda and Marlene standing behind him, Brodie broke out in a sweat. The items were on display as the man made change of his bill.

"Uh, hi." Brodie did his best to block the view of the counter.

"Out here on your own?" Glenda pouted.

"Uh, no. Yes. No." Brodie looked over his shoulder as a paper bag was filled. Taking his change, he thanked the man, curling the bag in his fist.

Marlene giggled, "Yes, no? You don't know?"

"I, I met a friend. See ya at dinner."

"Some lucky lady?" Glenda tried not to snarl.

"See ya." Brodie waved and raced out of the shop.

Julian was waiting one door down at a gallery with Native American paintings in it. When their eyes met, Julian stood up from the wall he was leaning against. "You got it?"

"Yeah. What a fucking performance."

"Not as easy as you thought?"

Brodie shoved the bag at him, hitting him in the chest. "I bought it, you carry it."

Feeling the bottom of the bag, Julian asked, "What the hell else is in here?" He opened the top and peeked in. "I thought we both had rubbers…chewing tobacco?"

"Shut up. Throw the shit out." Brodie spied behind him quickly.

Julian removed the flat round can from the bag, starting to laugh. "Macho Man chewing tobacco?"

"Yeah, and ribbed rubbers, for 'her' pleasure. At least I got the damn lube."

Passing a trashcan, Julian was about to toss the tin in, instead set it on top of the receptacle. "Hey, maybe a poor local will want it."

"Yech. That shit's nasty." Brodie curled his nose. "Okay, we got what we needed. Wanna head back to my cabin and see how it works?"

Julian checked his watch.

"Come on," Brodie whined. "What if you were on a fucking tour bus? You wouldn't be back 'til four."

"Yeah, but Jenny and Paul know I'm not."

"For cryin' out loud!" Brodie shouted.

"Shh!" Julian peered around in panic.

"Who do you care more about, her or me?" Brodie put his hands on his hips, challenging him.

"Don't pull that. Please, Brodie." Julian shook his head.

Hearing what he had asked echoing in his own brain, Brodie felt very strange suddenly. Seeing a public bench, he made for it, needing to sit down. Once he was, he slouched low over his lap, covering his face in his hands.

~

Julian felt miserable. Planting himself next to Brodie, the tiny paper bag sitting on the opposite side of him, Julian made a good scan of their surroundings before he said anything. After what seemed like a long period of silence, Julian whispered, "You, okay? You—"

"I'm sorry I'm such an ass." Brodie rubbed his eyes until they were red. "I hate it when women become possessive, and I shouldn't be doing it to you. I have no idea why I asked you that."

Julian stuffed his hands into his jacket pockets deeply, his legs falling into a wide straddle. People came and went, some looking at them others not.

"I'm stuck at the moment, Brodie."

"I know." Brodie didn't stop rubbing his head and hair as if he had a headache and was massaging himself to relieve it.

"I can't even look at her anymore. I feel as if I'm betraying you."

That got Brodie's attention.

When Julian met his watery eyes, he nodded, "Yes!"

"Oh, baby," Brodie moaned, his hand moving as if to touch his leg, reconsidering and settling on his own.

Julian exhaled in a loud blast. "We've been on this cruise two days, Brodie, which leaves eight more to come. I have got to act normal for her. I know it sounds lame, but I don't want to kill her the way Melanie killed you. I can't be that mean."

"No. I know."

"Once we're back in Seattle, I can let her down easier."

Brodie nudged his arm.

Julian connected to his eyes again.

"You want to see me when we get home?"

His lip trembling slightly at the thought that Brodie didn't, Julian asked weakly, "Isn't that kind of what we're discussing?"

Brodie twisted on the bench to face Julian full on, his leg tucked under him. "I don't know. So, this isn't just some crazy onboard fling?"

Julian didn't realize how crushed he would feel. "Is that how you see it?"

After what appeared to be an internal debate, Brodie seemed to burst when he said, "No!"

It was so loud, two passersby paused to stare. Julian averted their gaze. When they had left, he whispered, "You dork."

Brodie began giggling. "I didn't mean that. I mean, I did mean it. Shit, just shoot me."

Julian snuck a squeeze of Brodie's leg. "Look, Brodie, originally I didn't really expect much more than a little fun, maybe some mutual jerking off…"

"And?"

"Well…the problem I'm having is I keep wanting to try more." Julian felt his cheeks grow warm.

"Yes. Exactly. I want to feel your dick up my ass."

"Shh!" Julian covered his laughter. "You realize they probably skin homosexuals alive up here?"

"Julian, it's more than that."

Hearing a serious tone coming from Brodie, Julian looked him in the eyes again. "What do you mean, more? Like in…"

Nodding, Brodie whispered, "Like in, I like you. A lot. Not just for your body, though I'm addicted to it now. But I think you're awesome. I just feel as though we click. Am I nuts?"

Smiling shyly from the compliment, Julian replied, "If you're nuts, so am I. I just worry about it. You know. I didn't intend on coming on a cruise, losing my virginity to a man, and falling for him."

Brodie blinked his eyes in surprise. "Yeah? Falling?"

"Yeah. Asshole."

Brodie let out a hissing whistle, sat facing the street, slouching on the bench with his legs spread wide. "Falling?"

"Shut up. Don't let it go to your head."

"It already is. The head of my dick. I'm hard as a rock."

Julian's cock twitched at the comment. "Don't get us started. We're in Juneau, for God's sake. We ain't in Kansas anymore, Dorothy."

"I want to shove you down on your face on my bed and stick my dick so far up your ass you taste my come in your mouth when I orgasm."

"Sounds painful." Julian winced.

"Oh no, it won't hurt. I promise."

Julian pushed at his crotch as it swelled.

Brodie's eyes darted to the act. He jumped to his feet, reaching out his hand. "Let's go."

Julian stood.

"Get that bag." Brodie pointed to it. "I risked life and limb for the thing."

Grabbing it, stuffing it into his jacket pocket, Julian nodded. "If we do it, we better be quick. It's after one and I know Amelia will be up and looking for me, or throwing darts into a picture of me. One or the other."

"We'll be quick. I'll get you worked over in an hour."

"Wow." Julian shivered. "Sounds like you have a plan."

"I do." Brodie grabbed Julian at the elbow to hurry him up.

Julian kept his eyes alert to anyone who sat at their dining table. He felt as if he was playing with fire.

~

Brodie pushed Julian up the gangplank, rushing him. At one point Julian's ass was in front of his face and it was all he could do to not nip at it. Showing their boarding pass to the man at the top, they slipped quickly into the elevator and pushed the button down to the main floor cabins. The door opened, Brodie poked his head out, looked both ways, grabbed Julian's hand, and began running down the long corridor.

Coming to a crashing stop at his door, Brodie panted as he shoved the key into the slot, opened the door, yanking Julian inside. The beds were made with a fresh towel shaped as a swan on each.

"That's cool." Julian pointed to one.

Brodie pushed Julian's jacket off his shoulders anxiously. "Get naked."

Julian tossed the paper bag on the bed, hurrying to shed his clothing. Brodie stripped first, shoving the terrycloth bird to the floor and peeling back the spread. With his hands trembling in excitement, he dug inside the bag for the rubbers and the box of lubrication. Standing in between the twin beds, Brodie removed the large tube out of its outer box, and took two rubbers off the strip of twelve.

A warm hand cupped his ass. Brodie smiled broadly. "Hello."

"Hiya, big fella. Come here often?"

"I will be 'coming' here any minute." Brodie rotated around to face Julian. "Get over here." He reached for a kiss. When their lips connected, Brodie felt his cock bobbing eagerly. Savoring the dancing of tongues, spinning around each other, licking teeth, sucking hard, Brodie pressed Julian from behind, using his hand as it dug through his hair, feeling the kiss deepen to overt sexual foreplay. *God, kissing him feels so good!* Brodie couldn't get enough of Julian's mouth. His attention was brought lower as their cocks rubbed together, since they matched in height, they met side by side between their humping hips. Brodie pulled back from their kiss, arching his back, lifting Julian off his feet. "God, I can't get enough of you!"

Julian started laughing, "Put me down, you dork."

Brodie threw him back on the bed. "Let me fuck you, Julian. Please."

"Yes! I want it. I'm not stopping you." Julian spread his legs, asking, "Uh, like this? Face up?"

"Let me see." Brodie crawled between Julian's legs. "You have to be higher. Use a pillow under your back."

Julian grabbed two and stuffed them under his hips.

"Perfect." Brodie grinned at the sight between Julian's legs. "Oh, fuck it." Brodie was going to get on with the anal sex, but the lovely view distracted him. Nuzzling into Julian's balls, Brodie moaned and inhaled him in pleasure. "You hot mother fucker…"

Julian raised his hips in reflex, groaning in reply.

Stroking Julian's cock, slipping it in and out of his mouth quickly, Brodie sat back to stare at it again, wet and engorged. "Shit. I have to fuck you." He reached for the condom first. Pumping his own cock a few times to heighten his excitement, Brodie rolled the rubber on, picking up the tube to inspect. As Julian watched, panting, his hands flat on the bed beneath him, Brodie figured out how to open the seal. "Jesus, childproofing lube?"

"Huh?"

"Nothing." Having no idea what he was doing, Brodie squeezed the tube into his hand. A huge blob came out. He greased up his cock first. Since he had so much extra on his fingers, Brodie used some to spread on the rim of Julian's ass.

"*Ah...*" Julian raised his hips.

"Wow. I'm not even in you yet." Brodie's cock jumped in excitement.

Pushing his finger inside Julian, smoothing the slippery ointment in, Brodie watched Julian's face as his eyes shut and his mouth opened. Julian began rising and falling on Brodie's index finger. "Holy shit. Does it really feel that good?"

"Fuck yes."

Brodie removed his finger, positioning his cock to replace it. "Ready?"

"Yes."

Brodie pushed the head of his penis passed the tight ring of muscle. "Jesus Christ," Brodie moaned. Moving until he was completely inside Julian's body, Brodie felt so thrilled at the act he was stunned with the intensity, the pleasure, the closeness, everything that made making love the most amazing thing two people could share. As his hips stilled, Julian's came alive. As if he couldn't resist, Julian pumped up and down on Brodie's cock. Throaty gasps came out of Julian's lips. As if waking from a dream, Brodie got busy, thrusting deep and long into Julian's body.

"Christ, touch my cock, touch my cock," Julian begged.

"No! You are going to fuck me." Brodie clenched his teeth as the sensation rose in him to unbelievable heights. Looking down at Julian's swollen dick, his expression of complete bliss, Brodie convulsed in an ejaculation that rocked him to the core. Pushing in as deeply as he could, Brodie felt his cock throbbing inside Julian's hot hole. Grinding his jaw, imagining the veins in his neck bulging from his climax, Brodie finally exhaled as if he were holding his breath. "Oh my God..." He hung his head, feeling the aftershocks washing over him.

Opening his eyes, pulling out gently, Brodie whispered, "You have got to feel that."

"Are you kidding me?" Julian laughed. "You have any idea what it feels like to be fucked like that?"

"No, but I will." Brodie tore off the rubber, dropping it on the floor. "Get up, swap places."

Julian rolled over, standing on the floor as Brodie lay down eagerly. The pillows under his hips, Brodie nodded. "Go for it."

Sitting on the bed, Julian unwrapped a rubber, putting it on himself quickly. When he knelt between Brodie's legs, Julian smiled wickedly.

"Nice view, huh?"

"Yes." Julian held his own cock by the base.

"Lube!"

"Oh, right." Julian reached for the tube. "Sorry."

Brodie laughed at him. "Used to wet women, I know."

"Shut up." Julian squeezed the tube and it made a spitting noise. "That was the tube. Not me."

"Duh."

"Hang on." Julian bit his lip and Brodie felt his cool slippery finger being inserted inside him.

Brodie's eyes sprang open. "Holy crap!"

"See!" Julian finger-fucked him faster.

"Oh my God." Brodie felt his cock go rock hard again as the chills washed over his body like a tsunami. "Use your cock!"

"My pleasure." Julian spread Brodie's legs wide, placing the tip of himself against Brodie's ass. "Okay?"

"Yes." Brodie waited. Soon a sensation of heat passed inside him. With it was intense pleasure. "I am absolutely amazed, Julian. No one tells you about it."

"No. A well kept secret." Julian pushed in deeper. "Ah...*ooh* yes."

Brodie closed his eyes as Julian established a rhythm. Riding it with him, his hips moving on their own, Brodie closed his eyes as the connection made him want to weep. He loved this guy. No one made him feel like this. *Love? Lust? Who cares, I want him!*

Unable to prevent it, Brodie grabbed his own dick and began jerking it. It seemed the minute Julian witnessed that action the hotter he became. The penetration became deeper and harder. Hearing Julian's pre-orgasmic grunts, which Brodie was beginning to recognize and cherish, he quickened his hand, spraying his come all over his chest just as Julian pumped it into his body. A chorus of oohs and ahs followed. Slowly Brodie felt Julian disconnect from him. As Julian removed the used condom, Brodie kept stroking himself gently, feeling the last vibration continuing to rattle his genitals.

They were dripping in sweat.

Julian gathered his breath, sitting back on his heels. He ran his hand inside Brodie's thigh, caressing it lovingly. "You believe this?"

"No."

Julian shook his head. "I love it. I must be completely gay, because I can't imagine touching a woman after touching you."

"Good."

"You trying to get that thing hard again? Three?" Julian laughed tiredly.

"Looking at you is such a fucking turn on." Brodie smoothed his hand up and down his own cock gently.

A demonic expression appeared on Julian's handsome face. He leaned over Brodie's hips and began licking the spent come off his chest.

Brodie lit on fire, a raging inferno of passion. Closing his eyes, tilting his head into the blankets, Brodie felt like sobbing at the strong sexual attraction he felt for Julian and didn't know why.

~

Julian knew it was growing late and he needed to go. Amelia would be worried, fretting, angry, furious.

Licking the puddles of come off Brodie's taut chest and stomach, tasting the essence of his masculinity, Julian just couldn't leave. Not yet. What was another ten minutes?

Once he had lapped up every drop, he sat up, smiling in satisfaction. His smile drooped when he noticed the single tear running down Brodie's cheek. A dagger passed through Julian's chest. Julian lay his body down on top of Brodie's, kissing his neck and ear. "What is it? What happened?"

"Nothing."

Julian ran kisses along Brodie's jaw, his high cheekbone where the salty drop had come to a halt. He kissed it too, tasting it off his lips. "Tell me."

Slowly Brodie moved his head so they could see one another's eyes. The expression on Brodie's face made the breath catch in Julian's throat. Brodie didn't have to say it. Julian could read it so clearly. "Don't worry."

A sad smile curled the edges of Brodie's lips.

"I mean it." Julian hugged him, wriggling playfully on Brodie's soft cock.

"Don't you have to get going?"

It was a dry comment, but it cut deep. Julian lowered his eyes. "Eight days." He sat up, moving to the side of the bed.

"What happens then?" Brodie challenged, "We live happily ever after? A gay couple?"

Julian shrugged. "I suppose that's up for debate."

Brodie reached out for him, sitting upright next to him. Julian held him against his chest. "Why do you worry yourself? We're still on a stinking ship. Don't do this now. Look, at least we live close to each other. I mean, you're not Canadian."

Feeling Brodie nod, Julian parted from their hug. "I do have to go. I know she'll rip me a new one."

"I know."

Julian stood, looking down at his body. "Geez, I need a shower, I have to smell like sex."

"Go. Rinse."

"You mind?"

"No."

"Wanna join me?"

Smiling, Brodie shook his head. "It'll take too long. You just go."

His grin falling to a pout, Julian nodded, stepping into the bathroom.

~

Hearing the water run, Brodie wiped at his eyes and wondered what was wrong with him. Why was he becoming so emotional? He'd never reacted this way with a woman. Never. He never told a woman he loved her either. The urge to say those three dreaded words to Julian was overwhelming him. "I'm such an idiot." He hated the fact that this wasn't just some fling, some experiment.

The entire idea of doing the "gay thing" from now on terrified him. It just didn't fit the image of who he thought he was.

He wanted Julian. There was no question there. Imagine that in your bed every night. Brodie groaned in agony and his cock once again attempted an erection, though he was exhausted. "You're gay. So what? Lots of guys are." Brodie argued with his own internal dialogue. What was the big deal?

~

Julian didn't wet his hair. That would be impossible to explain. Toweling off, he dried himself and wiped the steam off the mirror. His face was red. Taking a closer look, he found a slight rawness where Brodie's scratchy jaw had roughed him up during their kisses. Was it noticeable? He paused, backing up from his reflection. He could say it was windburn. Yes. That was it.

Stepping out of the bathroom, he spotted Brodie still in the same position on the bed. Quietly, knowing they both felt let down, Julian found his clothing in a pile on the floor and got dressed. When he was done, he picked up the two used condoms and threw them out. Grabbing his leather jacket, draping it over his arm, he stood next to Brodie by the bed. "I'll see you at dinner."

"Okay. Don't forget your workout clothes."

"Shit. Right." Julian knelt down to pick up the tiny damp pile by the door. "Maybe I can convince her to go clubbing without me tonight."

"Okay."

Julian sat down, rubbing his hand over the soft dark hair of Brodie's leg. "I feel terrible."

"Don't. I understand."

"I won't touch her. It's over that way between us."

Brodie didn't reply, but his eyes never left Julian's.

"I mean it."

"Okay," Brodie repeated tiredly.

"What are you going to do?"

"Catch a nap."

"I need one desperately. But I doubt I'll be that lucky."

Brodie didn't answer.

"I'll see you later." Julian leaned over and kissed him, noticing the same redness on Brodie's face. Rubbing his own jaw, Julian whispered, "We need to shave. We look raw from the kissing."

"Do we?" Brodie touched his upper lip.

"Yes. Windburn, got it?"

He smiled tiredly.

"See ya."

"See ya." Julian stood at the door, looking back at Brodie's beautiful, naked body. Brodie had curled into the pillows, shutting his eyes. Julian lowered his head, and left.

Walking to his cabin, he peeked in. It was vacant. Tossing the damp running clothing on the bed, he hung up his jacket, looking for a note of some kind. There was none. Sighing tiredly, Julian wanted a nap very badly, but figured he owed it to Amelia to look for her first. Having no clue where she would be, he yawned in exhaustion, beginning his search in the salon and shops.

At four o'clock a loud blast of the ship's horn sounded, letting everyone know they were heading out to sea. Julian looked everywhere. No luck. Dragging his feet, he returned to his room, shut off the lights, and dropped down on the bed, sleeping in an instant.

~

Deep inside a dream, Julian felt something intruding on his slumber. About to say Brodie's name, the scent of strong floral perfume filled his nostrils. Coming around, he found Amelia next to him on the bed, opening his trousers. "No, babe, I'm exhausted."

"Where were you all day? Did you take a tour?"

"No. I just walked around Juneau a little."

"On your own?"

"No. Some other people were there. Jenny, Paul..."

"I had a massage from a guy masseuse. I can't believe how horny it made me." She tugged open his slacks.

"No way, Amelia. I'm really tired."

"Aw, come on, Julian. We haven't had sex since we've been on the boat." She nuzzled into his neck.

"No, please." He closed his pants.

"What's with you?"

"I told you. I slept like shit last night. You came in at one, woke me up, and I couldn't get back to sleep again."

"Then why did you wake up so early? I slept in 'til eleven. You could have just slept in longer."

"I want to keep the running routine up."

"Well, screw you. Don't blame me then."

"I'm not blaming anyone. I just wanted a nap before dinner."

She crossed her arms and lay flat on her own side of the bed. "I'm not tired."

"Then go have fun and I'll meet you for the meal."

"You sure?"

"Of course."

"I was thinking about the casino. Once we're at sea they open it up."

"Okay. You have enough money to play with?"

"I'll just use your credit card."

He flinched slightly. "Uh, no more than a hundred, okay?"

"Fuddy duddy." She kissed his cheek. "See ya later."

"See ya." The door closed. He rolled to his back and wondered how he was going to keep making excuses not to have sex. Sooner or later she was going to suspect something. Rubbing his face tiredly, he felt his stiff sandpaper jaw. Sitting up, he motivated himself enough to get out of bed and shave.

~

After stepping out of the shower, Brodie stood at the sink and used a towel to wipe off the steam from the mirror. Checking his jaw, seeing the growth of new beard, he smeared cream on his face and shaved it off. Once he had splashed water to rinse the rest of the foam, he applied moisturizer on his skin. It still had a slight redness to it from Julian's dark shadow, but it only made him smile at the thought. "Windburn, my ass."

Brushing his wet hair, dabbing on some cologne, Brodie read the slip of paper that had come through the door for the evening's dress code. Formal. "Crap." Taking out his black suit, dreading a tie, Brodie decided to forgo formality, and put on a mock turtleneck instead of his white, starched dress shirt and neck tie. In his opinion the suit jacket looked perfect on top of the dark, soft shirt. Stepping into his slacks, Brodie felt excited at the prospect of seeing Julian decked out in his suit. Zipped, his belt fastened, his leather shoes on his feet, Brodie checked out his reflection in the mirror over the dresser. Touching his sideburns, smoothing a hand back through his thick, brown hair, Brodie stood back, twisting around and trying to check out his ass. "Nice, Mr. Richards? Tempting you? I hope now that you've been in it, you find it irresistible. I know I feel that way about yours." Pocketing the room key, Brodie wondered if the time Julian spent with Amelia reinforced his heterosexual side, and turned him against the idea of becoming a full time queer. "I have no idea what I would be doing in your shoes, Julian. But it must be mind-bending."

~

Still groggy from his nap, Julian rinsed his face of shaving cream. Stepping into the room he noticed the daily announcement sheet had been shoved under his door. "Formal. Fuck." Setting the paper on the dresser, he sighed tiredly and took his suit out of the closet. "I better not hear another word about a tuxedo. Not one word." As he changed into his suit, he checked his watch, wondering if Amelia would figure out on her own that it was another formal night and she had to dress accordingly. She had a selection of gowns that would shame a prom queen. Obviously Amelia knew what to expect on this cruise. He hadn't a clue they had nights that demanded that type of attire. If it were up to him, he'd never change out of his jeans or gym shorts.

Knotting his tie in the mirror, noticing that slight redness still present on his face, Julian couldn't help but smile. "Windburn, ha. Yeah, right. Beard burn, baby. Beard burn."

Just as those thoughts rushed to his cock, the door swung open. Amelia smiled smugly. "Won a hundred bucks!" She waved the cash.

"Cool. Break even?"

"Uh, no." She set the money down sheepishly.

"No? How much did you lose?" She mumbled a number under her breath. Julian didn't hear it, wondering if he was meant to. "Amelia?"

"Three."

"Three? Three hundred? You lost three hundred?"

"Well, here's one back." She handed it to him.

He shook his head at her in disapproval, sticking the cash into his wallet. Avoiding the scream he felt welling up in his chest at how easily she abused his bankroll, he grumbled, "It's formal tonight."

"I know! You needed a tuxedo!"

Throwing up his hands in frustration, he snarled, "I'm getting a drink. See you up there."

"See ya!" she sneered back. As he shut the door he heard her mutter, "Asshole."

The urge to push the door back and shout, *Asshole? You mean the asshole who paid for this cruise and who just lost two hundred from your little gambling session?* Instead, he shut the door and walked down the hall.

Knowing he was early and they didn't open the dining room doors until six, Julian headed to the nearest bar. On the same level as the dining room there were two lounges. Julian didn't care which, he just chose the closest. Walking across a wooden floor to the bar, he stopped short at the sight of a tall, dark, handsome man, all in black. His jacket covered a mock turtleneck shirt that showed off two powerful pecs underneath its soft material. His legs were long and the thighs of the slacks fit snugly over them. Julian had to tear himself away from the sight of Brodie's ass before his engines revved up so high he was stripping the hunk down and sucking his cock deeply into his throat.

As Julian approached from behind, unseen, he noticed two women chatting flirtatiously with him. Poor Brodie seemed slightly pinched at having to behave like a charmer. Something Julian knew must come very naturally to the delectable creature when in the right company.

Moving behind the object of his sexual appetite, Julian slid up to the bar almost, but not quite, rubbing up against the oblivious, Mr. Duncan.

"I loved Juneau. I thought it was very quaint." One of the large women sipped her colorful cocktail.

"It's so funny they have a Starbucks!" the smaller of the two giggled.

Brodie's deep tone sent the hairs standing on Julian's arms.

"I know. They're everywhere. I suppose you'd even find one in Moscow."

"Yes, a glass of red wine please." As Julian made his request, Brodie spun around quickly at the sound of his voice.

"Hello," Brodie purred.

"Mr. Duncan." Julian smiled, tongue in cheek.

"Alone?" Brodie looked around.

"For now." Julian signed his receipt, thanking the bartender, slipping the paperwork into his pocket.

Brodie stepped aside, introducing Julian. "These are two of my table-mates, Glenda and Marlene."

"Yes. Hello." Julian shook their hands.

Glenda leaned closer to Julian, saying, "You have the same windburn as Brodie. You should be careful. It's as bad as sunburn."

Julian hid his smile behind his glass of wine. "Yes. I should be more careful."

Brodie leaned against Julian's side, "Maybe some soft, slick cream would help?"

"Do you have some?" Julian asked innocently.

"Yes. I can let you borrow some. Maybe later? Come to my room?"

"That's very kind of you, Brodie." Julian pressed against Brodie harder, connected their shoulders and arms.

Marlene fanned herself and giggled. "I don't know if it's the margarita or just the sight of the two best looking men on the ship standing and talking to us!"

Brodie made an exaggerated gesture to look Julian over. "You think he's good looking?"

Marlene blushed, nodding.

"Huh." Brodie scratched his chin. "I suppose, in a pretty-boy sort of way."

"Don't start," Julian warned.

"Believe me, I haven't. Uh," Brodie put on his thinking face again, "there was something I wanted to show you in the gallery. A great snapshot of you and your girlfriend."

"Oh?" Julian smiled sweetly. "Are they up now?"

Glenda replied, "Yes. The ones from when we boarded. They're up."

Julian nodded. "Can you show me where they are, Brodie?"

"I'd be happy to. See you in a few minutes, ladies."

"Bye." They waved excitedly, turning to whisper into each other's ears excitedly.

Brodie hooked Julian's elbow, "You saved my life."

"Come on, they're sweet and harmless."

"True." Brodie sucked down his scotch, leaving the glass on a vacant table. "Which men's room?"

"The least crowded."

"I found one, a floor down. I had a good look around last night."

"Did you?" Julian finished his wine and set it on a table as he was ushered out of the lounge.

"Yes, you wouldn't believe the hidden nooks and crannies on this ship." Brodie nudged Julian to hurry.

They jogged down the stairs to a long narrow corridor. "There," Brodie whispered, "at the end."

Julian could sense the isolation of the spot. "Hey, not bad."

"Shut up and get in." Brodie opened the door.

Julian found it vacant. "We should still use a stall, just in case."

Brodie pushed open the last door. They jammed into it. The moment they did, Julian wrapped around Brodie's neck and connected to his lips. "I shaved," he panted between kisses.

"Me too." Brodie opened Julian's slacks, kissing him.

"Windburn," Julian chuckled.

"I'm going to give you palm burn in a second."

"Oh yes." Julian thrust his hips forward as Brodie reached inside his briefs.

"Christ, you have the most amazing cock," Brodie moaned.

"Compared to?"

"Shut up." Brodie kissed him again, trying not to laugh.

"Suck it."

Without another word, Brodie crouched down, wrapping his lips around Julian's dick. Bracing himself on the walls of the stall, Julian closed his eyes in reflex, having to force himself to open them to stare down at that fabulous man doing the sucking. "Oh, you are unbelievable, Brodie."

Brodie hummed in reply, sending a vibration along Julian's cock that sent his toes curling. Brodie paused, wetting his finger. Knowing what that meant, Julian prepared for the rocket launch. As that hand wormed its way between his legs, under his nuts, and inside his ass, Julian's cock throbbed in delight and yearned for that hot orifice once more. Poking Brodie with the head of his dick, Julian moaned pathetically.

Laughing, Brodie said, "Hang on. I'm here."

Julian realized Brody had taken his own cock out of his slacks. Just the sight of it dangling exposed sent chills washing over Julian's body. In the most incredible example of multi-tasking Julian had ever witnessed, Brodie had one finger up Julian's ass, sliding in and out, his other hand on his own cock, jerking off, and his mouth on Julian's penis, sucking it. Julian felt like a puppet to this man's mastery of the art. "I'm there."

Brodie quickened his hand in both places, shoving up into Julian's ass and fisting his own dick.

Arching, throwing back his head, Julian came as Brodie grunted with his mouth full. Slowly that index finger slid out, but Brodie kept his mouth on Julian's cock, sucking it dry.

Julian opened his eyes, blinking, looking down. A spatter of Brodie's come was on the tiled floor. "Christ, you're getting good at this."

After kissing the head of Julian's cock tenderly, Brodie stood upright, panting to catch his breath. "Did I get come on my pants?"

Julian leaned down to look, took a big lick of Brodie's cock to taste the oozing drop still lingering on the tip, shaking his head. "Nope. You're perfect."

Before they could close their pants, Brodie grabbed Julian's face and kissed him, licking at the mixture of wine, scotch, and come.

Then to Julian's astonishment, Brodie whispered, "I love you," in between his insatiable kisses.

The shock of those words rattled around Julian's head. Did he hear straight? Did he just hear what he thought he heard? Or was it wishful thinking? Or was it what was on the tip of his own tongue?

Wrapping around Brodie as tightly as he could, Julian connected their bodies together. Going mad for him, running kisses all over his face, his hair, his neck, Julian felt like he was burning up in flames.

Brodie slowed them down, holding Julian's hands in his. When their eyes met, it sent a shiver down Julian's length. "How can it be?"

"I don't know." Brodie shook his head.

"Are we insane?"

"Yes!"

"Brodie, you are so amazing."

Smoothing his hand over Julian's exposed cock, Brodie whispered, "You too."

"You don't think this is some trick of the cruise, you know, some holiday feeling?"

Brodie's face soured.

"No. I don't mean it that way," Julian explained quickly, grabbing Brodie's jaw. "I'm just scared."

"Me too. My fucking heart is pounding."

They heard a noise. Freezing where they were, the sound of someone's scuffing heels on the tile became audible. Water hitting a urinal. The urinal flushing. The sink. The blower. Then the door.

Exhaling, Brodie quickly closed his pants, tucking in his shirt as Julian did the same. They opened the door, peering out. It was vacant.

Standing side by side at the sink washing their hands, Julian looking over his appearance in the mirror.

"Shit."

Julian turned to ask why when he noticed Brodie wiping at a tiny drop of cream on his black trousers.

"Windburn."

Brodie looked up, caught his eyes, roaring with laughter. "Oh, baby, I adore you."

Crouching down to help, Julian licked his finger, rubbing at the spot. "I'd suck it off, but I'd leave a wet stain."

"Stop talking about sucking off or I'll be hard again."

"It's gone. Honest. You can't see it." Julian brushed his hand over it, getting a good feel of Brodie's cock underneath. "You are hard again."

"Whose fault is that?"

"Shit, it's after six. They've opened the dining room doors."

"Okay. Let's go."

Julian watched Brodie's ass as he walked down the hall. "You look absolutely incredible in that outfit."

"I was hoping to impress you."

"You have. Jesus, Brodie. You are so damn good looking."

"You took the words out of my mouth, babe." Brodie paused.

"Don't kiss me. I know it's right there, but don't." Julian pressed his hand against Brodie's solid chest.

"I won't. See ya."

"See ya." Julian frowned despite himself as Brodie jogged off, into the dining room. Inhaling, running his hand back through his hair to make sure it wasn't sticking up from their little tousle, Julian noticed the back of Amelia as she sat in their assigned seats. Hoping he wasn't in for a tongue-lashing, knowing nothing could compare to the one he had already gotten, he pulled out his chair and sat down.

"Where were you? I thought you'd be waiting for me. Why is your skin all red?"

"Windburn." He thanked the waiter for the wine as he poured.

"Windburn? You sure?"

"Yes. Now stop pestering me. What's the selection for tonight?"

She handed him the menu. As he took it, he looked across two tables to see a set of aqua eyes staring back.

~

"There you are!" Glenda waved as Brodie joined them. "I told you he would be here."

"I'm here." He smiled sweetly.

"Did you buy a photo?"

"Hm?" Brodie thanked the waiter for the glass of wine.

"You know," Glenda prodded, "you and that man, Julian? You were going to the gallery."

"Right. No, we didn't see any we liked."

Marlene leaned over Glenda to say, "There's a comedian and a magic act in the showroom tonight."

"Ooh, sounds great!" Brodie said sarcastically but it was lost on them. He picked up a roll from a basket, buttering it.

"You want to join us?"

"I'll let you know." He bit the roll, chewing, starving. A set of light blue eyes was watching him. He smiled knowingly, raising his glass to him.

Glenda looked around the room. "There's Julian!" She waved. "He has a pretty wife. Is that his wife?"

"No." Brodie sipped his wine.

"Oh." Glenda swallowed a piece of bread. "What are you getting?"

"Something tasty, no doubt." Brodie leveled his gaze at the gorgeous male brunette who couldn't keep his eyes off him this evening.

"I know. Everything is so good!" Marlene moaned.

"It is indeed." Brodie finished his wine.

When the waiter topped up his glass, Brodie remembered his promise. He stuffed a ten dollar bill into the young man's hand. "Thank you."

"My pleasure, sir."

Chapter Seven

Brodie decided on checking out the nightclub act. He did love stand-up comedy. Killing some time at the casino, he spent his twenty dollar quota and downed another scotch in the process. It wasn't so bad now. Being on his own. Knowing Julian had a noose around his neck, Brodie felt like he was the fortunate one out of the two. If, in fact, Julian was telling him the truth, and Amelia no longer had a claim on his body, Brodie wouldn't want to be the one having to make up excuses for the long week as to why they wouldn't make love, or even kiss. At least he hoped Julian was making those excuses. He trusted him. No way. If Melanie was with him, would he touch her now? *Uh, no.*

A thought occurred to him. He headed back to his room and tried his mobile phone. It was dead. He plugged it into the charger and stared at it in frustration. Leaving the room again, he remembered something else he had found on the night he made a complete survey of the ship, the internet.

One floor above the promenade deck was the library and internet service. Seeing a few passengers already on line, he looked around for an open chair. One left. He sat down, booted up the computer, sticking his credit card into the slot for some air time. Getting to Yahoo quickly, Brodie was surprised at how many emails were sitting unread in his box. He scanned the names, knowing some were work colleagues and could wait. He typed one to Paden, just to boast and tease him.

Hey, babe. I met a charmer on board. What a hunk, you would die. We've been delving into the Greek way of love. I love the chance to experiment with him with no strings attached. It's given me the chance to try out my wild side. I'll fill you in when I get home. Please, don't breathe a word to anyone. I would die of embarrassment, and after all, the women in my life wouldn't understand, would they? Pausing, biting his nail, trying to be funny, he ended it. *It's been a very interesting experiment. See you soon.* He hit send, smiling happily.

Before he logged out, he read the one from his mother. He had just bought her a computer for her fiftieth birthday and taught her the basics of email. His dad had a little knowledge of how to use computers from his job, but his mother had resisted until recently.

Hi, Brodie! I hope you and Melanie are enjoying your trip to Alaska. We should have joined you. I told your father it's one of the few vacations we could have done together. Next time. Give my best to Melanie. Call me when you get back. Love you!

Brodie couldn't even imagine typing her a message to explain what had happened. He reread hers again, biting his lip in frustration. "Oh, what the hell." Hitting the reply button, he wrote, "Having a great time, wish you were here. Kidding! Love you too." That was it. He hit send, logged off, and sat there staring at the icons as they vanished.

~

Julian searched for Brodie wherever they went.

"Oh, look!" Amelia gushed, "They have the photos up from when we boarded." She released his hand and craned her neck at the mass of pictures.

"Here we are! Oh, Julian, it's a nice one!" She took it down from the board. "What do you think? We should buy it."

"Sure." Julian shook his head sadly. It wasn't fair to the poor woman. He felt like the worst heel.

As she announced their room number to the attendant at the cash register, Julian noticed another photo. Brodie. Brodie boarding the boat with Melanie. "Holy shit." Moving to investigate it, he could see via their body language how bad it already was even at first board. Neither looked at the camera, or even knew it existed. They were both scowling and looking away from each other.

Amelia stood behind him. "I got it."

"Okay."

"Whatcha looking at?"

"Just checking out some others."

"I've seen that guy." She pointed right to Brodie.

Julian's gut tightened.

"He's cute. I didn't see her though. Doesn't he sit alone at that table a couple of rows back from ours? There's an empty seat next to him every night."

"My, aren't you observant," Julian said dryly.

"Can't help it. I notice every gorgeous man in the room."

Julian bit his lip. "Really?"

"Don't worry, I only have eyes for you, baby." She threw him a kiss, waving her envelope at him. "There's a great nightclub I found with a dance floor and piano bar."

"Is that a fact?"

"You want to dance?"

"I actually wanted to see the stand-up comedian."

She wrinkled her nose. "Oh, come on."

"I like comedy. Beats those corny cabaret acts."

"I'd rather dance."

"Can't we compromise?"

"We did last night. And I was still alone after the show!"

"You managed fine without me. You must have found someone to hang out with."

She put her hands on her hips in anger. "You kidding me?"

"Look, Amelia, I get the feeling we don't have much in common."

"What's that supposed to mean?"

"It means what I said. We don't like the same things."

"So? You're breaking up with me?"

There it was. Take it! Snatch her arm off! But where were they supposed to go. They were on a damn boat.

"Don't be ridiculous. I just don't see why we have to be attached at the hip."

"Fine! See ya."

"Amelia!" he shouted as she stormed off.

She gave him the finger as she left.

Standing still, trying to decide how much damage that little scene had caused, Julian waited until she vanished. Moving back to the gallery, he took the picture of Brodie off the wall, purchasing it.

With it in his hot hand, he imagined using a scissor to cut off the pouting Melanie, and keeping Brodie close to his heart.

~

Brodie was surprised at the crowd already gathered inside the auditorium. Reading the name of the comedian, Brodie had never heard of him and doubted he did anything more than the cruise line circuit. Most of the acts were about the same quality as the local casinos or ragtag productions of the fringe theaters. Very few lived up to expectations of a Broadway or Vegas type experience. But they were fun, and the old people loved them.

A glass of water in his hand, Brodie found an unoccupied table and relaxed, sipping water, knowing he had to get up early and run laps in the morning.

After a half hour the room darkened and the lights lit the tiny stage. Someone sat next to him. He glanced quickly to see who it was. "Hello."

"Heya, big boy."

"Where's, uh?"

Julian shrugged. "What are you drinking?" he whispered as he flagged a waitress down.

"Water."

"No shit?"

"No shit."

The waitress leaned close. Brodie heard Julian request, "Ice water, please." Brodie smiled. He did adore the man.

Julian shifted his chair so they were connected, side by side. Brodie found his hand, held it, keeping it low under the tiny round table.

"Is it just starting?"

"Yes."

Julian shook off Brodie's hand as the waitress returned with his water. After he sipped it and set it down, he laced his fingers into Brodie's again.

The comedian was introduced, a spate of clapping followed, and a man stood nervously at a microphone. The minute he opened his mouth to speak, the pronounced lisp and wiggle gave him away instantly. From then on, the gay gags kept rolling.

"Inside Passage?" The man acted shocked, touching his face. "I thought they were joking? Do I want to go on the inside passage? Oh, honey, they had to ask?"

Brodie started laughing, squeezing Julian's hand tightly.

"Did I want to know anything about it?" The comedian flipped his wrist, "Honey! I wrote the manual!"

Sipping his water, Brodie felt Julian inch closer. A whisper filled his ear. "I love you."

Brodie spun around, staring in the dimness at that expression on Julian's face. "Oh God, baby…"

"Don't kiss me," Julian giggled.

"Later." Brodie wagged his finger at him. "Later."

Julian winked.

"…and then the man said something about sperm whales. Sperm? Did I want to know about sperm?" The comedian rolled his eyes. "Who did this man think I was?"

Brodie snuck a quick kiss on Julian's knuckles, so pleased they were sharing the show. It wouldn't have been the same without him.

~

Staying for the magic act, Brodie enjoyed it, enjoying Julian's companionship even more. When the magician took his final bow, waving and throwing kisses to the audience, Brodie stared at Julian's profile, savoring the straight line of his nose, the curve of his lips, and his square jaw. "Christ, I want to lick your face."

"Shh!" Julian scolded. "You'll shock Granny."

Brodie looked to where he was indicating. More than one gray-haired individual was getting up to go back to their cabin. Brodie had held Julian's hand during the entire performance. It was under the table, discreet, invisible to anyone else. Now, with everyone getting up and the lights coming on, they released the hold. "Do you have to get back to your cabin? Where's Amelia?'

Julian shrugged. "I'm slowly not giving a shit."

"What happened to only a few more days?"

"She hates my fucking guts."

"Bullshit."

Julian sighed, his eyes wandering around the emptying room.

"You're just saying that because you feel guilty."

"I don't know. She and I don't connect, not on any sort of real level."

"Real level? Like us?" Brodie relaxed in his chair, his legs in a comfortable straddle, his hands clasped on his lap.

Julian met his gaze. "Yes. Like us."

"Come to my room."

"*Oh,* I want to." Julian's face contorted with sensual longing.

"So? Amelia hates your guts. Do you owe her anything anymore?"

"I don't know. I'm just saying stupid things."

Brodie grew angry. "Don't fucking tease me."

That made Julian sit up and pay attention. "I'm not doing that!"

"Then come to my room."

"How about this…" Julian looked around first, asking in a soft voice, "What if we just have a quick check of the clubs? Hm? See where she is?"

Brodie moved out his chair. "Sure."

They exited the empty theater. Brodie couldn't stop staring at the sway of Julian's hips as he walked. Completely sober, having done nothing but drink water for the last three hours, Brodie was ready for anything, except an early night.

The first club Julian found was on the promenade deck. The casino was hopping with the sound of slot machines cranking away, frantically stealing passengers' money. She wasn't there. Next the Riviera level, a dark bar, a disco with a disc jockey playing 80s and 90s hip tunes. Brodie wanted to barf.

"Wait." Julian tapped him. "She's there."

Brodie looked over Julian's shoulder. Amelia was dancing the hustle with another man. "Look out, *Saturday Night Fever*." Brodie smiled despite himself.

"Christ, you believe this?"

"Oh, come on. Let her have some fun. She didn't expect you to become an old man and leave her to find some young stud to swing with."

"She better not be swinging."

"Huh?" Brodie grabbed his arm and jerked him around to face him. "You still care about what she does? What the hell's that suppose to mean to me?"

Shaking his head, Julian replied, "Never mind. It's just a gut reflex."

"Fine. She's dancing with a Travolta impersonator, so? Time for you and me to fuck." Brodie grabbed Julian's arm.

When Julian kept staring at his girlfriend gyrating on the colorful dance floor, Brodie became irritated. "Go dance with the witch."

Julian raced to catch up with him as he stormed away. "Brodie, wait."

Inhaling to stop his fury, Brodie stood his ground.

"I'm sorry. Let's go to your room."

"You sure?" Brodie was about to explode.

"Yes."

Brodie checked Julian's expression carefully, turned on his heels, and started the long trek to his cabin.

~

Julian felt like shit. Jealous at seeing his girlfriend dance with another man and angering Brodie by his jealousy, he felt like he was screwing himself twice. Passing some people as they marched down the never-ending hallway of the main deck, Julian peeked behind him first, seeing it was clear, cupping his hand over that marvelous set of gluteus maximus in front of him. He felt Brodie jolt from the contact but keep moving. By the time they stood before Brodie's cabin door, Julian was already in a lather, rubbing his bottom, suddenly not caring who noticed. "I want to fuck you. Fuck you balls deep. I want to be in this gorgeous ass."

Brodie peered over his shoulder skeptically at him, opening the door. As they entered the dark room, Julian sung, "Fuck your ass, fuck your ass..." ramming his hips into Brodie's butt.

Brodie flipped on a light, tossing his key on the dresser.

Julian paused, "Is my subtle method of seduction not working tonight?"

"I can tell you're trying too hard." Brodie took off his jacket, hanging it up in the closet.

"No. That's crap and you know it."

Brodie faced him, hands on hips. "You were jealous."

"Just for a second. Look, Brodie, I'm cheating on her, do I really care if she's cheating on me?"

"Only you can answer that."

"I don't. Okay? There's your answer. I pretty much told her it was over."

Brodie cocked his head to the side, interested.

"I did." Julian nodded. "I told her we had nothing in common, other than her need to spend my money."

A slight smile curled Brodie's mouth.

"If I could, I'd stay the rest of the week here."

"So? Do it."

Julian regretted that line. It was a dare he wasn't prepared to take.

Brodie settled on the bed heavily, running his hand through his hair. "I'm beat."

"No, baby...don't be like that." Julian sat next to him, wrapping his arms around him. "I know I've upset you. Let me make it up to you."

"Bi? Straight? Gay? What are we, Julian?"

"Gay. Gay with all our hearts."

"Sure. Keep telling yourself that."

Julian rested his forehead on Brodie's shoulder. Inhaling his cologne, Julian closed his eyes. "I imagine us together." He sighed. "I'm in my kitchen, cooking you a nice meal."

"You cook?"

"Yes. I'm pretty good."

"Okay, what happens after dinner?"

"Uh, we chat, we sip some sherry, perhaps. I put the stereo on, maybe some jazz, or blues. We sway in a soft dance."

"Yeah?'

"Yeah." Julian hugged him tighter. "I kiss your neck. Your ear. Sniff at you." Julian did, showing him what he would do. "You smell divine."

"Then what?"

"We'd dance a little more, our hips connected. Your cock hard and rubbing against mine."

"Mm."

"Maybe we'd waltz our way to my bedroom. I'd keep the lights low, you know. Ambiance."

"Mm. Then what?"

"I'd move you to my bed. Undress you slowly, very slowly." Julian ran his hand over Brodie's chest, feeling his muscles through the soft black fabric.

"Then what?"

"Once you were naked, I'd ask you to lie on my bed, then maybe I'd lick you, all over."

Brodie twisted on the mattress, cupping Julian's face. "Do it now."

"Oh, Brodie," Julian moaned, opening his mouth, receiving Brodie's tongue. At the taste of his lips, Julian moaned, closing his eyes. Brodie gently urged them to lie back across the single bed.

"Sleep with me."

"Brodie…" Julian felt a slight shiver of stress wash over him.

"Sleep here."

As Brodie's hand dug down the front of Julian's slacks, Julian felt his body release, giving into pleasure. "Take it."

"I intend to."

~

Brodie rolled over, on top of Julian, pinning him down on the bed. Clasping his hands, pressing them above his head, Brodie sucked on Julian's mouth as if his life depended on it. Writhing against Julian's hard body, Brodie wrapped his tongue seductively around Julian's showing him exactly what he was going to do with it. Julian squirmed under him, moaning.

"You hot mother fucker," Brodie hissed. "You tease, you fucking tease."

"No," Julian panted between kissed. "Not teasing."

"Let me fuck you."

"Fuck me."

Brodie sat up, stripping Julian's slacks off as Julian unraveled his tie. His shoes, socks, shirt, everything fell to the floor. Brodie stood up, panting, staring down at Julian's naked body. After absorbing it, lusting after it, Brodie stepped out of his own black slacks and pulled off the soft turtleneck. Standing over Julian, pumping his own cock as he admired his muscular physique, Brodie commanded, "Roll over."

Immediately Julian flipped to his stomach on the bed. Brodie found the rubbers and lube still sitting on the nightstand from their earlier bout. Tearing the package with his teeth, Brodie unraveled a condom, preparing himself, liberally applying the lubrication. Without asking, Brodie gripped Julian's waist, wrapping one hand around him, raising him off the bed. Hearing Julian's gasp, Brodie smiled in delight, impaling Julian's ass with his cock. As the heat and tightness surrounded him, Brodie shivered, his dick tensing as it reacted to the penetration. Humping Julian's ass, his balls slapping Julian's butt as he had imagined they would do, Brodie clenched his jaw and came, closing his eyes and grinding his teeth at the intensity.

Underneath him, Julian was moaning, his body tensing and reaching out on the bed.

Trying to catch his breath, Brodie backed up, pulling out, standing still, amazed at the extreme heat that seemed to always be there on their contact.

~

Julian spun around. Looking at that posture, seeing the seraphic expression on Brodie's face, he wanted it. Fuck Amelia. Amelia who?

Wrestling Brodie to the bed, Julian took advantage of his swoon, shoving him down on his face. "Nice one, Brodie?"

"*Oh, yes...*" Brodie moaned, his face pressed into the pillows.

Julian tore one of the condoms open. Sliding it on, remembering at the last minute to use lube, Julian spread Brodie's heavy legs apart, thrusting between them. At the penetration, they both tensed up instantly. "Holy shit." Julian closed his eyes and tried to control the spasm of pleasure that rushed over him. Once the chill had subsided, he pumped hard into that masculine treat, his balls slapping Brodie's ass just as Brodie had done to him. Moaning loudly, unashamed he felt so much pleasure, Julian came, shoving his dick deeper into Brodie. Once the throbbing subsided, Julian hung his head, catching his breath, pulling out slowly. "Oh Jesus Christ, I love you so much."

As if hearing those words woke him up, Brodie rolled over to see Julian's face. Once he removed the spent rubber, Julian nodded, "I do. Don't look at me that way."

"Come here."

Julian dropped down beside Brodie. They kissed, slow, lazy, and full of satisfaction.

"Sleep with me."

"Yes." Julian nodded, too tired to refuse.

Brodie urged them under the blankets, and they both fell fast asleep.

Chapter Eight

Julian woke. It was dark in the room. Stretching his back, feeling another warm body intertwined with his own on the narrow bed, he suddenly realized he had indeed slept in Brodie's cabin. "Shit. I am so dead."

Trying to see the time, finding a digital alarm clock that read seven ten, Julian adjusted his position under the blanket to face the dark ceiling. "Brodie?" He waited, nudging him. "Brodie?"

"Hm?" a deep grumbling sound answered him.

"Wake up."

As if it took a supreme effort, Brodie stirred. "What time is it?"

"Just after seven."

"You want to run?"

"Uh, it depends how screwed I am."

Brodie leaned up on his side, reached behind him to a light switch on the headboard and turned it on. They both flinched at the brightness until their eyes grew used to the glare. "You want to go and check?"

Julian exhaled deeply. "Yes, and no."

"You have to go to your cabin to get your running clothes anyway."

"I know." Julian turned on the narrow mattress to see Brodie's face. His jaw was dark and rough, his hair tussled and covering his forehead. He looked absolutely edible. There was a light pressure on the side of Julian's hip. Brodie's morning hard-on was resting against him.

"What do you want to do?" Brodie asked.

"I have no idea." Brodie's warm hand smoothed over Julian's stomach gently. "I wish I could just tell her it's over and stay here the rest of the cruise."

"Why can't you?"

"Come on, Brodie. Could you do it? Think about it." In the pause, Julian imagined he was thinking about the nasty idea. "What am I supposed to do? Move my shit into your cabin? Sit with you at dinner, pretend she's not there?" When Brodie's expression lit up, Julian shook his head. "Sure, Brodie. It would be *so* easy," he said sarcastically.

"No. It would be the hardest thing you ever had to do. I don't know if I could do it."

"Thank you," Julian exhaled in relief.

"But I sure would love it." Brodie wrapped his hand around Julian's stiff cock.

Julian shivered at the touch. "She's probably thrown my clothing overboard, or at least out into the hall. I bet she's seeing red this morning, Brodie."

"I wouldn't mind seeing come." Brodie pumped Julian's cock a few times.

Shivering at the sensations of chills rippling over his skin, Julian closed his eyes. "It's the sex. It's like a drug."

Brodie pushed the blanket back, exposing what had been hidden. Julian peered down at Brodie's hand as it continued to jerk him off. "Oh, why fight it?"

"Exactly." Brodie lowered himself onto the bed, taking Julian into his mouth.

"*Ooh*," Julian howled in delight. "Your mouth...oh, Brodie, your fucking mouth." In response, Brodie hummed in agreement, sending a shock up Julian's spine from the vibrations. Spreading his legs, Julian wanted Brodie's hand between them. As if his message was spoken, Brodie began stroking Julian's balls and ass. His hips elevating, fucking Brodie's mouth, Julian rose quickly, yearning for that morning ejaculation.

~

Within a few moments Brodie felt the skin of Julian's cock tighten, his balls squeeze, and the taste of come on his tongue. Wriggling in pleasure, Brodie continued to press that magic come button between Julian's legs, sucking the tip of his cock, savoring every drop as the pulsing slowed but didn't stop.

Sitting up to stare down at Julian contentedly, Brodie began masturbating over Julian's spent cock. As Julian slowly came back from his swoon, Brodie shot come all over Julian's pubic hair.

"If you'd have given me a second, I'd have sucked it for you."

"I know. Next time." Brodie wiped at the tip of his own dick as a drop oozed out. "Come on, let's get that run out of the way."

Brodie crawled over Julian to get out of bed. Standing up next to him, he reached out his hand. Julian took it, looking down at the creamy spatter on his dark, curly hair. "Nice."

"Glad you like it," Brodie chuckled, heading to the bathroom. As he turned on the water in the sink, he noticed Julian standing behind him, wiping himself clean with a washcloth. "You okay?"

"Hm?" Julian caught his eyes in the mirror. "Yeah. Look, whatever happens, I'll deal with it."

"I'm here to back you." Brodie loaded up his toothbrush with paste.

Julian relieved himself in the toilet behind him. "I know."

Once they had washed up, and Brodie was in his running shorts, Julian slipped on his slacks and white shirt, holding his tie and jacket over his arm. "Here we go."

"What should I do?"

"Just wait here." Julian opened the cabin door.

"Okay, babe. Good luck."

~

Julian nodded, gave Brodie a thumbs-up, and bravely made that trek down the hall and across the width of the boat to the other side. Inhaling, holding out his keycard, Julian inserted it, opened the door and pushed it back, waiting for the shouting.

It was vacant. The two beds were still made, those silly towel swans were resting on them so their necks formed a heart-shape in the middle of the bed. "What the fuck?" Julian stepped inside. "She never slept here?" Half in relief, half in fury, Julian looked around for a note. Nothing was there. He hung up his suit jacket, changing into his running clothes. Before he left, as an afterthought, he rolled down the bedspread, messing up the covers and pillows, to make it look as though he had slept there, even sitting on it to cause the sheets to crease. "There. Now I can blame you."

Just as he was tucking his key into his gym shorts the door opened. Waiting in expectation, Julian watched Amelia peek in, looking like something the cat had dragged around all night. "Oops."

"Oops?" Julian put his hands on his hips.

"Hi."

"Hello."

"Uh, sorry."

"Sorry?" Julian tilted his head in disbelief.

"I swear, nothing happened. I just fell asleep."

"Where?" *Sure, Amelia, and I'm not fucking someone else either.*

"Uh, I don't remember." She tossed the room key on the dresser, pushing her hair back from her face.

"Oh? How convenient."

"You going running?"

"Yes."

"Are you mad?"

Julian didn't know how to answer that question. He sat down on the edge of the bed to think. "Did you meet someone?"

"No!" she shouted, only to sheepishly add, "Maybe? Am I dead?"

Totally flustered by her confession, Julian ran his hand through his hair to buy him time.

She sat next to him on the bed, leaning on his shoulder. "You said we didn't have anything in common. Remember? Like you were sort of breaking up with me. Remember?"

"Yes. I remember."

"Well, I had a little time to think about it. And you were right."

Julian tilted his head so he could see her eyes. "And?"

She bit her lip nervously.

"You met someone more your type?"

"Er…are you going to kill me?"

Shaking his head sadly, Julian sighed. "No."

"I thought when I didn't show up last night you would throw all of my clothing overboard."

That made him chuckle.

"What?" She nudged him.

"Nothing."

"So, uh…I suppose this is really awkward, huh?"

"Amelia," he asked in a serious tone, "what is it you really want to do?"

"I don't know. I don't want to hurt your feelings."

"I appreciate that. So, this guy you met, does he share a room with someone?"

"No."

"Do you want to stay with him now?"

Her eyes widened, her mascara smeared down the corners. "You're being very casual about this? I mean, I thought you'd be furious. You sure you get what actually happened last night?"

"Do you think I'm an idiot?"

"No! Maybe just naïve?"

He shook his head. "I'm asking you a question."

"What?"

"Are you intending on sleeping in this other man's cabin now?"

"Not if it pisses you off. I can always sleep here." She gestured to the bed they were sitting on. "Is that what you want?"

"So, this guy you met, he came alone?"

"No. He's with his parents, his sister and brother, his cousins…"

Julian held up his hand. "Don't give me the gory details. Is he with a partner?"

"No."

"Then I will ask you again. Are you going to sleep with him in his cabin from now on?"

"I don't know how you want me to answer that."

Julian rubbed his eyes tiredly. "How about honestly."

It was as if she needed a moment to assess that comment. Sitting up, straightening her back, she replied, "I'd like that. If it won't like crush you to death. You know, losing me."

He tried not to smile. "It won't *like* crush me to death."

"You're being very cool about this, Julian. You really don't give a shit about us, do you?" She stared at him. When he didn't reply she threw his own line in his face, "How about honesty?"

Biting his lip, he whispered, "I do care about you. I don't want

103

to hurt you. But I don't think we're getting along anymore."

"Oh. Good."

Julian waited. "So?"

"So?"

"So, you're going to move your things into his cabin?"

"Are you sure you're okay with this? I mean, you paid for my fare, Julian. I mean, I feel really funny about this."

"I don't mind. What about the dinners? Are you going to be able to sit at his table?"

"Uh, yes. I won't if you don't want me to."

"No. I'd prefer you did. So we don't have to keep up the charade."

Her expression went blank. "What will you tell Jenny and Paul, and Joe and Elaine?"

"What do you want me to tell them?"

"I don't know. That we broke up?"

"Okay."

"But you'll be all on your lonesome." Amelia wrapped her arm around his waist.

"I'll manage."

"I can't do that to you. I feel really bad."

"I said I can manage."

"You sure?"

"Absolutely." He rose up and tucked his shirt into his running shorts. "So, you'll be out when I get back?"

"I don't know how long it'll take me."

"Call one of the staff to help you with your things."

She faced him, holding onto his shoulders. "I know this is crushing you, Julian. I feel really horrible."

"It's not crushing me. Will you just do what's best for you?"

"I do like Harry. He's a pisser. You should see him dance."

Julian withheld comment on that.

"He's a blast, and his family is really nice. They're like Polish or something. But he's great. I really like him."

"Okay."

She crossed her arms over her chest. "You sure?"

"Yes."

"Wow. Strange how this ended up. I never would have imagined leaving you alone onboard and shacking up with another guy. It sounds really rotten. I mean, if you met another woman, and did it to me, I'd want to cut your balls off."

He flinched. "Uh, nice thought, Amelia."

"I'm serious, Julian. I can't imagine being dumped onboard, having to see you having fun with someone else while I was alone."

"Well, it hasn't happened that way."

"But it has, and you're the lonesome loser."

"What a sweet thing to say," he snarled, heading to the door.

"I didn't mean it that way. It came out wrong."

"I know what you meant."

"So, I'll try not to rub it in your face. I mean, we still have several more days on this boat, and now we'll be running into each other all over the place."

"I'll try my best not to let it matter." Julian opened the door, checking his watch.

"Let me tell the guys at the table. Okay? I want to be the one to explain it. You'll probably make me sound like a real bitch or something."

"You do what you want." Julian stepped out into the hall.

"I'm sorry, Julian. Honest. I didn't mean for it to end like this."

"Maybe it's for the best. Maybe you and Harry are right for each other."

"He's great! I really like him. And his family seems to really like me as well."

"Good. I'm happy for you." He felt like he needed to chew his arm off to get away from her snaring trap.

"You sure? I mean, I'd be really upset. I'm just shocked you're taking it so well."

"I'm a big boy. Can I go?" He pointed down the hall.

"The run." She rolled her eyes. "You see? That's the kind of stuff Harry would never do. He's on vacation!"

"Okay. See ya. Bye." He waved, walking away as she kept talking. Nodding, waving, walking, Julian finally couldn't hear her incessant babbling. He hurried to Brodie's room, knocking.

~

Brodie grew tired of waiting. Having no idea if they had some kind of joyous reunion and were making up, he grumbled in irritation as the time past and Julian never showed up. Throwing up his hands, impatient as a child waiting for Christmas morning, Brodie left his cabin, heading to the sports deck. If Julian needed him, he knew where to find him.

Done with his warm up lap, Brodie lengthened his stride, hitting his full speed. Just as he was passing one of the doors to the interior, it opened and Julian stepped out, looking for him. The minute they caught eyes, Julian hurried to match his stride.

Brodie didn't say anything, continuing to pass the slower movers as they lapped them.

"Sorry."

Brodie peeked over at him quickly, not answering.

"She wouldn't shut up."

Brodie wiped at his forehead and temples as the drips of sweat began to run down to his eyes.

"She met someone."

Whipping his head around, Brodie gasped, "What?'

"Watch it." Julian grabbed him to move around an old lady power-walking. "I said she met some guy last night. You remember the Travolta look-alike?"

"So? What the hell does that mean? Is she still in your cabin?"

"No. She's moving into his. Thank fuck. Do you believe this?"

"No!" Brodie grinned broadly, running faster in excitement. "Holy shit."

"I know. Ironic, huh? She's the one with the guilt trip."

"But what the hell does it mean? Are you going to stay in your cabin alone? What about dinner time?"

"Christ, slow down!" Julian gasped as the speed went to a full sprint.

"Keep up, old man."

"Old? How old do you think I am?"

"I don't know. Twenty-eight, nine?"

"I'm twenty-seven, you dork!"

"Ouch! Sorry. I suck guessing ages. I hate it when chicks ask me that question. I always insult them and err on the older side. That means you're a year younger than I am, you should be able to keep up!" Brodie began racing him.

Julian raced passed him momentarily. Pushing his legs harder, clenching his teeth, Brodie caught up. It was an all out dash and he knew he couldn't keep it up much longer.

Finally Julian gave out first, slowing to a stop. Brodie halted, spinning around and running back towards him. "Sorry. We can continue slower."

"You butthead!" Julian gasped for breath.

"Come on. Granny pace." Brodie touched his back as he hunched over to gasp for air.

Straightening up, Julian jogged slowly next to him.

Feeling elated, Brodie asked, "So, uh, you moving into my cabin, or me into yours?"

"Let me move into yours. I guess it's easier in case she gets into a fight with the new guy and needs to move back."

"Cool. There's an empty seat at my table."

"I know. Do you think it'll look obvious we're a couple of queers if I sit there with you?"

The smile fell from Brodie's face. "Shit."

"Yeah, exactly."

"Can't I just say we're friends?"

"*Oh*, special friends!" Julian teased, lisping.

Brodie felt insulted. "Whatever." He increased his speed again as punishment.

Julian kept up, laboring, checking his watch. "Haven't we gone three miles yet?"

"I've no idea. I lost count."

"Well, has it been twenty minutes?"

"I don't know that either."

"When did you start running?" Julian panted.

Brodie shrugged.

"Five more minutes. Then I'm stopping." Julian held up his hand, spreading out his fingers as if to reinforce the number five.

"Okay. Then we run faster." Brodie edged past him.

"Bastard!"

Laughing, Brodie pushed himself on the last lap, stopping when they were in front of one of the doors. Bent over hands on knees, he gulped for oxygen loudly.

Julian dropped to his back, holding his chest as it rose and fell like a bellows. "You suck."

"You didn't have to keep up."

"Yeah, right."

Using his shirt to wipe his face, Brodie peeked down to see Julian staring, licking his lips. "Come on, Mr. Richards. Let's get you packed and into my domain."

Julian reached for his outstretched hand, allowing Brodie to haul him to his feet. "She may still be doing that exact thing. Let's give it 'til after lunch."

"Okay. You want to stop there for some clean clothing."

"Yeah, okay." Julian held open the door for them to enter the hallway. "We're supposed to see Glacier Bay today."

"That's right. That should be cool."

"Cool?" Julian raised an eyebrow.

"No pun intended." Brodie chuckled under his breath. They walked down the staircase to the main deck. Brodie followed Julian to his room, intending on waiting outside for him to collect his things.

Julian paused before he inserted his key.

"What?" Brodie asked, wiping at the sweat that continued to pour off him as he cooled off.

"What will I say if she sees you?"

"I don't know. That we run together?"

"Yeah, but why am I taking clean clothes with me?"

Glaring at him, Brodie spun on his heels. "See ya later."

"I'll be there in a minute," Julian shouted after him.

Waving as he walked, Brodie dragged the edge of his shirt over his face again. Was it that bad? Admitting they were friends? Friends with benefits?

Pushing his key into the slot, Brodie found the room cleaned up, a paper had been pushed under the door. Informal dinner tonight, casino night, the nightclub show was songs from the 50s and 60s. He set the sheet of paper on the dresser, tossing his key on top of it. Pausing, looking in the mirror, Brodie found his hair stuck to his face from his perspiration. His five o'clock shadow was dark on his jaw, his eyes seemed to laser back at him with a look of anger. "Come out with me, Julian," he hissed. "Come out onboard. Let's show the passengers we're not afraid." But even as he told his reflection that command, he shivered in doubt and fear. "How humiliating. Why? Why is it embarrassing?" he demanded to know that answer, but his reflection wasn't talking at the moment. A knock echoed through the tiny cabin. Brodie jumped to open the door. Sweaty, delicious Julian was there, his clothing in his arms. "Hey."

"Hey." Brodie swung the door wider, letting him pass. Julian set his clean things down. "We need to push them together." He pointed to the separate twin beds.

"We do." Brodie let the door close on its own, locking it.

"So? Shower?" Julian rubbed his hands together.

"Yes. Shower." Brodie smiled sweetly at him.

Yanking the damp shirt over his head, Brodie started the water running in the shower stall. Glancing over his shoulder he noticed Julian stripping off his clothing, piling it on the floor.

"Do they have a washer and dryer onboard?" Julian asked.

"I think they do it for you. Just stuff it in a bag and leave it by the door. Something like that."

"Really?"

Brodie stepped out of his shorts and into the hot water. Julian followed, waiting, arms crossed over his chest as Brodie wet down. They were quiet. Strangely quiet.

Too many thoughts were going through Brodie's head. *Okay, now what? We have free rein to be ourselves, we can sleep together, dine together, have unlimited guilt free sex. What's really going on?* But he already knew the answer to the question. Fear. Labeling. Reality. It was one thing to sneak, hide, have sex in the dark, and another to *come out*, look like a gay couple, have everyone see them together to make assumptions and answer their curious questions if asked. *Yes, we're together.* He knew immediately Glenda and Marlene would suspect it. Or would they? Julian would move from his assigned seat at his dining table, where he was coupled with a beautiful woman, to sit where? With him?

"Christ."

"What?" Julian seemed to wake out of his daydream, shampooing his hair.

"Nothing." Brodie rinsed off, finished in the shower. He opened the door, grabbed a towel and stepped out.

"Brodie? What's going on?"

Wrapping the white terrycloth around his hips, Brodie wiped at the foggy mirror preparing to shave. A minute later the water stopped and Julian pushed back the sliding door. Another burst of steam filled the room and coated the mirror. Brodie swiped at the glass again, trying to see as he shaved.

"You suddenly turn off to me as well?"

"No." Brodie ran the razor under his jaw in swift confident strokes.

Julian stepped out, wiping his back with a towel. "What then? We were both naked in the shower. You didn't so much as make eye contact with me. Am I imagining this, or did something happen I should know about?"

Exhaling, lowering the razor to the sink, Brodie had no idea how to answer him.

Julian rubbed Brodie's damp back with a warm hand. "Brodie. Please."

Regaining his composure, Brodie shaved his top lip. Once he had finished, he rinsed the razor in the sink. "So? We're a couple now?"

Silence.

Brodie splashed his face, washing off the rest of the shave cream. "Dining together, socializing together, sharing a room."

"Uh, isn't that what we were after?"

Using his towel to wipe his chin, Brodie faced him. The sadness in Julian's eyes crushed him. Draping the towel over his shoulder, Brodie reached out to hold Julian. "Will it mean to everyone on the ship that we're a couple? A gay couple?"

"No. Why would they assume that? Can't guys be friends?"

"If you were at a table, all couples, one dude. And suddenly a second man sits with him every night, on a cruise boat, what would you think?"

Julian turned his eyes away, as if he were considering that question very seriously.

"I know what I would think."

"Do we care? We'll never see these people again. And I don't really give a shit about Amelia. She'd never believe it for a minute anyway."

It was back in his court now. Did he care? Brodie didn't know. "So, you're okay if people whisper behind our backs that we may be a gay couple?"

Julian twisted out of Brodie's grasp, storming out of the tiny bathroom.

It wasn't the reaction he expected. Racing after him, Brodie paused when he found Julian dressing, obviously angry.

"I'll stay in my own fucking room."

"No." Brodie stopped him. "No. I don't want that. That's not an option."

Julian threw his shirt onto the bed in a huff. "I can't tell you how you should feel, Brodie. If you can't do it, you can't. I get it."

Brodie felt torn in half. Why did it come easy for Paden and Tim? They did it. They survived.

"You cut yourself, you dork," Julian reached up to touch Brodie's chin. At the contact, Brodie embraced him, wrapping around him. "I'm sorry. I'm just fucking nervous, that's all."

Holding him tight, Julian sighed, "You don't think I am? My luck Amelia will jump right to that conclusion and call my mother and tell her."

Brodie crushed Julian in his arms, closing his eyes and pressing against his neck and wet hair, wanting to find strength in their bond. "Who gives a shit, right? It's what we want that matters."

"We should feel that way, yes."

Brodie set back to see Julian's eyes. Kissing him, contacting his mouth and tongue, Brodie began to feel the power of the attraction connecting them, urging them to unite as one. Sucking deeply at Julian's mouth, his hands smoothing down Julian's silky skin of his back to his jeans, Brodie dug hungrily into the waistband of those jeans. Julian unzipped them, tugging them partway down his hips. As the jeans loosened, Brodie cupped both of Julian's bare ass cheeks in his palms. Molding them, running in circles around them, Brodie moaned, shifting their position so they could fall back onto one of the beds. Once Julian was horizontal, Brodie tugged off his jeans.

"I didn't shave yet," Julian whispered between kisses.

"I don't care." Brodie sucked at his lips, his tongue, feeling that sandpaper grit.

"Brodie...when we do this, I don't give a crap who knows."

"I know. I feel the same." Brodie ran his hands down Julian's muscular sides to his pelvis, sneaking his hands between them to touch Julian's cock with his fingertips. In the process he felt his own, resting beside Julian's. Straddling Julian's thighs, Brodie pressed his cock to drop between Julian's legs, rubbing under his balls. "I want in."

"Where's the lube?"

Instantly Brodie spun around to the nightstand, reaching blindly inside. Tossing the two items he needed next to them, he dragged Julian to the edge of the bed, pushing back his knees to expose his ass. His eyes glued to the sight of Julian's engorged cock, tight sack, and anus, Brodie began panting in excitement. Tearing open a condom with his teeth, he rolled it on, trying not to tremble at the anticipation. Coating himself with lube, pushing his finger into Julian eagerly, Brodie loved the moan of pleasure Julian made on contact. "Christ, you have any idea how much I love you?"

Julian chuckled, "You love me more when you're staring at my ass."

Trying not to laugh, Brodie replied, "Shut up." He pushed the tip of his cock in and felt a chill pass over his body length. Julian held onto his legs, keeping them high and straddled. Standing on the floor in front of him, Brodie rode him, deep and slow. His teeth clenched and his eyes shut involuntarily as the climb to an orgasm began. Quickening his thrusts, feeling his balls slap Julian's body, Brodie forced his eyes open, looked down at the expression of bliss on Julian's face and came, opening his mouth to grunt like an animal at the strength of the climax. Waiting until the last tremor subsided, Brodie pulled out, staring down at his cock as it bobbed gently. "Christ, I'm so hard I can't pull this thing off."

"You're hard and big."

Trying to catch his breath, Brodie said, "Thanks, that's a compliment no matter how you interpret it."

"My pleasure."

Finally getting the stubborn thing off, Brodie dropped it to the floor, replying, "No, *this* is for your pleasure." He crouched down, taking Julian's cock into his mouth.

~

Julian released his grasp on his legs, letting them settle in a gentle straddle, his feet on the edge of the bed. Closing his eyes, he rested his hand on his chest, feeling his own heartbeat pounding like thunder beneath it. Brodie's tongue was going wild under the head of his cock, sending shockwaves throughout his body. Every flick of the tip of his tongue made Julian's hips flinch, dying to thrust up and in. When that hot tongue moved to lick his balls, Julian almost cried. "Don't stop."

"I want you to wait."

"Why?" Julian whimpered.

"It'll make it more intense."

"I already waited for you to come."

Brodie pushed Julian's hand away as he sought to grip his own dick. Julian shook his head in protest, closing his eyes as Brodie sucked one of his testicles into his mouth, rolling it around on his tongue. Julian loved it, but it was exquisite agony. Leaning up, watching Brodie's expression as he licked the base of his cock, Julian placed his hands behind his head so he could have a better view. Witnessing Brodie in action, seeing the joy he took in what he was doing was worth the wait. Just as Brodie made his way back to the tip of his penis again, Brodie opened his eyes. The electric blue color made Julian's breath catch in his throat. "Holy Christ."

Brodie's lips curled to a wicked smile. Moving Julian's cock toward his mouth, he licked the glistening drop that emerged from the tip, pushing his tongue into the slit. Julian dropped his hands to his sides, groaned in anguish and let his head fall back on the bed. When the contact stopped again, Julian was about to scream about the torture until he found Brodie sliding a rubber on him. "Sit up." Julian obeyed Brodie's command. Once Brodie had coated Julian with lubrication, he knelt, straddling Julian's lap, impaling himself. Getting over the shock of the penetration, Julian lost himself completely until Brodie reached for his hands, placing them on his re-hardened cock. The minute Julian had a good grasp, Brodie rode Julian's dick up and down. Blinking, amazed at Brodie's ingenuity and talent, he gasped as his body began to shiver with chills. Almost forgetting to move his hands, Julian felt Brodie helping him, gripping over his to pump it in the right direction. As if coming into focus, Julian took over, jerking Brodie's cock with more force.

"That's it," Brodie hissed.

"I'm close." Julian closed his eyes, humping him, getting deeper.

"Faster," Brodie breathed.

Julian sped up his hand. As he did, the climax rushed over him like a tidal wave. He grunted in pleasure and his hand dripped with come. Sliding over that sticky head a few times first, Julian dropped back to the mattress in exhaustion.

~

Brodie disengaged himself from Julian's hips. When he looked, Brodie found a very demonic grin on Julian's face. Pausing to watch him, he blinked in awe as Julian licked the come from his fingers. In excitement, Brodie dove on top of him, grabbing his jaw and sucking at his lips. "I love you, you gorgeous mother fucker."

"Mr. Duncan, you said a mouthful." Julian laughed wearily.

Digging his arms underneath Julian's back, Brodie squeezed him as tight as he could, closing his eyes and savoring the warmth of the emotion they shared. He'd never felt anything like it before in his life.

Chapter Nine

Glacier Bay appeared off the stern of the ship. Dressed warmly in their jackets and jeans, Brodie moved to the rail to get a closer look. A mass of people were photographing and videotaping the sight. An ice floe,, aqua blue in color, had oozed its way between two mountainsides. It was thick, slick and appeared ancient, as if it were as old as the earth under it.

Stuffing his cold hands into his pockets, Brodie leaned against Julian. "It's really amazing."

"I know. Someone said if a chunk falls off into the sea it's called calving. How weird is that?"

"No. Really?"

Julian shrugged. "I thought that's what I heard."

"I thought with this global warming, chunks were supposedly falling off all over."

"It's not the arctic, Brodie, maybe it doesn't happen here."

"Weren't there supposed to be whales here too?"

"I really have no clue. I feel like I've been preoccupied."

Brodie caught his wink. "Ya think?"

"Duh!" Julian laughed. "Too much sex has turned me into an idiot."

"You losing brain cells in that delicious sperm of yours?"

"Shh! You dirty boy!" Julian looked around them.

"You have no idea."

"Yeah?" Julian's interest perked up. "Got a kinky streak in you? Mr. Mild Mannered Microsoftman?"

"That's for you to find out." Brodie grinned wickedly.

"Christ, either you're giving me the chills, or it's freezing out here." Julian hopped up and down.

"Both, hopefully." Brodie looked back at the glacier as they drew closer. "Shouldn't there be penguins on it?"

"I have no clue."

"You'd think someone would tell us something about it."

"They did mention some naturalist was going to be here. I can't recall. My brain is fried from too much sex."

Brodie started laughing. "Is that your new excuse for everything?"

"Yes. Why? Doesn't it work for you?"

"Brodie!"

They turned around to see Glenda and Marlene waving at them. Brodie asked, "Should we mention you'll be at our table tonight?"

"Shit. I don't know."

The women rushed up to them excitedly. "Isn't it cool!" Marlene shouted, a camera in her hand.

"Cool!" Brodie rubbed his hands together. "It's freezing."

"I didn't mean that. Hi, Julian."

"You remembered my name." Julian smiled.

"Of course!"

Glenda held up her camera lens at them. "Can I take one of you guys in front of the glacier?"

Brodie was about to nod agreeably when Julian gripped him around the shoulder and pulled him tight to his body.

"Say cheese!" Glenda giggled, just as Marlene took the same shot.

"Got it!"

"You want me to take one of you two?" Brodie offered.

Glenda handed him her camera. As he looked down at it to figure out how it worked, Marlene asked Julian to do the same for her.

The women stood side by side, smiles plastered on their faces. "Say cheese," Brodie sang, clicking the shutter. Hearing Julian mumbling, "How do I work this thing?" Brodie leaned over to have a look. "Push that button once you find them in that screen."

"Oh, duh."

Out of the corner of his mouth, Brodie whispered, "Too much sex, I know."

Trying not to laugh, Julian yelled, "Hang on! Almost there!

Smile!" He took the picture, looking down at the frozen frame.

The women ran over to take a peek. "Oh, that's nice." Marlene showed Glenda. "Look, here's the one I took of you guys." She handed the camera to Brodie.

Brodie paused, taking the tiny camera to inspect. There, on the miniature monitor was he and his gorgeous lover, together. "Wow."

Julian connected to him to see it over his shoulder. "That is nice."

"I can email you a copy, if you give me your email address."

"Yes. Thank you." Brodie handed her back her camera. "Tonight at dinner. Remind me."

Glenda showed them her copy, not wanting to be left out. "I can send you this one as well."

"Okay. Thanks." Brodie felt his cheeks blushing from the attention.

"Where's your girlfriend?" Marlene asked Julian, looking around the deck.

Brodie and Julian exchanged looks, as if deciding how to answer that question. Brodie nodded, encouraging Julian to tell her.

"We've parted ways."

"Have you?" Marlene didn't hide her pleasure at the news.

"Yes. Uh, would you mind if I joined you at your table from now on? It's really awkward with Amelia now."

Brodie was floored at how easily this was coming out of Julian's mouth. It sounded very normal for some reason, nothing out of the ordinary.

Glenda poked her head into their tight circle. "Did you say both you and Julian were going to sit with us at dinner?"

Brodie could imagine her enthusiasm at the idea that they were somehow going to be on a double date.

"Yes," Julian shivered, jumping up and down to keep warm. "Is that okay?"

"Yes!" Glenda responded excitedly. "You guys are welcome to hang out with us. We're on our own here as well. And you know, it's always all couples on these things."

Brodie felt upset at where this was going. He made eye contact with Julian, trying to communicate that he wanted to say something.

Julian met his eyes briefly, but didn't indicate he understood Brodie's thought wave. "Uh..." Brodie had it on the tip of his tongue, telling the women they were a couple, a gay couple.

"We could join you for the shows and the dancing. I know how hard it is to go solo." Marlene gave Brodie an inviting smile.

"Uh," Brodie nudged Julian, who had been distracted by the glacier again.

"What?" Julian asked, still hopping like a pogo stick. "Isn't anyone else freezing?"

"Julian," Brodie said calmly though he wanted to raise his voice from his frustration, "they think we're going to be a quartet now."

"What?" He stopped hopping, looking at the women's hopeful expressions. "Oh."

Glenda added, "We don't mind. It'll be fun."

Julian looked at Brodie helplessly.

Brodie tilted his head, as if saying, "Tell them."

"Oh?" Julian seemed to get the message. "No."

"Why not?" Brodie asked.

Glenda and Marlene exchanged curious gazes. "Sorry. What are we talking about?"

Marlene's expression dropped. "I hope we're not overstepping our bounds."

"Brodie," Julian chided, shaking his head.

Throwing up his hands in frustration, Brodie walked away from them to the rail again.

"What happened?" Glenda asked. "Did we say something wrong?"

"No, I did. Excuse me, ladies."

Brodie overheard their conversation. As Julian fell back in at his side, Brodie squinted his eyes at the bright blue ice.

"You really wanted to tell them we were a couple?"

Brodie shrugged, not taking his gaze off the view.

"What do you think they would have done if you told them?" Julian began hopping to keep warm again.

"I don't know. I think they would have been cool. I don't think they would have given a shit."

"Come on, they're giving out signs all over the place they want us to pair off. Don't be stupid."

"Too much sex has made me stupid."

After a pause, Julian nudged Brodie. "Let's go inside, I'm freezing my nuts off."

Nodding, Brodie followed Julian through the metal doors to the ship's hallway, waving goodbye to Marlene and Glenda who stared at them curiously.

"Let's get a cup of coffee," Brodie breathed in Julian's ear as they passed a group of people hurrying out. Someone said there was a whale sighting and caused a rush to the promenade deck.

Filling a cup with coffee, Brodie tipped in some milk as he watched Julian stir in one packet of sugar in his. Relaxing at a café table with a view of the water and glacier beyond, Brodie took off his jacket, draping it on the chair behind him. Warming his hands on the cup, he stared at Julian as he sipped the hot liquid, still obviously too cold to take off his jacket.

"You should have gone to the Bahamas."

"Ha ha." Julian rolled his eyes.

"We could, next time."

"I don't like cruising. I'm not sure I'd want to do this again. I feel as if I don't own my own time."

Nodding, sipping his coffee, Brodie agreed. "Yes, but you do get to see different ports without shifting from one hotel to the next."

"True." Julian set his cup down, finally removing his coat.

"What the hell's that?" Brodie asked.

"What's what?"

"Out there. Is that a fucking whale?"

Julian glued his face to the glass. "Holy cow!"

Brodie stood up, trying to see out in the distance. "That is so incredible."

Pausing, watching an enormous Humpback whale breech, splash, and vanish, Brodie caught his breath at the amazing sight. Sitting back down, he smiled as he finished his cup of coffee. "I love shit like that."

Julian joined him in his glee, grinning like a little boy. "I have seen whales before. There are killer whales all along the coast of the San Juan's."

"I've heard that. I saw one once when I was on the ferry."

"No way."

"I swear. I thought the boat would tip over so many people rushed to see it." Brodie set his cup aside, reaching across the table.

Julian had a peek around. "You don't intend to hold my hand, do you?"

"Yes."

"Uh, maybe later? In a dark auditorium."

"Chicken shit." Brodie sat back.

"A little. You feel ready for that?"

Brodie shrugged, moving his legs underneath the table to make contact. "I'm not embarrassed by you. You're not that horribly ugly."

Julian laughed into his coffee cup. "I don't mean it that way, ya dork."

Again Brodie shrugged. "Why not? Julian, do you really give a shit what these other passengers think? Really?"

"Sort of. I thought you did as well." He set his empty cup aside, leaning over the table.

Brodie took the opportunity to mirror him, bringing their lips close together. Brodie expected Julian to recoil and pull back, but he didn't. An inch apart, Brodie whispered, "I don't care. I thought long and hard over it, pretty boy, and I'm tired of living a lie."

"Pretty boy?"

Feeling the puff of breath from Julian's lips, Brodie smiled wickedly. "Oh yes. Very, very pretty."

"Shut up, you dork."

"Kiss me."

"I can't. Christ, just look at the way we're sitting. Any moron would figure it out. Straight guys don't talk with their noses almost touching. Isn't this enough?"

"No."

"Brodie…" Julian chided.

"Julian?"

At the sound of Amelia's voice, both men recoiled and parted to their respective corners.

"What?" Julian asked casually.

Brodie stared at her as she studied him carefully.

"You just looked like you were going to kiss this guy." She pointed her red fingernail at Brodie.

"What the hell do you care?" Julian replied.

That made Brodie's eyebrows rise up in surprise.

"Julian!" she snorted. "Don't embarrass yourself in public. Sheesh! It's bad enough you got dumped, don't make people think you're a fucking queer."

Brodie held his breath. The look of rage that flashed over Julian's handsome face was explosive. Before Brodie knew what had happened, Julian had lunged across the table, grabbed his face in his hands, and planted a rich opened-mouth smooch right on his lips. Grunting in surprise, his eyes blinking wide, Brodie choked in shock.

"Julian Richards! You stop that this instant!"

Breaking the kiss, Julian faced her, snarling, "I am queer. Okay? One relationship with an idiot like you would make anyone gay."

Brodie's mouth reverberated with Julian's kiss. Frozen to his chair, he had no idea who had spied it, and the fluttering in his gut was like someone had opened up a can of moths in it.

"Don't be disgusting!" Amelia spat out. "You're just playing some stupid game to get me upset. And it won't work. So stop acting like a moron." She looked around behind her, shouting, "Harry? Harry, where are you?"

Brodie touched his mouth lightly. When he looked at Julian, he was grinning demonically.

The dancing disco man made an appearance. "Come on, Harry, this jerk is making me sick to my stomach."

Harry gave Julian a nasty scowl, held onto Amelia tightly, and walked her away.

Julian exhaled, dropping back in the seat tiredly.

Brodie was still recovering from the stunt. "I thought you didn't want to kiss me in public."

"Sorry. I just wanted to get a dig in at her."

Brodie leaned back across the table. "You sure? Just a joke? Nothing more?"

A strange gleam appeared in Julian's light eyes.

When he met him in the middle of the table, mirroring him, Brodie began to laugh.

"Get over here, Mr. Duncan," Julian purred.

Stretching over the Formica topped table, Brodie closed his eyes as those warm, masculine lips connected to his. As they kissed he could hear a slight, disapproving murmur rumbling around them. Passengers expressing their opinions no doubt. Did he care? Half of him wanted to shout out, "I'm gay! and I don't give a shit who knows it." But still deep inside, a tinge of fear kept worming its way around his gut. Could he ever get used to this?

~

Julian lavished in the kiss. It was insane, it would cause a scandal and he didn't care. Screw these idiots. He'd never see them again. Parting from that set of seductive lips, Julian smiled at Brodie dreamily. "I adore you."

"You are something else." Brodie shook his head.

"How about a hot Jacuzzi? Sauna heat!"

"You bet." Brodie stood up, reaching out his hand.

Taking it into his, Julian clasped it tight, following him down the crowded corridor. So what if people gawked. It was their problem. Wasn't it?

They stopped at Julian's room first. He peered in. "She's cleared out."

"Good. Pack." Brodie threw his coat down, looking for Julian's suitcase. The two of them working to empty the room, they had his things into his bags in a few minutes. Julian did a last check into each drawer and closet. "Okay."

Brodie carried the large suitcase with him as Julian took his toiletry case. Walking down the long corridor, and across the width of the ship, avoiding eye contact with anyone who stared too long, Julian had made up his mind this wasn't going to be a big deal. Gay couples went on cruises. No one seemed to find it illegal, immoral maybe, but you couldn't get thrown into jail for it. What? Did they segregate gay men? Make them take their own vacations? Well, maybe. There were gay cruises. Julian couldn't decide if this was okay or not.

Brodie opened his cabin door, bringing the case inside. He

dumped it on the bed, removing Julian's suits from it to hang up. Julian brought his shaving bag into the bathroom, tossing it on the counter by the sink.

Stepping out of the toilet, he watched Brodie unpack his things efficiently. "You find my bathing suit in there yet?"

Brodie held up a pair of Speedos. "You mean this little thing?"

Julian snatched it out of Brodie's hand. "Yeah, what about it."

"Can't wait to see you in it."

"What did you bring?"

Moving to a drawer, Brodie held up a set of swim trunks.

"Oh."

"Oh." Brodie laughed at him.

"Fuck you. You're not going to make me self-conscious."

"Not until I tease you hard, you mean."

"You wouldn't."

"Wouldn't I?" Brodie took off his shirt.

"No. Because you know it'll embarrass the crap out of me."

Brodie raised his eyebrow in reply.

Shaking his head, Julian removed his jeans. "You do that to me, and you are so dead."

Brodie slipped his swim trunks on. "So dead? That's your threat?"

Julian moaned, dragging down his briefs and jeans to slip on his bathing suit. Once he had it on, he adjusted his cock to fit, seeing it was already hard and showing through the material. "Perfect." He threw up his hands in disbelief.

Moving to kneel in front of him, Brodie peeled the soft, shiny material back, exposing him. "Yes. Perfect." He opened his mouth and surrounded Julian's cock. Stumbling to sit on the bed, Julian fell back, digging his fingers into Brodie's auburn hair, combing through its length.

~

Closing his eyes, Brodie loved sucking on this man's cock. It could easily become his favorite hobby. Screw tennis and volleyball.

Hearing Julian moan, tasting the pre-come drop on his tongue, Brodie deepened the penetration, wondering how far he could go before the gag reflex kicked in. He was almost down to the base as it was. Using his fingers to form a ring around the bottom of Julian's cock, he squeezed it tightly, moving his mouth up so his lips rolled over Julian's head, then back to touching his fingers again, long, deep, and slow sucking until Julian raised his hips in yearning, and that throaty groaning began. Making a pattern to the act, Brodie squeezed, sucked, licked, and repeated. Each time he did, Julian elevated his hips and whimpered. Brodie knew he was prolonging Julian's orgasm. Why not? They had all day, and he loved it. Moving that tiny black bathing suit down Julian's legs to his ankles, lifting one leg out of it, Brodie pushed Julian's thighs wide apart. Another agonizing moan erupted from Julian's lips.

Smoothing his fingers around Julian's testicles, Brodie continued the slow, deep sucking, the tight squeeze around the base and added anal penetration to the mix.

A loud gasp met his ears, making him smile. The rippling of Julian's muscles began at his balls. Brodie released the tight grip he had on his cock and it began to throb instantly. Julian's hips rose off the bed, thrusting deeper into Brodie's mouth. Come shot out of the tip, hot and thick, as Brodie swallowed down the treat.

"Oh. My. God."

Brodie sat back, stroking Julian's balls gently, watching them move in their sack.

"You are a fucking master. I cannot believe how well you suck dick. You sure I'm your first male partner?"

"Yes! Shut up!" Brodie laughed shyly. "I just like it."

"I'm completely spent. You sucked the life out of me."

"Mm, I sucked the juice out of you," Brodie purred, nuzzling Julian's thigh.

"What do you want? Hm? Name it."

Brodie stood, looking down at him. "You just said you were exhausted."

As if finding the energy, Julian patted the bed next to him. "Bring it here. I'm not going to leave you unsatisfied."

Brodie removed his bathing suit, lying on the bed next to him. Julian edged closer, going for a kiss. Wrapping his arms around Julian, bringing him in contact, Brodie closed his eyes and savored those lips. Hands instantly fondled him, running up and down his length, cupping his balls gently. Brodie squirmed on the bed, his breathing quickening. Parting from their kiss, Julian edged downward. His excitement growing, watching Julian get into position, Brodie panted, unable to slow down his lungs. Making himself comfortable between Brodie's legs, Julian leaned up on his elbows, stroking Brodie's cock a few times, admiring it. Pinching the tip, a glistening drop appeared. As Julian licked it off, Brodie's head spun. Soon he felt completely enveloped and a swirling tongue against his cock. Dropping back to lie flat on the bed, Brodie's focus was on that technique, slightly different from his own, but effective, very effective. A wet finger inched its way inside him. Brodie felt a charge of electricity rush to the tip of his dick. As that slick finger fucked him, he felt Julian trying to fit all of him into his throat. When wet heat surrounded him to the very base, Brodie released his seed, arching his back, grinding his jaw.

Julian quickened his pace, sucking hard, painfully hard, using his teeth to slide across Brodie's silky skin lightly. "*Ah*," Brodie moaned in ecstasy. "And you say I give good head? Holy crap."

Sitting up, wiping his chin with his hand, Julian grinned wickedly.

"Am I the first guy you've been with?" Brodie asked in a silly voice, echoing Julian's earlier comment.

"First and last."

Brodie sat up slowly, trying to recuperate from the intense climax. "First and last?"

"Yes." Julian stood, sliding his Speedos back into place on his hips. "Ready for a swim?"

"Wait." Brodie reached out to him. "I didn't get that last comment."

Julian tilted his head at him in awe. "Man, too much sex is making us stupid."

Managing to stand and pull up his bathing suit, Brodie asked again, "What did you mean?"

"I mean, you and me! Duh!"

"You and me what?"

"I cannot believe you are making me spell this out for you.

Brodie, get some blood back into your gray cells and out of your dick."

Laughing, Brodie replied, "I'm trying but my dick is still hard from your amazing mouth."

Julian grabbed him by the face and said in very measured words, "You. Me. Only. Get it?"

"Yeah?" Brodie's heart pumped in joy.

"Yeah. Now, where do we get towels? Do we take the ones from the shower?"

"No. They have them down there."

"Good." Julian slipped a t-shirt over his torso, which covered his bathing suit. "Grab a key."

Brodie put on a shirt, tucking the key into the front of his bathing suit. As they walked down the hall, Brodie reached back for his hand. It was clasped. "You. Me. Only."

He heard Julian chuckle.

"I like that." Brodie puffed out his chest proudly. "I like that a lot."

"You're such a dork."

~

The whirlpools were hopping with passengers eager to warm up after the cold shot on deck. When they entered the room, Julian noticed Glenda point them out to Marlene in excitement.

He and Brodie were still holding hands. Against his impulse, he didn't shake off his grip. "Brodie."

"What?"

"Over there."

Brodie looked to where Julian was gesturing. The women had obviously spied the connection and were whispering together, staring at them.

"Oh well." Brodie moved to the least crowded hot tub. Taking off his shirt, he set it with his key on a ledge away from the water.

As Brodie climbed into the pool, Julian took off his top, dropping it on Brodie's. He heard Glenda shouting his name, waving. He smiled, waving back, lowering himself to sit next to Brodie on the tiled ledge. "That feels so good. I hate being cold."

"They're coming over."

"So what?" Julian waited as they approached.

"Hi, guys!" Marlene waved. She was wearing a one-piece pink bathing suit that made her look slightly like a sausage.

"Ladies." Brodie smiled sweetly.

"Can we join you?" Glenda asked.

Julian gestured with his hand for her to come in. They settled down near them, between five others who had been bubbling in the cauldron.

"Feels nice to be warm," Glenda giggled, poking her toes out of the water.

"I know. I was freezing up on deck," Julian replied.

Marlene was studying them curiously. "Did you guys just meet here on the ship?"

Julian exchanged looks with Brodie. Brodie answered, "Yes. Why?"

"That is so cool." She shook her head, as if she was showing her approval.

"What?" Glenda didn't catch it.

Marlene leaned to her ear, but Julian could hear her whisper, "They're gay!" And it seemed everyone else in the pool heard it as well. Suddenly they were all staring at Brodie and Julian.

"Oh!" Glenda gulped, frowning. "Darn."

"Sorry, sweetie." Brodie found Julian's hand under the water, holding it.

"It's okay. I think it's nice. Really."

Marlene edged closer, trying not to shout in the loud noise. "You left that woman? The one at your table? To be with Brodie?"

Julian felt his cheeks heat up and he didn't know if it was embarrassment or the hot water he was soaking in. "Yes."

"Wow. That took guts."

Brodie looked back at him, smiling proudly.

Averting his eyes shyly, Julian said, "Yes. Nerves of steel. Believe me."

"I'm proud of you guys. Really. I know that must have been really hard."

"Thank you, Marlene." Brodie appeared genuinely surprised at her support.

"So? Are you a real couple now?" Glenda asked as two of the people suddenly needed to get out of the water.

Julian watched them leave, trying not to take offense.

Nodding, Brodie replied, "Yes. I guess so. We haven't planned too far ahead yet."

"Do you live close by each other?" Marlene asked.

"Yes. We do."

"That's incredible." Marlene nodded in awe.

Julian noticed now they were the only four left in the whirlpool. "Do you think we chased everyone away?"

"No!" Marlene waved her hand at him. "They've been in the damn thing for a half hour. They probably feel like prunes."

"What did your girlfriend do when you told her?" Glenda asked.

Opening his mouth, but unable to actually answer that question, Julian was glad when Marlene scolded her friend. "Glenda, give the guy a break. Don't start the twenty questions."

"Sorry." She smiled impishly.

Thankful someone found tact in the uncomfortable conversation, Julian lowered down in the water, closing his eyes to relax. As he floated above the churning heat in a state of complete contentment, Julian felt as if the first layer of fear had vanished from him. All he could think about was Brodie's hand holding his.

~

After the soak and a few minutes to sweat in the sauna, they showered, changed, and caught a light lunch at one of the cafés. Brodie asked, "Anything you'd like to do?"

Julian shrugged. "Any suggestions?"

"Did you know they have an internet room near the library?"

"I think I remember seeing that listed somewhere. Why? Do you need to check your email?"

Brodie smiled shyly. "It would help kill some time. Don't you want to?"

"I don't know. I kind of told myself I'd leave everything alone for the week. You know, cell phones, computers."

"I have a friend I've been corresponding with."

"Really?" Julian's eyebrows rose in response.

"He's gay. His name is Paden. He's my closest friend, or should

I say *was* my closest friend."

Hesitating in their walk down the hall, Julian blinked and asked, "You have a close gay friend?"

Slightly put out by the accusatory tone, Brodie's smile faded. "So?"

"Christ, Brodie. That should have been a sign."

"Shut the fuck up. You sound like one of the bimbos I've been dating."

Shaking his head and holding up his hands, Julian apologized, "Sorry. Old habits. It was a stupid thing to say."

"Ya think?" Brodie snarled.

"Never mind. So? You want to email this gay guy? Tell him you've joined his club?"

"Forget it," Brodie grumbled, walking away from him down the hall.

Julian grabbed his arm, stopping him. "Where's the library?"

Trying not to feel hurt by Julian's careless words, Brodie led him to the Atlantic deck, past a prayer chapel, and through the library. Several computers were available. After Brodie sat down, Julian pulled a vacant chair next to him. Removing his wallet, Brodie slipped his credit card into the slot and the computer allowed him to access his Yahoo account. Instantly he found one from Paden, replying to his revelation. "I already mentioned you to him."

"Did you?"

"Yup." Brodie opened it up.

"Should I not look?"

"No. I don't mind. Paden is a pretty funny guy. I assume his reply will be humorous. Nothing I have to be embarrassed about, cutie."

At the comment, Julian pecked Brodie's cheek quickly. Loving the little zing of pleasure it created, Brodie shifted in his chair.

"A hard-on? From that?" Julian teased.

"Yes. Shut up and let me read." Brodie noticed his own email was still visible underneath Paden's and suddenly had a pang of regret, wondering what Julian would think if he read it. Forgetting it for the time being, Brodie read Paden's reply. *Well! Mr. Duncan!*

What can I say? I'm shocked. I thought you were the consummate ladies' man. You never let on otherwise. Are you just experimenting? Or is this some life-altering decision on your part? You better call me when you get home. I need to find out what's going on. It's a little surprising considering your female conquests, Brodie. Are you sure you know what you're doing? Please don't hurt the poor man by leading him on. Some of us poor schmucks actually grow attached. Be careful. See you soon.

It wasn't what he expected. He assumed Paden would be raving about how it was about time and why did it take Brodie so long. Thinking about the slight reprimanding tone, Brodie relaxed in the chair, noticing Julian reading it with rapt interest.

"I'm a charmer who you're experimenting with? No strings attached?" Julian asked, "Is that what this is all about?"

Brodie signed off, closing the screen. He didn't know why but he regretted this idea deeply. Stuffing his credit card into his wallet, Brodie watched the icons vanish as the computer shut down.

Seeing someone else in the next cubby hole, Brodie stood, pushing in the chair.

"Brodie?"

He walked out of the room, through the library before Julian caught up to him and stopped his progress.

Julian looked around the immediate area. There were plenty of bookworms reading quietly. Julian directed Brodie into the chapel. It was a miniature church with pew benches and a small crucifix on the wall hanging over several different versions of the bible.

Forcing him to sit down, Julian kept a firm grip on his arm so he couldn't run away. In the utter silence of the room, Julian whispered, "Are you just using me for some idle curiosity? Some stupid fling to see if you could do it?"

"No. Julian, give me a break. Okay? When I first met you I got excited and wanted to tell someone, that's all. And you're not some idle curiosity, you're more than that and I shouldn't have to repeat it."

"You called me a charmer? Delving into the Greek way of love with no strings attached?"

"Why are you making such an issue out of it?" Brodie lowered his voice as it echoed in the empty room. The tormented plaster sculpture of Christ on the cross seemed oppressive in its depiction of agony.

Julian moved his posture so he was facing that tortured deity. Resting his elbows on his lap, Julian rubbed at his face as if he were very weary suddenly.

Brodie stared at Christ's crown of thorns, the way his body hung helplessly. "I..." Brodie's voice filled the tiny chapel. "I was excited. I guess I just wanted to tell someone." Julian didn't respond, resting his face in his hands. "I know I've always been a bit of a womanizer. But deep inside I knew what really turned me on."

Julian removed his jaw from his palms, looking over at him.

"I'm not using you, Julian. I'm not. You know exactly what I'm going through. You dated nothing but women before me. I could say the same thing to you. But I don't. I know you want me as a companion. Not a conquest or experiment."

Reclining on the hard, wooden bench, Julian stared down at his hands as they lay limp on his lap.

Brodie reached out to touch Julian's freshly shaven cheek. Using his knuckles, he smoothed against the soft supple skin the razor left behind. "I love you. I really do." Brodie bit back some lump of emotion that rushed up his throat. "I'd ask you to marry me if I could."

That brought Julian's undivided attention.

Brodie chewed on his bottom lip, fighting an urge to weep, as if the sacred sanctuary of that chapel allowed them their chance to express deep sentiments and be safe. "You think I've ever considered asking a woman to marry me? I haven't. It's never been something I entertained on a serious level. It's about trust, Julian. Trust. Laying your heart on the line and taking a chance. I have to admit, I never did it before. Do you think I've loved anyone like this? Like I would be torn in half if they left?" Brodie felt hot tears sting his eyes. He shut up, staring back at that crucifix again. All the religion of his youth was fighting back at his immoral urges to hump a man.

Julian reached for Brodie's hand. When he clasped it, Julian brought it to his lips.

Brodie fell apart. Wrapping around him, he hugged him, resting his chin on Julian's shoulder. And he wept. He had no idea why. Fear? Religion? Love? He couldn't remember crying like this. Ever.

"Shh, all right, baby." Julian rubbed his back, cooing gently.

Brodie didn't know whether to die from embarrassment or rejoice in the fact that he did have a heart in his chest. He'd felt so bland about relationships for so long, the sensation of a real love was petrifying him in its vulnerability. He could genuinely get hurt by this man. If Julian had second thoughts when they returned to Seattle, Brodie had no idea how he would cope.

Parting from the embrace, Brodie wiped at his eyes roughly. "I'm such an idiot."

"No." Julian caressed Brodie's hair, petting it back gently against him, like stroking a cat to make it purr.

Getting a better grip on his emotions, Brodie inhaled deeply, looking back at the solemn face of Christ, seeking some comfort or strength, though he'd never looked to God before for those things.

Once again, Julian clasped his hands, tightly. "Brodie."

Brodie peered up from his funk to see those crystal clear blue eyes.

"I'm not going anywhere."

"Are you sure?" Brodie searched his light irises for sincerity. He'd made so many mistakes in his life up to now.

"As sure as I can be. This is uncharted territory for me as well. Do you really think there's some gay switch inside men where you flip it and you're a homosexual?"

"How the hell am I supposed to answer that question?" Brodie felt his body shiver involuntarily as he began thinking the worst of the comments.

"We're still in some kind of pseudo-society here." Julian gripped Brodie's hands tighter. "Our families are somewhere else, our work is back home, our friends, our commitments…"

"And?"

"I'm not going to lie to you and tell you I'm not apprehensive about our future as a couple."

"Oh God. No. I knew it." Brodie tried to tug his hands back.

Julian didn't let him. "Stop jumping to conclusions."

"How can I? Listen to yourself."

"Brodie! I'm trying to be honest with you. I'm shitting a brick, babe." Julian peeked around the room, as if making sure they were still alone. "You think I feel good about telling my parents I'm gay? They kissed me and Amelia goodbye last Monday as we went away on our little cruise. My goddamn mother constantly hints to me about marrying someone, settling down, having kids."

"Stop. Please don't put me through this." Brodie felt like throwing up. He managed to free his hands from Julian's grip.

The minute he did, Julian grabbed Brodie's face, turning it to look at him. "But!" Julian shouted in a muted roar. "I'm not letting go. No way. You think once I'm back home, suddenly I'll have some memory blackout of what we've done? Of the sex? The closeness we've shared? Brodie, I couldn't. I'd cry in my pillows every night craving you, your body, your taste, your scent."

Brodie's lip trembled. Why was this so hard?

"I couldn't do it." Julian shook his head. "It's like I've tasted something extraordinary and from now on I'm supposed to go back to bland food."

Trying to find some humor, Brodie forced himself to smile, but it fell quickly.

"You said this was about trust." Julian grabbed Brodie's shoulders, making him look into his eyes.

Wanting to reply, all Brodie could do was nod.

"Trust me. Brodie, I know the kind of relationships we've been dealing with, and honesty and trust weren't high on our list of character traits. But it is now. And you have got to have some faith in me."

"Promise?"

Julian held up his hand, gestured to Jesus Christ, and said, "As God is my witness."

That horrible emotional tidal wave washed over Brodie again. Holding back a sob with every fiber in his body, he reached out for Julian. Julian gladly accepted his hug, squeezing him tight. "I love you, Brodie. I swear I do."

"Oh God, baby..." Brodie choked up.

Julian kissed Brodie's face as tears rolled down it. When he contacted his mouth, Brodie sucked the salty taste from Julian's lips. Their passion rising, they jolted as a gasp echoed in the tiny chapel.

Spinning around, Brodie found an elderly woman standing in the doorway, a rosary bead necklace in her hand.

Instantly the men got to their feet, leaving the room. As they walked down the hall, Julian held Brodie's hand. "You all right?"

"Yes."

"How about a drink?"

"Definitely." Brodie smiled.

~

They relaxed in a lounge on the busy promenade level. It was the area of the ship that seemed to have the most going for it; the casino, two bars, cafés, the dining hall, everything to entertain two bored men.

Julian sipped his Irish coffee as Brodie nursed a scotch. "I think the only thing I haven't done so far on this boat is the swimming pools and the movie theater."

As if coming out of a daydream, Brodie replied, "The movies are slightly late releases. I've seen most of them. And the outdoor pool is too damn cold."

"There's one inside, on the lido deck." Julian finished his strong coffee, craving another.

"That's right." Brodie nodded. "By the sauna area."

"We could take a dip later."

"You know there's a midnight chocolate extravaganza tonight."

Julian chuckled in surprise. "A chocoholic? I thought that was reserved for women?"

Giving him a scolding look, Brodie shook his head. "Always taking a jab."

"Yeah, so what? Wanna deck me?" Julian grinned.

"Anyway..." Brodie rolled his eyes. "Think we could motivate ourselves to check it out?"

"And get up and run early the next morning?"

"We could sleep in. Take one day off. I haven't had a day off in..." Brodie put on a thinking face. "It has to be at least ten days in a row now."

"I suppose we could pass on one day." Julian flagged a waitress down. "Could you get me another Irish coffee? Brodie?"

"No. I'm still working on this one." He raised his glass.

"Thank you," Julian smiled at the nice woman as she took his empty mug.

"Are you still cold?"

"A little. Funny. I feel a craving for hot coffee. But the whiskey is really kicking in." Julian wiggled in his soft chair happily. After a pause he sighed, "I dread getting back to work and dealing with Amelia. I can't tell you how much I needed this break."

"So, stock trading?" Brodie asked.

"Not really. I do more personal advising for clients. If someone wants to invest their savings I work on getting them into different accounts, CDs, you know."

"Huh. Maybe you can do it for me."

"Sure."

"I've got a savings account but the interest rate has really sucked lately."

"Yes. It has been in the dumps because the US economy is in the toilet." Julian sat up as his fresh drink arrived. "Thank you."

The waitress set it down on their small round table first, holding out a pen and paper for Julian to sign. He did, handing her back the pen. As Julian elevated the coffee to his lips, he muttered, "I have a feeling Amelia is still using my credit account."

"No."

Julian shrugged. "She's registered to my room, my credit card."

"Go to the reception desk and change it. That's unfair."

"I don't know how much damage she can do. Maybe I should just leave it." Julian suddenly remembered her spending spree on the casino. "On second thought…"

Brodie leaned closer to him. "She'll nail you. Spite is a nasty thing when you're dealing with the opposite sex."

"I should find her and ask her about it. I was hoping Harry had some pride and would insist he buy her what she needs."

"Don't count on it, babe." Brodie took another sip of his drink. "Does that Harry have a really big head, or am I just imagining it."

Julian chuckled. "No. He has a big head. I wonder if he can find a hat to fit it. Anyway, is it a formal dinner tonight?"

"No. It was formal last night. They can't do it every night."

Julian nodded, dazing off again. After a quiet moment, Brodie got his attention, pointing to the entrance. Amelia and Harry had entered the dim lounge.

"Now's your chance to see if she's milking you," Brodie whispered.

"Shit." Julian dreaded any contact with her at all.

She noticed him as she drew closer to the bar. Immediately she rolled her eyes.

Julian set his mug down on the table, as if he needed his hands free to defend himself.

"You know," she sneered, "if you guys keep hanging around together, people will really think you are queer."

Out of the corner of his eye, Julian noticed Brodie stiffen in anger. "Uh, Amelia." He stood up. "Can I have a word with you?" Julian looked at Harry as the new beau curled his lip.

"If you want to get back together, the answer is no." She grinned with superiority, glancing back at Harry.

"Uh, no. It's about my credit card."

"What about it?" She took up a posture of defense.

"You're not still signing your spending to our room, are you?" Julian caught Harry's eye, trying to convey something to him as well.

"Screw you, Julian. You owe me."

"I owe you?" Julian touched his chest.

"That's rich," Brodie laughed sadly.

"Why do I owe you, Amelia?" Julian tried to keep calm. "If I recall, you told me you didn't want to be with me anymore."

"That was after your speech on us not having anything in common."

"Wait a minute," Brodie shouted.

Julian held out his hand to keep him quiet. "Amelia, can we speak in private?"

"I don't know what you have to say to me that Harry can't hear. Right, Harry?"

The silent, unusual looking man glared at Julian with homicidal intent. "She doesn't hide anything from me."

"Then I'm sure you won't mind paying her way from now on." Julian put his hands on his hips.

"She said she insisted she pay." Harry tilted his large head at her.

"It's my credit card. She's not paying. I am."

"Julian," Brodie prompted, "just go to the reception desk and straighten it out."

Amelia bristled. "Why does he care, Julian? Are you two really together now?"

"That's not the point here, Amelia." Julian felt a nervous pang in his gut.

"You mean you're not just trying to jerk my chain to piss me off about leaving you?" She gasped. "You're really gay?"

Julian felt ill, as if he needed to sit down.

"Your mother is going to kill you." Amelia shook her head. "Does she know?" Before Julian could answer, Amelia sneered, "No, I bet she doesn't know what you've been doing onboard. You told me you weren't going to use your cell phone or the computer while we were on vacation. Man, I can't wait to inform her she's got a queer son."

"Don't you dare, Amelia." Julian's knees grew weak.

"How about this? I use your credit card, and I don't tell your mommy."

Brodie jumped to his feet, approaching them, steam pouring out of his ears. "You blackmailing bitch."

She gave Brodie a good once over. "I thought you were cute. Now you make me sick."

"I'm going to punch her," Brodie snarled.

Growing dizzy with the anxiety, Julian grabbed Amelia's arm, bringing her away from Harry and Brodie.

"Don't touch me, you nasty faggot. I can't believe I had sex with you. Now I need a fucking AIDS test." She recoiled.

Imagining strangling her, Julian peeked back at Brodie quickly. He was arguing with Harry, but Julian couldn't hear what they were saying. "Amelia. Be rational. First of all, we always used protection, okay?" Julian felt his heart in his throat. "And," he made sure she was looking at him, "Brodie is the first man I've ever been with."

"Then you *are* having sex with him?" she gasped loudly. "Ew!"

"Shut up!" Julian was struggling to keep his voice down. Some of the passengers were beginning to take notice. "Listen to me. I will not be manipulated by your threats. Okay? First of all, stop using my money. We're not together any longer. And even you know that's not right. You're far from poor, Amelia, and I'm sure your new boyfriend would be happy to pay for anything you need." Before she interrupted he added, "And about telling my family about me, you wouldn't be that cruel."

A cold expression washed over her face. "How do you think I feel, huh, Julian? My ex-boyfriend turned gay on me."

"It didn't happen that way. You left me. Why are you turning this on me? You asked to move out. You spent a night with him before we broke up. Why is this now about me?"

"Because homosexuals make me sick."

"Since when?" he challenged. "You work with gay men in the bank. You never even flinched."

"I can't. It's not politically correct." She rolled her eyes.

"I won't let you hurt me. Not financially, nor emotionally. You made a clean break with me, Amelia. Your decision. Don't act as if you have an ax to grind."

"What if I didn't find Harry? You probably have been seeing that faggot behind my back. All your talk about nothing in common? I bet it was just so you could sneak away and suck his cock."

Hating the reality of that, and the expression of revulsion on her face, Julian bit his lip on more fury. A glimpse at Brodie and he could see by his body language their debate was heating up as well. Inhaling, calming himself forcefully, Julian threw up his hands in defeat. "Fine. How much are you going to blow?"

Looking satisfied, Amelia replied, "Only a thousand or so."

"Fine." Julian wanted to smack her.

"Good. Nice doing business with you."

As she walked away, Julian rubbed his face in agony.

~

"You moron," Brodie snarled at Harry, "join the fucking twenty-first century."

Harry retorted, "It's in the Bible, asshole. Your kind are damned."

Brodie noticed Amelia returning, hooking Harry's arm. "Come on, Harry, I can't stand the sight of these guys."

Giving Brodie a last sneer, Harry turned his back on him and escorted Amelia away.

Brodie hurried to where Julian was standing. "What happened?"

"This sucks, big time." Julian rubbed at his eyes.

"Sit down." Brodie touched his arm, indicating their chairs.

Dropping down on his, Julian reached to finish his coffee.

As he waited, Brodie knew it wasn't going to be good news. "You let the bitch blackmail you, didn't you?"

"Yes." Julian replaced the mug on the table.

"Why?"

"Because I'm shitting a brick she'll call my mother, okay?"

Holding up his hands at the venting hostility, Brodie shook his head. "Don't take it out on me."

"I'm sorry."

Chewing on his lip in frustration, Brodie wanted to scream. Instead, he rose up, walked to the bar, ordering two shots of tequila, it always worked in the past. After he signed for them, he returned to his seat. A second later the waitress brought over the order, two limes accompanying it. Brodie thanked her. He handed Julian a lime, and a glass. In sync, they sucked down the shot and gnawed the lime. Julian coughed, shaking his head at the sting.

Brodie tossed the rind and empty glass back on the table. "Another?"

"No. Not yet. I've already got a good start from the whiskey."

"Then let's get the fuck out of here." Brodie stood up.

Julian got to his feet, head down, following him.

There was a simple solution. All Julian had to do was tell his parents first. *Maybe that isn't so simple after all.*

Though Brodie suggested they leave the lounge, he didn't know where to go. Checking his watch, seeing it was only four and dinner wouldn't be served until six, he instinctively led them to his cabin. It was quiet, dark, and private. When he stood before his door, sliding in the key, he looked over his shoulder. Either Julian was beginning to feel the effects of the booze, or he was brooding. Or both.

Tossing the white card down on the dresser, Brodie kicked off his shoes and reclined on the bed. A frown plastered on his face, Julian disappeared into the bathroom. Brodie heard his stream hitting the water. It made him feel the urge. Standing with an effort, Brodie stood at the door as Julian finished.

"Don't flush, I've got to go."

Julian peered over his shoulder, moving to the sink to wash his hands.

Brodie yanked down his zipper, relieving himself. After giving it a shake, he tucked himself in, but didn't zip his jeans. As Julian left the bathroom, Brodie washed his hands and face, trying not to look into his own eyes. He knew he was reflecting Julian's dower mood. Returning to the bed, he found Julian lying on it, his back facing him. Brodie imagined taking off his jeans and getting under the blankets for a nap. Not wanting to disturb Julian, he climbed behind him, spooning him, hugging him tight.

Without intending on initiating sex, longing for a nap, Brodie felt his body respond regardless of his plan. His cock was inching its way out of his open zipper as it hardened. Trying to ignore it, shutting his eyes, Brodie inhaled deeply. The scent of Julian's hair, his skin, and his cologne made his skin tingle. *Oh, this is so useless!* He was helpless to control his attraction. *Leave the man alone for five minutes.*

Knowing part of the problem was his contact against Julian's back, Brodie lay flat, staring at the ceiling. Last minute before he closed his eyes, he reached for that switch on the headboard. The room went black. In the pitch darkness Brodie heard the hum of the massive ship's engine, felt the sway of the waves under them. Julian rolled over, towards him, his arm lay across Brodie's chest. Julian's face pressed against his hair and neck. Blinking his eyes open, Brodie's cock twitched in excitement. Just being next to this man drove him insane. He was insatiable, constantly craving to suck him, touch him. It was madness. He wondered if it was like heroin addiction, chronic withdrawals and intense craving.

Julian sighed, or yawned, Brodie couldn't hear it too well over that loud rumbling hum. In a sleepy, casual way, Julian rubbed his palm against Brodie's chest, as if he was comforting himself that Brodie was there with him. Slowly Brodie moved his own hand, touching his exposed cock. Imagining jerking off, Brodie wondered if he had lost his mind. Couldn't he wait? Surely when they woke up from their nap they would fool around.

But Julian felt so good. Smelled divine. That wandering hand of Julian's was definitely moving south in the darkness. Very soon Brodie's secret would be discovered.

~

Julian savored the comfort of Brodie's body. Though his mind gave him no rest from the episode with Amelia in the lounge, Julian tried to sleep. A nap before dinner would be perfect. The buzz from the alcohol made him drowsy. Humming to himself contentedly at the feel of Brodie's muscled chest, his narrow waist, Julian blinked his eyes wide as he ran into Brodie's hand. And it was holding his cock. Even though it was completely dark in the room, Julian leaned up, trying to make out what was happening. If he could, it was with a picture in his mind, because there was no light in the cabin. Using his fingertips, like reading Braille, he got a good sense of exactly what was going on. Smiling, Julian pushed Brodie's shirt high on his chest, fingering his way up to Brodie's nipple and back down to the head of his cock, knocking into it gently as Brodie held it tight.

Taking his time, pinching Brodie's nipples until they were erect like his dick, Julian made his way to one to lick. Above that hum of the engine, Julian heard Brodie's masculine sigh. Running his tongue over it, imagining what it looked like, Julian closed his eyes to allow his working senses to take over. Once he had gnawed that nipple to his heart's content, another impulse drew him away.

Sliding his cheek along Brodie's warm skin, down his sternum, belly button, toward his pubic hair, Julian ran face first into the spongy head of Brodie's cock. Nudging Brodie's hand away from it, Julian replaced it with his own. His eyes still closed, he moved that erection so the tip brushed over his dry lips. A drop oozed out of it moistening them. He licked at the taste of it, moving to push the head of Brodie's cock inside his mouth. Instantly Brodie stiffened his back. Julian was amazed how he could sense every muscle of Brodie's body contract, even without the lights on. Resting his cheek on Brodie's belly, Julian raced his tongue around that mushroom shaped head, always ending up at the slit to lap at the juices. Brodie's hand found Julian's hair, massaging his scalp through it. It felt so relaxing Julian almost forgot what he was doing. But not quite.

Sinking down, taking Brodie's cock deeper into his mouth, Julian hummed with the ship's engine, deep and low. It made Brodie raise his hips off the bed. Smiling, even with his mouth full, Julian pushed down until his lips met Brodie's pelvis. He had Brodie's entire cock enveloped in his mouth. A rapid pulse raced over it. Sliding it back out, Julian pushed at those tight jeans. Instantly, Brodie wrestled them down his hips. The moment Brodie's balls were exposed, Julian went for them, kneading them softly in his left hand. Over the rumbling noise, Julian heard Brodie's groan, felt his legs go tense. *You always make me wait. What's the rush?*

Throating Brodie's cock again, holding it there while he ran his tongue up and down its slick length rapidly, Julian felt Brodie writhe under him. Withdrawing, licking up and down the sides of Brodie's erection, mostly underneath to the head, Julian wondered if he could do this for an hour. It was soothing yet extremely stimulating. His own cock had grown hard down the side of his pant leg, and twitched and throbbed every time Brodie moaned, or elevated his hips from his pleasure.

Julian toyed gently with Brodie's wet dick, snuffling at Brodie's balls, rubbing his face into them,. Again that whimpering moan emerged, hips pushing off the bed and into his palm, as if the urge was too strong to keep putting off. Julian knew it. Yes. The agony and the ecstasy. Brodie had taught him well.

Sitting up in the pitch blackness, Julian gripped Brodie's jeans and tugged. Down they came. Feeling and hearing Brodie stepping out of them, Julian reached out to touch Brodie's long, hairy legs.

They spread as wide as they could with Julian next to him. Julian took off his shirt, kicking off his slacks, pushing everything over the side of the mattress. It seemed Brodie knew what he was doing because he sat up, taking off his shirt until they were both naked. As if making sure, Julian felt Brodie's hands reaching out, feeling his skin. In that deep darkness, Julian heard Brodie's deep breathy voice, "Julian…"

It was filled with so much passion and craving, it made Julian's skin run with chills. Without a verbal reply, Julian maneuvered himself between those large quadriceps. Once he had made himself comfortable, he leaned up to get that cooling wet dick back into his hot mouth. As he did, Brodie groaned loudly and gripped Julian's hair in his fists. Brodie had waited long enough. Julian wanted to taste him now. No more teasing. Resting on Brodie's leg, Julian gripped the base of Brodie's cock tightly, and sucked like he meant it. His hips came alive, pumping, his muscles twitching and clenching.

Keeping a steady pace up and down, biting tight with his lip-covered teeth, Julian went after those testicles again, grabbing them in his palm, rubbing underneath them until he felt them tighten. Adding the movement of his hand on the base of Brodie's cock in harmony with his mouth, Julian knew it only would take one last touch. Pushing his finger against Brodie's ass, he felt him explode. A rushing of pulsating waves possessed Brodie's body as he shot into Julian's mouth. A loud, erotic cry of desire echoed in the cave-like room.

~

Brodie heard his own voice coming back to his ears. It sounded like an animal in heat. It was!

"*Ah…ah…*" Brodie continued to groan as the aftershocks rocked him to the core. He couldn't see a thing, but he didn't have to. "Julian! Julian…" he gasped. Nothing could express the feelings, the experience of intense affection coupled with outstanding sexual gratification. It was indescribable.

"I'm here, baby."

Grasping for him, trying to orient himself in his blindness, Brodie managed to find Julian sitting up next to him. Grabbing his arms, Brodie pushed him down, lying on top of him, squirming on his hot body, finally managing to pin down his mouth. His body still rock hard, Brodie sucked wildly at Julian's tongue, touching him all over at once in the dark. "I love you. Holy Christ, I love you so much."

Julian's deep gentle chuckle floated in the air. "You love the way I suck your cock."

"Yes! Are you kidding me?" Brodie laughed with him. Running kisses all over Julian's face, cupping his jaw, Brodie kept crooning, "I adore you, adore you…"

Feeling Julian relax, Brodie slowed down his enthusiastic reaction from his amazing orgasm, and grew more passionate, wanting to reciprocate. "What do you want? Name it."

"To nap."

"Are you sure? You're hard as a rock." Brodie ran his hand along Julian's cock.

"Yes. Let me close my eyes. When we wake up before dinner, I'll savor you."

"You sure?"

"Yes."

Brodie wrapped around him, tangling their limbs. Resting his head on the pillows, hearing Julian's breathing deepen, Brodie allowed them their rest.

Chapter Ten

Brodie wore black slacks and a soft, black, wool v-neck sweater. Stepping into his shoes, he perked up when Julian came out of the bathroom. A flash of their intercourse, Julian riding him like a pony ten minutes prior to them getting showered and changed, rushed over him like a streamroller. "Wow."

Julian smiled sweetly in reply. "Acceptable for our casual-dress night?"

Strongly attracted to him, Brodie couldn't resist approaching him on the pretext of straightening his chocolate-colored shirt collar. "You are so incredible. I am so fucking lucky."

"If you toy with me, I'll show." Julian pointed to his light brown slacks. "I should have brought my black ones like you did. Unfortunately Amelia picked out my wardrobe. I can't say she included any of my favorites, but she was determined to pick out hers."

"They have a men's shop onboard. You want me to pick you up a pair?" Brodie stuffed his room key into his pocket. When he didn't hear an answer, he spun around. Julian had a screwed up expression on his face. "What?"

"I can buy my own clothes."

"Don't take it that way." Brodie wanted to be able to give him things. When Julian's expression was slow to change, Brodie stood nose to nose with him, hanging his arms around Julian's neck. "You're not my kept boy. I love you and the idea of buying you gifts makes me feel nice."

Julian's pout relented. "I know. I'm sorry. I'm used to playing the man in my relationships."

Brodie waited. Julian's sharp grin finally appeared. "You were the man. In bed a minute ago."

"I was, wasn't I?" Julian puffed out his chest proudly.

Unable to help it, Brodie ran his hand over Julian's crotch.

"Shit, is the men's shop open? You're going to tease me all night."

"We can have a look before dinner." Brodie checked his watch. "Because I will tease you."

"Go." Julian nudged him to the door, shaking his head.

Grinning at getting that wicked gleam in Julian's eye, Brodie stood in the hall, closing the door behind them. "Uh, shops are on…" he tapped his lip as he tried to remember, "one level below the promenade deck."

"Lead the way."

They took the stairs, avoiding the long lines at the elevators. As Brodie tried to find the shortest route, he came upon a large roadblock of passengers. Excusing himself through them, Brodie noticed a photographer taking posed shots. Couples smiled happily, families grouped for portraits, and friends stood side by side as the lens captured their gleaming smiles.

Brodie lowered his head, making his way beyond them to the empty hall where the shops were located. He felt Julian tug on his hand. Stopping, Brodie tilted back to see him.

"Ya…uh, you want a photo?" Julian asked.

"Like that?" Brodie pointed behind them.

Julian shrugged shyly.

"Glenda and Marlene took one of us in front of the glacier." Brodie tried to read Julian's expression. "You sure you want to stand there like that?" A flutter of nerves passed through Brodie's stomach.

"No. It's all right." Julian waved at him to keep going.

Imagining posing in front of that huge crowd, together while they were snapped by the ship's photographer for some reason unnerved Brodie. Gesturing to the men's clothing shop, Brodie paused, looking back at the crowded hallway and the bright lights as Julian entered the store. There were too many people there all standing and watching the sappy heterosexual couples and their children. He wasn't sure he was ready for that.

Shaking himself out of the slight feeling of terror it had created, he found Julian inspecting a pair of black pants on a hanger. Moving behind him, Brodie asked, "You trying them on?"

"I should, but I always wear the same size, thirty-six waist, forty length."

"Up to you."

"I'll try them on quick."

"Okay."

Julian disappeared into the dressing room. While he waited, Brodie investigated a few items but had little interest in them. The curtain parted and Julian stepped out. "They look all right?"

"Yes. Fine." Brodie wanted him again. Would he ever feel he'd had enough?

"I figured. Okay." Julian allowed the curtain to fall in front of him.

"Can I help you?" A woman approached Brodie.

"Yes. There's a man trying on a pair of slacks in that dressing room. I want you to put it on my room number. I want to give them to him as a gift."

"Certainly, sir." She walked behind the register and took out a familiar looking slip of paper, one he'd seen every time he ordered a drink. He told her his cabin number, adding, "He'll give you his room number. Just ignore him."

She smiled in a conspiratorial way. "He'll see the wrong room number on the paper."

"Use a blank one. Let me sign it now. Toss out the one he signs."

"Good thinking."

Brodie scribbled his name quickly, standing back as Julian approached.

"I'll take these." He set them on the counter.

"Certainly, sir. Your cabin number?"

As Julian gave her his information and signed the slip, she placed his slacks in a bag and handed them to him. Before they left the store, Brodie winked at her. She showed him the paper she was tearing up. Smiling happily, Brodie knew Amelia was already putting a dent into the poor man's budget. It was the least he could do.

"I need to head back to the room to drop these off."

"Okay."

They avoided the jam in the hallway with the photographer and used a different route back. Since it was clear on the other side of the boat it took ten minutes to walk to the room. Brodie used the key, pushing back the door when they finally arrived.

Julian hung the slacks up in the closet.

"Not going to wear them?"

"No. Tomorrow night. Bet it's another formal." Julian took the receipt and tucked it into his suitcase.

As he paused, Brodie wondered what was taking so long. Sneaking up behind him, he was surprised to see a photograph of him and Melanie in Julian's hand. "Where the heck did you get that?"

Julian spun around. "The gallery."

"Let me see it." Without hesitation, Julian handed it to him. Catching the complete indifference on their faces, the fact they didn't even know they were being photographed, hit Brodie over the head like a mallet. "Do you believe I didn't see it coming? Her walking out on me? Look at us. We look like combatants in a war zone."

"I know. But I couldn't resist."

Brodie lowered the photograph, looking at Julian's crisp blue eyes. After handing it back, Brodie asked, "You ready?"

"Yes." Julian stuffed the photo into his suitcase.

After he locked the door, Brodie held Julian's hand. When he bypassed the dining room level, Julian tugged at him. "Where are you going?"

"You'll see." Brodie found the line had dwindled down as the dining room had opened.

"Brodie?"

Smiling at Julian's surprised expression, he asked, "Yes?"

"You sure? It'll be up in the gallery. Everyone will see it."

"I know. Make sure you get to it before Amelia does. She'll most likely tear it up."

"Shit." Julian shook his head. "You're right."

When their turn came, Brodie swallowed his intimidation and

asked, "Can we go next?"

"Yes, of course." The photographer looked up from his camera and his smile appeared strained. "Just you two? Or are we waiting for two more people?"

Knowing what he was insinuating, Brodie replied flatly, "Us two. You got a problem with that?"

"No!" came the quick response. "Step in front of the backdrop."

Knowing he was now scowling in annoyance, Brodie waited for Julian to stand next to him.

Once they were where they needed to be, Brodie heard Julian whisper, "Say cocksucker."

Instantly a big grin found its way to Brodie's cheeks. The man snapped his camera lens. Still laughing, Brodie gave the photographer his room number. Julian reached out for his hand and Brodie took it.

"You ready for our debut? Hand in hand?" Julian asked, moving towards the dining hall.

"Uh, no. But I'm starving."

Julian released his grip on Brodie's fingers. "We don't have to prove anything, right?"

"Nope." He was glad Julian had done that. He wasn't quite ready for another public spectacle. Leading the way, passed Julian's old table where everyone stared at him as they passed, Brodie wondered how Julian was holding up.

~

Oh God. Julian didn't know what to do. Jenny and Paul, Joe and Elaine, all four of his co-dining couples were gawking at him. The two chairs where he and Amelia had sat for the last few nights stood vacant. Julian hadn't a clue where Harry and his big Polish family were located, and he didn't want to know. Forcing himself to smile, though he could imagine it was as pinched as he felt, he nodded as he walked beyond them to another table. It wasn't much better. Though Glenda and Marlene were there, greeting them, most of the company was gray and gnarled.

"Hello," Julian whispered to them shyly.

As he sat down, Brodie said, "This is Julian." That was it.

"Hi guys!" Marlene giggled in excitement. "I'm so glad you're joining us."

"Thanks, Marlene," Brodie said sincerely. The waiter immediately poured wine for them. Giving him a big smile, Brodie produced a ten and stuffed into the man's vest pocket. "He's the best," Brodie told Julian.

"Thank you, sir." The water nodded gracefully.

Gulping the wine as if he was dying of thirst, Julian hated the fact that he was facing his old table. They were staring at him, leaning over to talk amongst themselves. It didn't take a rocket scientist to figure out what they were discussing. The eye contact and pointing unnerved him.

Glenda asked, "Did you guys do anything after the sauna?"

"Not really," Brodie shrugged. "Are you taking one of the tours to Skagway tomorrow?"

"We just figured we'd wander around, like we did in Juneau. How about you?"

Brodie shrugged. "We haven't decided yet."

One of the old women asked Julian, "Did you just board the boat?"

Confused, Julian asked, "Excuse me?"

"I just wondered if you just came on. That seat's been empty before now."

Under his breath, Brodie snarled, "Shut up, you old crone."

Julian nudged him to be quiet. "No. I was seated at another table. You don't mind that I joined you, do you?"

Trying to help, Marlene said, "They're friends, Rita."

Before he could add anything, Julian watched the last couple sit with them at their table. He recognized them from somewhere.

As if Brodie read his mind, he whispered, "Hot tub."

"Oh, right." Julian nodded.

"They're on their honeymoon."

"Ah. That explains it." Julian finished his wine. A bottle appeared and filled his glass instantly. "Wow."

"I told you. We've got the best waiter in the room."

"Thank you, sir." The shy waiter nodded again.

"He certainly keeps our wine glasses full." Sandy laughed, gulping hers. "I'm Sandy, and this is my new husband, Bob."

"Hi. I'm Julian. Nice to meet you." Julian reached for their outstretched hands.

"Where did you come from?" Bob asked.

Tilting his head, Julian asked, "You mean originally?"

"No. I mean, did you board late?"

Hearing Brodie's exhale of disgust, Julian replied, "No. I just changed tables."

"Really? You can do that? Didn't you like who you were sitting with?" Bob asked.

Servers rolled out and the waiter delivered salads to the ring of diners.

Julian didn't know how to answer him.

Glenda said, "They're friends," as if that explained it. It made Bob's expression worse.

As if Brodie had enough, he set his fork down and said, "Look. We met on board. Okay? He wants to sit here with us. Is that going to be a problem?"

His face going red at the force in Brodie's voice, Julian felt like crawling under the table.

Marlene shouted, "Brodie! No one minds. Julian is welcome! Right?"

A slow murmur of consent rumbled around the circle.

Julian didn't meet anyone's eye. Lifting his full glass of red, he noticed Amelia had stopped at their old table. She leaned on it with both hands, talking to them, then to Julian's acute horror, she pointed straight at him. "I don't believe her."

"What?" Brodie leaned over to him, chewing his wild greens and blue cheese salad.

Julian nodded to where Amelia stood.

"What's she doing?" Brodie whispered.

"Outing me."

Brodie choked on his food.

With a satisfied grin on her face, Amelia stood tall, gazing at him. All eight people at the table twisted around in their chairs to look at him.

"Shoot me."

"Calm down," Brodie whispered.

"Christ, Brodie, she's coming this way."

Before she made it closer, Brodie intercepted her.

Julian went pale.

"What's going on?" Marlene asked Julian. "Is she making trouble?"

"Yes." Julian swallowed.

~

"Let go of me!" Amelia squirmed.

"Out. Now." Brodie dragged her to the corridor outside the dining room entrance.

Once they were past the gawkers, Brodie shoved her back. "Don't you fucking do it."

"Screw you, faggot."

Enraged, Brodie body-slammed her to pin her against the wall though he wanted to use his hands to strangle her. Breathing fire as he tried to control his temper, he warned, "Julian has something to fear from you, I don't. I'd just as soon wring your fucking neck."

"Get away from me."

"You're sucking his money from him. You've got yourself another loser to latch on to, leave Julian alone."

"What the hell's wrong with you? Both of you? I can't get why you good looking men don't like women."

"Ever look in the mirror?"

"That's rude. You think you're helping him?"

"Why are you doing this? What did he do to you? He paid for your cruise, didn't he? He didn't leave you, you left him."

"Come on. He wanted you before I left him. Don't give me that. All that bullshit about us not having anything in common. I'm not as stupid as you think I am."

"I'm asking you to leave him alone. This is hard enough."

"Why? Why should I do that? You don't think it humiliates me that he's shacking up with a guy?"

"Please. I'm asking you once. Nicely."

"Nicely? I'm pushed against a wall."

Brodie backed up.

She gave him a once over, pausing at his crotch. "Man. I can't believe you like men. What a waste."

"Amelia."

At the sound of her name, she met his eyes.

"Please. Have a little pity. You have no idea what hell this is."

"It's your own fault. Society doesn't really accept it. It's all just a front for the liberal democrats."

Brodie rubbed his face tiredly. "You've already told your own table. Let us tell ours. Okay?"

"Whatever." She walked away.

~

Julian had stopped eating. Waiting, he drank two more glasses of wine, which the waiter was so good about keeping full.

"Don't worry, Julian." Marlene smiled kindly at him.

"Thanks, Marlene. But you don't know Amelia. She's a woman hell bent on revenge."

"I can talk to her." Marlene set her napkin on the table, battle ready.

Julian smiled, patting her arm. "I think Brodie's got it handled. But thanks."

"What's going on?" Sandy asked, trying to see out of the door. "Why did Brodie leave?"

"He's coming back." Julian watched him strut in. Even the way the guy walked was a turn on.

Brodie glared at Julian's old table as he passed. Julian could tell he was making sure he met each set of eyes.

"Come on. Just sit down, Brodie." Julian wished he could hurry him up.

Moving out his chair, Brodie joined them, picking up where he left off on his salad.

"Everything okay?"

"Yup." Brodie chewed, washing it down with red wine.

"Good." Julian rubbed Brodie's thigh under the table.

"Don't worry about anything, Brodie." Marlene leaned over Julian to speak to him. "If you need someone to be on your side, I am."

"Me too!" Glenda added.

"Side?" Sandy set her glass down. "What's going on? Why are we taking sides?"

"Nothing." Julian tried to smile at her. When he looked across the table, four sets of senior citizens were staring at him suspiciously. "Oh great," Julian sighed, finishing his meal.

~

Thanks to Glenda and Marlene the dinner wasn't a total loss. The two women kept up happy chatter, distracting Julian from his bitter thoughts. Waving at them as they left the dining room, Brodie grabbed Julian's elbow to stop his progress down the hall.

"What?"

"Come with me," Brodie ordered and Julian followed. When Brodie ended up at the lobby and the reception desk, he asked, "Why am I here?"

Brodie physically brought Julian to stand at the desk.

"Can I help you?"

"Yes." Brodie pointed to Julian. "This man no longer wants to pay for his ex-girlfriend's way. Can you remove her from his credit card and get her to use her own?"

Julian bit his lip, knowing Amelia was determined on breaking him financially as well as emotionally.

"We can. Would you like us to send her a note, advising her that she can no longer use the room number?"

"I don't know which room she's staying in, Brodie."

"She's with a guy with a big head named Harry and his Polish family." Brodie leaned over the desk, as if he wanted to see some kind of list.

"Do you know their last name?"

Julian and Brodie exchanged helpless looks. "Forget it, Brodie."

"No. It's not fair, Julian. I'm not going to let her go on some sort of spending spree at your expense."

The attendant sighed. "Well, that is a problem. If we can't advise her, or notify her to come here and register her own card, there's really no way we can stop it. The hotel employees will just allow her to sign. I'm sorry."

"Brodie, we tried." Julian touched his arm.

"This sucks! What's she done so far? What's his balance?"

The man asked for Julian's room number. Julian supplied it, waiting in suspense.

"The current balance is nine hundred seventy-five dollars and fifty-three cents."

"Ouch." Brodie cringed.

"Come on." Julian urged him to walk away. As they left, Julian said, "I did it to myself, Brodie. I invited her. I paid her way. Forget it."

A deep, disapproving growl came from Brodie's throat.

"Where are we going? It's only eight." Julian paused, looking out a window on the black ocean.

"What's the show tonight?"

"I don't know." Julian's focus changed from the sea to the reflection. Brodie's silhouette outlined behind him. He stepped back, connecting them.

Brodie wrapped his arms around him, swaying with the movement of the ship.

Leaning back, enjoying the nuzzling of Brodie's mouth to his ear, Julian sighed.

"You want to screw around?"

Julian smiled dreamily. "We have all night."

"So?"

A hard cock rubbed against his ass.

Someone passed behind them. Julian almost pushed Brodie back in reflex. Reconsidering, he ignored them as they walked by. So what? Who cares? He relaxed in Brodie's arms, his eyes blurring at their image in the glass.

"Want to dance at a club?"

"Are you joking?" Julian laughed softly.

"Sort of."

Smiling, Julian replied, "I'm not much of a boogier. I don't do disco. It was one of Amelia's complaints."

"I'm thinking slow dancing." Brodie began moving them side to side.

"In public? No. In our room? Yes."

"Okay," Brodie said as he spun Julian to face him. "Dance, then a swim, then the chocolate extravaganza?"

"Okay." Julian held his hand as Brodie escorted him to the main deck and their little hideaway.

~

Brodie was growing weary. It was after eleven and swimming in the indoor pool was more challenging than he anticipated. They were at sea and the water in the pool rode up and down with the waves. It was entertaining at first, but soon became exhausting trying to fight being tossed out of the water. They had showered and changed back at the room. Taking a look at Julian, seeing the same tired expression on his face, Brodie asked, "You want to skip the chocolate thing?"

Julian met his gaze. "Up to you. We don't have to stay long."

Tucking in his shirt, Brodie replied, "All right, since we're showered and dressed, let's just go look at what they've got."

"I really don't feel like stuffing myself this late."

"No. I know. Come on, five minutes." Brodie opened the door.

The halls were vacant at that late hour, but as they headed to the lounge level and casino they could hear the night owls at it. The clubs were still hopping as the younger set was spinning their heels on the dance floors and the older passengers sipped bourbon in the supper club and played poker and roulette.

Brodie pointed to a sign signaling the location of the chocolate event. A buffet was on display like artwork along the counter where their lunch meal was usually served. "Wow." Brodie took in the delights visually.

"Yes." Julian picked up a refrigerated plate, handing it to him. "I changed my mind. This was a good idea."

Laughing, Brodie took the dish and began selecting from the delicacies. "Maybe we should run tomorrow after all."

"I know."

Truffles, tortes, chocolate fondue, it was so overindulgent it was sickening. Brodie stopped himself from being too greedy. Pausing at the end of the line, he looked around for a table. Suddenly he realized the room was ninety percent female. For some reason it made him blush.

"Right," Julian met him, "where to?"

"How about that table?" Brodie pointed to one near the dark windows.

"Fine."

After they relaxed, Brodie whispered, "You were right. This chocolate thing is definitely a woman's party."

Julian took a look around. "There are some men here."

"One, two..." Brodie counted.

"Who cares?" Julian picked up a very large strawberry from his plate. The tip had been dipped in milk chocolate. "Eat this." Brodie reached out his hand to take it. Julian drew it back. "Uh uh. I feed you."

Looking around the room in paranoia, Brodie asked, "You sure?"

"Yes. I remember you eating a strawberry in this café when I was still with Amelia. It was really hot."

Recalling it as well, Brodie leaned over the table. Parting his lips, Brodie felt Julian touch the chocolate to his bottom lip. Brodie opened slightly wider. Like a sex fiend, Julian poked the berry in and out of Brodie's mouth. Struggling to control his coming laughter, Brodie stretched closer, trying to get near enough to take a bite. His cock went ballistic in his pants, pulsating and twitching like mad.

Obviously entertained with his own antics, Julian kept berry-fucking Brodie's mouth. Finally Brodie had to turn away to laugh. Shaking his head, he said, "You'll get us into trouble."

"You have chocolate on your lips and I want to lick it off."

"Let's bring this to our room. I can't do this here." Brodie noticed some women staring at them with a little too much interest.

As if the idea was brilliant, Julian rose up, taking his plate with him.

Trying not to look obvious, Brodie scooted Julian out to stand at the elevators. They weren't alone in their descent, so they kept quiet and behaved. Once they were on the main floor, Brodie hurried up his pace. Opening his door, he tossed the key aside and sat on the bed.

Julian joined him. "Where were we?" He picked up the strawberry, hovering it in front of Brodie's mouth.

In the privacy of their cabin, Brodie felt less self-conscious. He licked at the chocolate tip, as if it were Julian's penis.

Julian pushed the juicy berry into Brodie's mouth, his attention enrapt at the act. Brodie bit it off at the stem, licking his lips. Before he swallowed, he grabbed Julian's jaw and connected to his mouth. Sucking Julian's tongue along with the sweet treat, Brodie moaned in pleasure. Swallowing, parting from their kiss, Brodie held up a truffle. He teased it over Julian's lips. It sent Julian over the edge. Grabbing both plates, Julian slapped them on the nightstand, dove on Brodie, and pinned him to the bed.

As Julian's hands sought to undress him, Brodie kept pushing the truffle into Julian's mouth, where he sucked and licked at it like a wild man. Finally enveloping the candy into his mouth, Julian yanked his own clothing off as if he couldn't do it quickly enough. Naked, feeling hornier than he imagined was humanly possible, Brodie watched as Julian snatched another strawberry from his plate. His chest expanding with his excited breath, Brodie stared in awe as Julian ran the chocolate tip along his cock. Once the chocolate had melted against Brodie's hot skin, Julian crushed the berry against Brodie's nipple, the juice running down his chest.

"Holy Christ," Brodie gasped as Julian licked at the sweet nectar first, flattening his tongue all over Brodie's torso where the drops ran in red sticky lines. Sitting up, Julian ate the remainder of the berry, flicking the stem onto the plate.

Brodie glimpsed down at his chocolate covered dick. "You going to clean up the mess you made?"

"Yes." Julian licked his fingers.

Brodie responded with lightning reflex, taking Julian by the wrist to suck those fingers himself. Starting with his index finger, Brodie drew it into his mouth, closing his eyes. As Brodie gave Julian's fingers head, Julian did the same to Brodie's cock.

As the oral sex began, Brodie sucked harder on Julian's digits, moving from one to the other, shoving Julian's middle finger deep into his mouth.

~

Julian lapped at the chocolate hungrily. Once he had cleaned him up, he sat back. Wicked thoughts were burning in him. Staring at Brodie's expression as he paid individual attention to each finger, Julian looked back at those full plates. A chocolate torte was calling to him. Once he could take back his hand from Brodie's grasp, he picked up the slice of mouse-like pie and held it over Brodie's crotch.

"What are you going to do with that?" Brodie panted to catch his breath. As if he just caught that satanic expression, Brodie shook his head. "Are you kidding me?"

Julian let out an evil laugh, smashing the thick cold chocolate all over Brodie's crotch.

Gasping in surprise, Brodie sat up to gape at him. "Are you insane?"

His excitement at such a high level, Julian felt as if he were on drugs, he massaged the rich fudge all over Brodie's cock and stomach. Using the coating as a lube, Julian pumped his hand over that sticky cock as Brodie gulped for air. Straddling Brodie's hips, Julian went in for the kill. He began eating that sumptuous dish off Brodie's body.

~

Brodie had no idea what to do. It was so fucking hot his entire being was primed to explode. The vigor in which Julian was eating him, literally, made Brodie shake with desire. Never in his life had sex been like this. He hadn't imagined it could be. It certainly took a special bond to do this. To be silly, unabashed, absurd, and certainly creative when it came to sexual arousal and foreplay. Julian was being very diligent in his job. Lapping up every morsel, every drop. Brodie felt his muscles go rigid as lips, tongue, even teeth caressed his crotch with the enthusiasm of an auditioning cheerleader. Julian paused, as if making sure he had devoured every last crumb. Brodie reached out, tugged him close, and began licking the chocolate off Julian's face. It was Julian's turn to moan and close his eyes. Brodie lapped at his chin, his upper lip, cleaning all the sugary taste off his skin. Capturing Julian's arms, Brodie rolled over to lie on top. His turn. Casting a discerning eye on what was left, Brodie cupped a cube of ice cream coated with chocolate, in his palm. As it melted, he dripped it onto Julian's chest, making a path of drops leading down his body.

Rolling to his side, once Brodie had created that slick line to Julian's pelvis, he rubbed the rest of the ice cream onto Julian's cock. Leaning over him, Brodie took long slow licks to follow that road to the ultimate treat.

~

Shivering at the chill from the ice cream, Julian had never done anything like this before. He didn't even know what possessed him to do it now. Smearing chocolate on someone? Where the hell did that come from?

As Brodie devoured Julian's ice cream-coated penis, Julian wondered what had come over them. They were two ordinary guys. How on earth did it come to this? This constant desire to keep having sex? He'd become obsessed with Brodie, his taste, his scent. Two testosterone filled bodies craving each other to the point of insanity. That's what they'd become. He never imagined doing this with another soul. He wasn't very sexually outgoing usually. He'd do what he had to do, then sleep. It's what couples did. Isn't it?

Knocked out of his dream by Brodie's expert mouth, Julian arched his back as Brodie sucked him to the base. As suddenly as it began, the blow job ceased. Brodie was reaching into the drawer. Julian knew what he was looking for.

In Brodie's shaking hands, he opened a condom, sliding it on his enormous penis. He squeezed the tube applying a liberal amount.. Julian smiled at Brodie's eager expression while he licking his lips, chomping at the bit. Julian relaxed as Brodie pushed back his legs, getting into position. As that hot body entered his, Julian hissed a breath between his teeth at the rush. While his head swam at the sensation of penetration, Julian felt Brodie grab his cock and begin pulling with purpose. With the mixture of sensations from his back to his front, intensified by the dynamic foreplay, Julian came. It took nothing he was so primed.

Another deep thrust and he heard that rumbling masculine voice. Julian knew Brodie was there. With his grip still tight on Julian's dick, Brodie hung his head to recuperate.

Glistening with sweat, Julian caught his breath as Brodie came around from his swoon and disengaged their bodies. Before Julian could say a word, Brodie leaned down to lap at the creamy spatter on Julian's abdomen.

"Oh. My. God. Brodie Duncan." He laughed, trying to breathe.

Brodie made sure he licked the tip of Julian's cock as well, cleaning off the last drip. Sitting back on his heels, Brodie stared at Julian, his face dewy with sweat.

That condom-covered cock still engorged, the end filled with sperm, Julian stared down at it in awe. "I'm glad we went to the chocolate extravaganza."

As if it was the funniest thing he ever heard, Brodie cracked up, holding his stomach.

"I have never had sex like this in my life, Brodie."

At the sleepy inflection of his voice, Brodie stopped chuckling long enough to catch his breath. "Neither have I."

"Unreal. Virtually, unreal." Julian shook his head.

Chapter Eleven

Having set the alarm for seven thirty, Brodie woke to the noise and slapped the snooze alarm. Snuggling against Julian for another five minutes of sleep, he wrapped around him tighter, using his leg to draw Julian close. The alarm buzzed again.

"Shut up." Brodie smacked it again.

"Run," Julian moaned.

"Run," Brodie agreed. Moaning in agony, Brodie hit the light switch after shielding his eyes. "Argh."

"Run." Julian sat up like a robot. "Must run."

"Argh." Brodie moved his feet to the floor. "I don't wanna," he whined.

"I don't wanna either," Julian joined him. "But we gotta. Too much chocolate."

"Waah," Brodie cried as he stood, scuffing to the bathroom to pee. Holding the wall as he went to the bathroom, Brodie noticed the boat shifting more than usual. "Geez." He flushed, standing at the sink to stare at himself. "Whoa!" he grabbed the sink. "Is this boat rocking?"

"Yes!" Julian appeared at the bathroom doorway, slightly wide-eyed. "Christ. My luck I'll throw up."

"Why is it so rough?" Brodie tried to stand on his own to brush his teeth. He kept reaching out to the sink to stay upright.

"Uh, I don't think I want to be on the sports deck when it's this rough. How the hell are we supposed to run? We'll fall overboard."

Spitting out the toothpaste, rinsing his mouth, Brodie held up his finger. "Wait." He walked to the desk, picking up the phone. "Hello? Reception? Why the heck is the boat shifting side to side like this?"

"Sorry, sir. There's just a slight rainstorm. We'll be through it momentarily. No need to worry."

"Thanks."

Julian stared at him curiously. "Well?"

"Come back to bed, pretty boy." Brodie reached out for him. Scrambling back under the covers, Brodie snuggled against him, turning out the light.

"What did they say?"

"It's raining. Screw that. I'm not getting soaked."

"Cool."

"Go back to sleep." Brodie sealed his body against Julian's. "Damn."

"What?"

"Now I'm horny."

Julian started to laugh. "You animal! After what we did last night?"

"I can't help it," Brodie moaned, rolling on top of Julian to trap him on the bed. "It's your fault."

"Is it?"

"Yes."

"So? I can't go back to sleep even for an hour?"

"No. Sleep. It's okay. I can wait." He poked Julian with is cock. "Wait a minute." He reached down. "You're hard too."

"And?"

Brodie moaned in agony.

"You never go to sleep with a hard-on?"

"No. I always jerk it off." Brodie clasped his hand around both of their dicks, pressing them together. "Oh, that is so nice."

"You're not going to let me get back to sleep, are you?"

"No. I am. Sorry." Brodie settled down, but his hand kept pulling on both their cocks.

Julian choked, trying to stop his hilarity.

Brodie smiled, joining him as they laughed. "Sorry. I can't help it."

"You dork." Julian wrapped his hand around Brodie's, encouraging him to move it faster.

"Yes..." Brodie jerked it with more intent. Both their hands, both their cocks, side by side and wrapped around each other. Brodie was already close. "You there?"

"Not yet."

Brodie swallowed to control himself. "You there?"

"Close."

"Ah!" Brodie gasped, biting his lip. "Shit." He couldn't stop it. "Sorry. Ah!"

"I'm there!" Julian gasped.

Brodie slowed his hand, but didn't stop moving it. "That was nice."

"You sleep on the wet spot."

"That's not fair."

"Tough. You wanted it."

"Like you hated it." Brodie had to fight back his laughter.

"You're an animal. Always grabbing my dick."

"It's your fault. You're too good looking."

"What are you doing? Don't wipe your hand on me."

"I thought you liked my come on you."

"Wipe it on the damn sheet. It's already covered."

Brodie did. "Wanna suck my fingers?"

"Later." Julian nestled into Brodie's neck.

"Later." Brodie echoed, closing his eyes.

~

They showered, washing the remnants of last night's chocolate insanity off their crotches. Dressed, feeling the boat had settled down, Julian waited for Brodie to get his key and nod he was ready.

"They need to change those sheets," Julian muttered as he walked down the lengthy corridor.

"They will. I left the spread down showing how messy it was."

"Gross. Poor maid. She'll think its shit, not chocolate."

"Ew, no she won't. It doesn't stink. We'll give her a good tip." Brodie pushed the elevator button in vain. "Take the stairs. We didn't run."

"Okay." Julian made his way up to the café, dying for a cup of coffee. The moment they passed through the door of the room, the scent of breakfast food smacked into them. Another buffet was spread out where the chocolate had been. Julian licked his lips, loading up on the pancakes and bacon.

"Look, there's a guy making omelets. Want one?" Brodie asked.

"No. I got enough here. I'll get us a table." Julian waited for his nod, moving to the window instinctively. They had docked in Skagway and the rough rocking had subsided completely. A waiter brought over a carafe of coffee. Julian thanked him, turning the two upside down cups right for him to fill. There was already sugar and cream on the table. "Thanks."

"My pleasure, sir." He left the full pot behind.

Shaking a packet of sugar into his cup, Julian watched Brodie approaching. Neither of them had shaved and Julian savored the scruffy, manly look of his lover. Once Brodie had begun eating his asparagus and crabmeat omelet, Julian gestured to the window. "It's still pissing down rain."

"Forget that. I'm not walking around Alaska in a downpour." Brodie leaned closer to the thick glass. "Not much to see anyway."

"I think most people book tours. I bet there are some nice places away from the boat dock."

"You want to try that again? We always seem to be too late to sign up."

"I know. I bet everyone has already done it the first day. I'm not that organized." Julian sipped his cup.

"And the sex is making us stupid."

Julian caught Brodie's tongue in his cheek. "Exactly." After eating in silence a little while, Julian cleared his throat. "What exactly came over us last night?"

Brodie laughed softly, devouring his food.

Refreshing their cups with the carafe, Julian revealed, "I've never done anything like that before."

"Me neither." Brodie tipped cream into both their cups.

"You ever see that Tom Jones' movie?"

"You mean the one with Albert Finney?"

"Yeah. I actually thought that food scene was really gross." Julian turned up his nose.

"It was." Brodie nudged his plate aside and a waiter took it away. "Thanks." After he left, Brodie whispered, "The service here is unbelievable."

"I know. So's the food." Julian gobbled his pancakes up.

"Anyway, about the chocolate thing..." Brodie covered his wicked grin with his coffee cup. "Hot or what?"

"Hot. Very hot." Julian finished eating, dabbing his lip with a napkin. His plate was removed efficiently.

"You going for seconds?"

"You kidding? After the calorie flood last night?" Julian shook his head as if Brodie were nuts. "I ate that whole torte."

"Yeah. Off my cock. You nut."

Blushing slightly, Julian whispered, "I have no idea why I did that."

"Neither do I. But holy shit, what an amazing bout. I'm still in shock."

Julian rested his cup in its saucer, leaning across the table so he could speak quietly. "Are we sex fiends?"

"Probably."

"I mean, is it normal?"

Brodie shrugged. "I don't know. Why? You think the novelty will wear off?"

"Not anytime soon. No way." Julian reclined in his seat, gazing at the pouring rain. "What the hell are we going to do all day?" When wicked laughter replied, Julian shook his head. "My dick will fall off. We have to slow down."

"Yeah, right." Brodie replied.

Marlene and Glenda appeared at their table. "Good morning," Marlene said cheerfully.

"Hiya." Brodie smiled.

"The weather sucks. We're not going to walk around in this." Glenda shook her head to emphasize her comment.

"Us either," Julian replied. "Did you already eat?"

"Yeah, we got up early." Marlene looked back at the food. "Though looking at it makes me hungry again."

"Isn't the food amazing?" Glenda asked.

"It is." Brodie leaned his elbow on the table. "We were just discussing that."

Julian looked at Brodie quickly. "You mind if they sit down?"

"No." Brodie scooted back.

They made room for the women to join them. Marlene sat next

to Julian and Glenda near Brodie.

"They had a chocolate extravaganza last night," Brodie hissed wickedly.

Julian instantly felt his face go red.

"I heard that. We considered trying to stay up for it, but we were too tired." Marlene gazed out of the window solemnly. "Anyway, how was it?"

"Decadent." Brodie grinned broadly.

"I can imagine." Glenda sighed. "I've probably already put on fifteen pounds during this trip."

"It's easy to do," Brodie replied. "We're trying to run every morning. But not in this." He pointed his thumb to the rain.

"They have a well equipped gym," Marlene offered. "Treadmills, row machines."

Brodie caught Julian's gaze. "Interested?"

"Maybe. After I digest breakfast."

"My guess, because of the weather, it'll be jammed." Marlene opened the top of the coffee pot, looking in.

"You want a cup?" Julian asked.

"Yeah, why not." She stood. "You want one, Glenda?"

"No. I'm coffeed out. Thanks."

When Marlene left the table, Julian tried to think of something to say in the awkward silence. Both Brodie and Glenda were staring out of the window with blank expressions.

"Formal tonight," Glenda said, her expression and stare not changing.

"Damn." Brodie rubbed his face tiredly. "It's getting old."

"I don't mind." Glenda became silent as Marlene sat back down, tipping the coffee into her cup.

"Sugar?" Julian offered.

"One. Thanks." Marlene emptied the packet into her mug, stirring it.

"What's this now? Women?"

Julian fell out of his stupor to see Amelia standing there, arms crossed.

"Here we go." Brodie shifted uncomfortably in the seat.

"Are you gay or are you straight, Julian?"

"Jesus," Marlene sneered. "What's with you?"

"Amelia," Brodie whined, "give it a fucking rest."

Glaring at her, Julian snarled, "You already spent almost a thousand dollars of my money. When will your vacuous personality be satisfied? You want a pint of blood?"

"Ew, not your contaminated blood."

"Get your skinny ass out of here," Marlene shouted. "Leave the guy alone."

Amelia's arms tightened into a knot. "Now you have a lesbian and a gay guy as your bodyguard?"

"Hey!" Marlene shot up, about to clobber her.

Julian grabbed Marlene's arm to sit her back down. "It isn't worth it, believe me."

Brodie commanded, "What's that asshole Harry's last name?"

"What's it got to do with you?"

"Why? You afraid we'll laugh at it?" Brodie goaded.

"Laugh? Who cares what you think?"

"Then what is it?"

Julian wondered if she would say it.

"Polkowskie. I'm not embarrassed to be with him. I'm not doing what you're doing."

"Polkowskie?" Brodie repeated. "How the hell do you spell that?"

"Brodie," Julian chided. "Forget it."

"No!" Brodie puffed up. "What fucking room are you two staying in?"

"I'm not telling you, you stupid queer."

Glenda flinched.

"Why? You afraid of a wimp like me? You think big-head-Harry can't take me?"

"Brodie." Julian shook his head.

"Big head? What's that supposed to mean?" No one replied. "We're in a better cabin than yours," she sneered. "He's got a window. We're two levels above your stupid cabin."

"Really?" Brodie urged. "Number?"

"Screw you." She walked away.

Brodie nodded. "I think it's enough. How many Harry

Polkowskies can there be on board?"

Marlene asked, "Why do you want to know? You going to punch him out?"

"No. Make him pay. Come on, Julian. Excuse me, ladies, we have something we have to do."

They stood up, allowing them to slide out.

"See ya later," Julian waved.

Following Brodie, who was like a man on a mission or perhaps a raging bull, Julian wondered if it was worth it. It was really noble, but growing pointless.

Waiting their turn at the reception desk, Brodie nudged Julian in front of him when their chance came.

"Can I help you?"

Julian rested his elbows on the counter tiredly. "I don't know if you can."

As if he was growing impatient, Brodie leaned over to the attendant. "Look, my friend's ex is racking up some big bills for him on his credit card. We don't know which room she's staying in, but we have a name. One of your co-workers said you can send her a letter telling her to use her own credit card."

"We can try, but it doesn't necessarily mean she'll comply."

"Try." Brodie's teeth showed as he snarled.

"What's the name?"

"Harry Polkowskie."

"How do you spell that?"

"I have no idea."

Julian listened, knowing it wasn't going to work. Amelia could ignore the note and continuing to use his room number.

After a few moments of typing into a computer, the man said, "He's on the veranda deck."

"Yes, that's right. Good." Brodie nodded.

"What room number was she in?"

Julian gave him his old room number, suddenly having a thought. "Wait. I'm not in that room any longer. Can you just cancel anything attached to that room?"

The man looked back at another attendant.

The second attendant asked, "What's going on?"

As the men conversed, Julian moaned, "Brodie, forget this. I can't deal with it anymore."

"Wanna bet she's racked up another few hundred?"

Rubbing his forehead in agony, Julian wished the trip would end and he could forget about Amelia spending his money.

The first man sat down in front of them again. "Okay. We'll put a stop on the card. It should show when the staff try to ring it up on the cash register."

Julian nodded. "Okay. But can I put my card on another room?"

Brodie shook his head. Don't worry about it."

"But..." Julian was about to object when Brodie asked, "What's his current balance?"

The man clicked at a keyboard. "Twelve hundred twenty-two dollars and fifteen cents."

"Jesus!" Brodie gasped. "What the hell's the bitch spending it on?"

"Uh," the man read the screen, "boutique shop, five hundred; casino, three hundred; massages—"

"Stop." Julian held up his hand. "I've had enough."

"Well, sir, at least it should stop now. Come back later and check to see if anything else has been added. But the computer should show the room number as invalid."

"Thank you," Brodie replied. He put his arm around Julian's shoulders as they walked to the elevator.

"I feel sick."

"You should." Brodie pushed the down button. "I'd make her pay you back."

Julian sighed sadly. "Yeah, huh? How am I going to do that?"

"You work together at a bank, garnish her wages."

The elevator opened. They waited for it to empty before they entered. "I somehow feel I deserve this."

Brodie rattled him roughly by the upper arms. "Cut that shit out."

As they descended Julian began to feel spent. Dropped off at their level, he scuffed his heels as they made their way down the never-ending corridor. Once Brodie had opened the door, Julian confronted him. "I'm not having you pay my way for the rest of the trip."

"I don't mind." Brodie laid his key on the dresser, looking at the made up bed.

"I do. Forget it, Brodie."

He moved to it, pulling back the spread. "Good, she changed the sheets."

Julian dropped down on the chair by the desk. "Brodie, stop ignoring me."

"I said forget it. You want to quibble over the cost of a few Irish coffees? Give me a fucking break."

Julian waved his hand at him, too tired to argue. When he looked up, Brodie was standing in front of him. At his touch, Julian rested his forehead against Brodie's abdomen. Two hands ran through his hair, caressing gently, massaging his scalp. Closing his eyes, Julian let the pressure of his anger slide off his shoulders. Reaching around Brodie's hips, Julian held him close.

~

Brodie loved the thick, feathery softness of Julian's brown hair. Using the tips of his fingers, he rubbed through that mane to erase his pain and weariness. From the front of Julian's forehead to the nape of his neck, Brodie massaged him, feeling Julian grow limp and lean heavily against him. Julian rolled his neck until his cheek was pressing against the flap of Brodie's zipper. Brodie felt his cock throb under that high cheekbone. He knew Julian did too. He didn't do it on purpose; it just happened on its own. When it twitched again, Julian looked up at him. Brodie whispered, "Sorry. Can't help it."

Julian kissed that bulge.

"You're not helping by doing that." Brodie chuckled softly. When Julian seemed to deflate, Brodie suggested, "Why don't we relax on the bed."

Nodding, Julian took off his shoes, flopping down on it heavily.

Brodie nudged him over, wrapping his arm around Julian's shoulders, as Julian rested his head on Brodie's chest. "You're still worried about it, aren't you?"

Julian exhaled a long sigh. "Sorry."

"What is causing the most anxiety right now?"

"Her telling my parents."

Considering the reply, Brodie thought about his own parents and his version of that conversation. He had no idea how they would react. It wasn't something he ever thought he'd have to tell them. "What are your parents like?"

Julian shrugged. "The usual, I suppose."

"Are they retired?"

"No. They're not there yet. They're only in their early fifties. Mom's a part-time teacher's aide and Dad is a lawyer."

"Do you have any brothers or sisters?"

"One sister, younger." Julian shifted on Brodie's chest, settling down again. "How about you?"

"One of each. Older brother, younger sister."

"What about your parents?"

"Mom's okay. She's a homemaker. Dad, on the other hand...maybe cool, maybe not."

"What?"

Brodie stroked Julian's hair again. "He's a lieutenant with the Bellevue police."

"Great."

"Uh, yeah, well, you know how it is." Brodie shivered imagining his father finding out and wondering if he'd get angry.

"Does he know you have a gay friend?"

"He knows of Paden, but he has no idea he's gay."

Julian groaned. Brodie felt the vibration in his ribcage. "We're so screwed."

"Cut it out, Julian." Brodie hated that kind of negativity.

As if with a supreme effort, Julian leaned up on his elbows to see Brodie's face. "A fucking police lieutenant?"

"So? He's still just a dad. I wonder if your dad being a lawyer is worse."

Dropping back down again, Julian groaned pathetically.

"Shut up." Brodie nudged him. "I seriously don't need this crap right now."

"You?" Julian choked in a sad laugh. "My ex-girlfriend just ripped me off for twelve hundred bucks."

"And you didn't want to stop her. At least now she's done."

"When she finds out we cut her off she'll call my mom. You wait and see."

"Call her first."

"Not now. Not while I'm here. I'm not going to call her from a boat and tell her something like that."

Brodie shrugged. "Then you're fucked."

"Exactly."

Chapter Twelve

After a nap, Julian roused them so they could get some lunch. Feeling lethargic from lying in a dark room for the last two hours, Julian craved light and movement. A slip of paper had been shoved under the cabin door. Formal tonight. Both men let out a weary sigh.

"We really should do something today."

"Why?" Brodie followed him down the carpeted hall.

"I don't know. I feel like a slug."

"I'm ready to finish this cruise. I'm starting to get cabin fever or something."

"I swear the mixed feelings I have about getting back to reality are making me sick." Seeing the look on Brodie's face, Julian regretted it instantly. "I didn't mean that, I just meant—"

"I know what you meant." Brodie shoved him to keep walking.

"Where am I going?"

"Food. I don't care what kind."

"I'm craving sushi." Julian began climbing the stairs.

"I didn't see that anywhere. There's a pizza place, a barbeque grille, a deli restaurant…"

Julian kept moving upwards robotically.

"You went one too many. We passed the promenade deck."

"Did I?" Julian read a directory on that level. "Well, we may as well check the gallery while we're up here."

"Good idea."

They stood in front of several walls of photos. A thousand faces smiling for the camera. Julian scanned left as Brodie searched right. Seeing Amelia with Harry, Julian cringed. Shaking the sensation of dread off his spine from the sight of her, Julian heard Brodie shout his name.

"Here it is."

Julian stood behind him. "That's not half bad. I thought I may have closed my eyes."

"Should we get it?"

"Yes."

Brodie brought it up to the cashier.

"Would you like copies? Wallet sizes? An enlargement? Magnets? T-shirts?"

As she rattled off the sales pitch, Julian laughed, "T-shirts?"

"I think I'll pass on that one," Brodie replied.

"I wouldn't mind an eight by ten."

She nodded, writing it down on an order slip. "Your room number, sir?"

Julian gave Brodie a pained expression.

"Shut up," Brodie said before Julian could complain. "Use ten seventy." She had Brodie sign the slip.

"It'll be ready tomorrow morning."

"Do we come here?" Brodie asked, taking the first photo from her.

"Yes."

Nodding, Brodie gestured for Julian to walk down the hall with him.

"I don't like this, Brodie."

"Now you're quibbling over five bucks? Please, forget about it."

"It was ten, but that's beside the point. It's not the money; it's the principle."

"Look, if it bothers you that much, keep a list and pay me back. I don't know how I'd manage without the ten fricken bucks."

"Shut up," Julian laughed, pushing him.

Brodie stumbled into the wall. In reaction to the roughness, Brodie body-slammed Julian against the opposite wall.

At the force, the air rushed out of Julian's lungs. Blinking in surprise, Julian went for him. He picked Brodie up off his feet, wrapping around his thighs.

Elevated up high, Brodie looked up and down the narrow hall. "Nice view."

"Me too." Julian snuck a nip of his jeans.

"Ouch! You pecker! You caught my skin."

"Good."

"Put me down. You proved you could lift me. So what?"

Julian allowed Brodie to slide down against him to his feet. "*Purr...*"

Unable to contain it, Brodie began laughing. "And you say I'm horny."

"Holy shit. I'm hard as a frickin' rock." Julian humped Brodie's leg.

Turning to see people making their way to the gallery, Brodie pushed back from Julian, trying to act discreet.

Julian didn't know what happened in that little episode but it was tantalizing. Urging Brodie to start walking down the hall, Julian hissed, "I'm fantasizing wrestling you naked, oiled."

Brodie covered his mouth to stop his roaring laughter.

"I'm serious!" Julian stuck his hand into his pocket to shove his cock down as it tormented him.

"You are unbelievable," Brodie mumbled.

"Go back to the room."

"We just came from there. I thought we'd—"

"The room." Julian grabbed Brodie's ass and squeezed it, making Brodie jump. "Now."

Chuckling the entire way, when the elevator opened at the level the cabin was on, Brodie began running down the enormous corridor. Julian was hot on his heels, sprinting like they did on the sports deck. As Brodie stopped short to impale the key entry slot with his card, Julian slammed him against the door making a loud racket.

Unfazed, Brodie opened the door, stumbling in with Julian attached to his back. The moment Brodie had tossed the bag with the photograph on the dresser with his key, the fight was on.

Brodie tried to trap Julian's arms behind his back. Twisting out of his grip, Julian grabbed him around the thighs, heaving Brodie onto the bed. Brodie sprung back up, grappling, getting his arms around Julian's chest, trying to spin them around so Julian was lying under him when they fell against the bed. Tensing his back, arching, and clenching his jaw, Julian broke free, diving onto

Brodie to nail him permanently to the mattress under him. They fought for superiority, rolling around, first one on top, then the other. Julian loved the way Brodie's muscles tensed under him, the roughness of the horseplay, the scent of sweat and pheromones.

Getting his hands into Brodie's jeans, Julian yanked open his button-fly. It made a noise as it opened, like fingers rushing down flat piano keys. As Brodie fought back, Julian crushed Brodie's shirt up his chest, his jeans and briefs down his thighs.

Giving a war cry, Brodie spun Julian over, so he was on top, going for Julian's zipper just as madly as Julian had gone for his.

Julian felt his slacks sliding down his hips. Growling like a wildcat, Julian shoved Brodie onto his back again, pushing down those jeans until he had exposed him.

"You son of a bitch," Brodie gasped for breath. With another rebel yell, he flipped Julian off him, stood up and faced him, prepared for anything.

Julian lay there, gulping oxygen, so hot and bothered he was about to combust. The sight of Brodie, ruffled and war-ready, made Julian want to devour him whole. Julian tensed up, trying to think of an attack tactic. Before he did, Brodie shoved him back violently so he dropped flat, grabbed the bottom of his slacks, and yanked hard, stripping them off Julian's body.

Shocked at being unable to stop him, Julian scrambled to his knees on the bed. Brodie threw the slacks to the floor, coming back for more. Just as Julian was about to spring up and jump him, Brodie aimed low, like a linebacker. He tackled Julian, knocking the wind out of him as he nailed him against the mattress.

Struggling to get his lungs back, Julian felt Brodie's mouth on him. Surrendering, lying back, Julian had so much adrenalin rushing through him it was making him faint. Julian closed his eyes as Brodie sucked hard on him, tearing his briefs down his hips, digging his hand under his balls.

His heart thundering beneath his ribs, the pleasure rushed up Julian's spine. He was so hyped up from the battle he knew it would take nothing to make him come. It appeared Brodie was pumped from the activity as well. The expression of lust on his face as he drew on Julian's cock like a Hoover ignited Julian's skin. That index finger found the magic button. When it pressed inside him, rimming the edge of his ass, Julian came, opening his mouth to shout out and gripping the bedspread in white knuckles.

Gasping for air, Julian opened his eyes to see Brodie going for the condoms and lube. "No way. Not this soon, and not when you're this keyed up."

Brodie shot him a fiery look. In response to that glare, Julian attacked him, throwing Brodie down on the bed. Stripping his jeans the rest of the way off, Julian used his hand against Brodie's sternum to press him down into submission opening his mouth to suck him, though all he wanted to do was gasp for air. The minute Brodie was inside Julian, he stopped fighting. Julian inhaled deeply through his nose, flaring his nostrils to gain oxygen. Sucking hard, the way Brodie had done to him, Julian gripped his testicles as if he meant to rip them off. As Brodie flinched in expectation of pain, Julian caressed them gently, soothingly, until Brodie settled back down again. Shoving between Brodie's legs, Julian mimicked Brodie's action, pushing, running his finger around the circle of his anus. Brodie shot into Julian's throat, gasping and thrusting his hips up and deep. Julian savored him, lapping at the tip, milking every last drop. Finally dripping with perspiration, Julian used his arm to wipe his forehead, and tried to slow down his pulse.

When he finally felt as if he could breathe normally, he looked down at Brodie. Brodie's blue eyes were glowing. "Hi," Julian said shyly.

"You are a god. A. God."

Laughing with his exhaled breath, Julian replied, "My, that's some high praise." His eyes swept over Brodie's exposed body from his belly button down. "Look at you. Jesus, Brodie, you're a pin-up boy."

Brodie moved his hand to clasp Julian's. "You know, I'm actually looking forward to telling my parents about you."

Making a noise in disbelief, Julian replied, "Yeah, right."

"I'm serious, Julian. You are the complete package. You're incredibly handsome, delightful company, successful, funny…they will adore you."

"Yeah?" Julian pushed his hand back through his hair to get it off his face. "I bet they'll want to give me away at our wedding."

"Don't be a jerk."

"Brodie, your parents will want to shoot me."

"Will you stop bursting my bubble?"

"Sorry. But Lt. Duncan will not be pleased. Okay? Believe me."

Brodie leaned up on his elbows. "Just because he's a cop, doesn't mean he's a pig. He's not one of those right-wing Nazis. He's more like Barney Miller than Detective Sipowicz."

"Yeah?" Julian mirrored Brodie's posture on the bed.

"Yeah. He's low-key. He's the kind of cop the other cops go to when they're in trouble."

Julian felt relief at those words. "Christ, I'm glad to hear it. I did imagine some staunch republican war-monger who worships Rush Limbaugh."

"No!" Brodie made a sour face. "God, no. You have him pegged completely wrong."

"So, you think he'll be all right?"

"Maybe." Brodie nodded. "Look, it's not what any dad wants to hear, but he's not going to kill me or disown me."

"Thank fuck."

"Is your dad like that? You know, a tough nut?"

Julian thought about it. "No. Not really. He's been pretty reasonable. I've never had an all out fight with him. My mother thought he cheated on her with his secretary once, but the accusation went nowhere, and the blonde bimbo ended up leaving his firm. I can always throw that in his face." Julian smiled, running his hand over Brodie's warm skin at his hip.

"Then what are we so worried about?"

"I don't know. I suppose it's natural to expect them to be disappointed. And we've never shown an interest in men before. It's like it'll come out of left field."

Brodie nodded, obviously thinking about it.

"If your dad is that cool, why doesn't he know about your best friend?"

"It was Paden's request. He thought my dad may think badly of him. I just did it as a favor to Paden."

Julian acknowledged him. "Too bad. It would have been a good litmus test to see your dad's reaction."

"Sometimes I just want to call them. Now. Just tell them and get it over with."

Julian looked back at the dresser where Brodie's phone and charger were laying. "No. Don't do it that way. Do it face to face."

Brodie checked his watch. "Formal tonight. And we missed lunch."

Groaning in agony, Julian dropped back on the bed.

Sitting up over him, Brodie whispered, "You can wear your new slacks."

"True."

"Bet you'll look hot in them."

Peering down, Julian blinked in awe. "I cannot believe you are hard again."

Brodie grinned wickedly. "I'm just a boy at heart."

"I'll say."

"We can wait 'til after dinner."

"Thank you. I'm starving and dying for a drink."

"Want to shower?"

"Yes." Julian stood up, taking off his shirt. When Brodie reached for his cock, Julian slapped his hand away playfully. "Behave."

"No."

"Yes." Julian walked to the shower, waving his hand like a tail to ward off Brodie's advances.

"No."

"Yes."

"Make me."

~

Both dressed in black, Brodie led the way to their table after a nice glass of scotch had soothed him inside, sating some of his hunger. Seeing Glenda and Marlene's happy faces, he greeted them warmly, sitting in their usual places.

"Wow, don't you both look sharp." Marlene clapped her hands in excitement. "Who needs a stupid tuxedo?"

Julian pointed his thumb at her. "I like her."

"Me too." Brodie smiled.

"Hi guys!" Sandy sat down, her blue sequins glittering. Bob wore a tux.

"Hello, Sandy, Bob." Julian smiled. "You both look very nice."

"Hate this thing." Bob tugged at the bow tie. "Stupid rental. It's snug. Been eating too much."

"I think you look handsome. Like the day of our wedding." Sandy kissed his nose.

"Thanks, schnookims."

Julian and Brodie exchanged glances at their saccharine exchange but kept quiet.

The waiter appeared, pouring their wine. Brodie held up a ten, waving it at him.

Julian looked on in amusement.

"Get over here," Brodie urged the waiter. "Closer."

The shy man approached him. Brodie stuffed the bill into his vest pocket.

"Thank you, sir."

"No. Thank you. You're amazing." Brodie raised his glass to him.

He bowed his head as he continued to move around the table, filling wine glasses.

"Think he's gay?" Julian whispered out of the side of his mouth.

"No." Brodie sipped the glass and moaned at how nice it tasted.

"Bet he'd like you."

"Shut up." Brodie shook his head, smiling.

"You can be his sugar daddy."

Brodie laughed so hard he choked on his wine.

Glenda leaned over Marlene. "What's so funny?"

"Nothing," Julian waved at her.

Marlene whispered, "They asked if the waiter was gay, and then Julian said Brodie could be his sugar daddy."

The men blinked in shock at being overheard as Glenda blushed and giggled.

"Sorry," Marlene replied smugly. "Good hearing."

"Wow. Impressive." Brodie raised his glass to her. After he took another drink, Brodie gave a quick look to the senior side of the table. They were ignoring them, which was probably for the best.

Ever since Julian had appeared, the pensioners decided to chat among themselves. *Oh well, six against four, screw them.*

They ate dinner, savoring the gourmet food as Marlene dominated the conversation only to be challenged by Sandy. Brodie didn't mind. He was growing fond of their little group. Right before dessert was served, the lights went dim and an announcement was made that their waiters were serving the baked Alaska now. A long line of smartly dressed men descended two staircases, each carrying a flaming pie loaded with sparklers. A roar of applause resounded around the room. Julian elbowed Brodie as they clapped, laughing at the corniness. Brodie knew it was silly but the wine and the good company elevated his mood. The kind waiter stood by, showing off the fluffy dessert as the sparklers shot off glittering ashes. Once the sparklers died back, he set it down, removed them, and efficiently sliced it into ten wedges.

"Wow." Glenda licked her lips.

"I am too stuffed," Julian moaned, rubbing his belly.

"Run tomorrow, rain or shine," Brodie announced as he stared at the whipped thing on his plate. He pushed his fork through the egg white topping. "Christ, there's ice cream in this as well."

"Shit, it's rich," Julian said with a mouthful.

"Screw the diet," Sandy snorted. "We're on our honeymoon!"

"Yeah, who cares." Bob gobbled it down.

Brodie leaned to Julian's ear. "I can take it back to the room and smear it all over you."

"Bad boy. Eat it here."

Marlene started laughing, covering her mouth so she didn't spit any out.

"Hey!" Julian gasped. "Tell me you didn't hear that."

She couldn't talk, still trying to swallow and stop laughing.

Brodie covered his mouth before he joined her laughter. "Christ, Marlene!" he shouted.

She finally managed to swallow and rolled in her chair in hilarity.

Sandy, Bob, and Glenda looked on in curiosity. "What?" Glenda asked.

"Nothing!" Marlene managed to squeak out, before choking.

They were all slightly buzzed on the never empty bottle of wine, but Julian still blushed. Brodie thought it was endearing when he spotted it. To tease him, he leaned over Julian to Marlene. "He's already tried the chocolate torte."

"Brodie!" Julian gasped.

As if Marlene was going to die, she pounded the table to hold back her roar but she couldn't, bursting with it. Brodie noticed the older set finally look down their snooty noses at them.

"I love you guys!" Marlene dabbed at her eyes. "You're both so incredibly macho that the image of you two doing things like that really amazes me."

"Doing what?" Glenda whined.

"Never mind." Marlene managed to eat more of her dessert.

Julian smiled at Brodie. "I'm glad I'm at your table instead of mine."

"Me too. These four are great," Brodie nodded to the two couples. "You see? Maybe it will be okay."

"Yes. Maybe you're right."

Brodie took a quick look around first before pecking Julian on the lips.

Marlene whooped it up, Glenda clapped, and Sandy and Bob started laughing, reaching to high five everyone.

"I love it!" Marlene dabbed at her eyes with a napkin. "You are too cool."

Julian smiled at them shyly while Brodie puffed out his chest in pride. *Yes. It's going to be all right.*

Chapter Thirteen

Lapping the slow runners on the sports deck, Brodie and Julian kept up a fast pace in the icy wind. Ketchikan was their final destination in Alaska, from there it was homeward bound, back through the Inside Passage to Victoria, BC, then Seattle.

Though Brodie was growing weary of cruise life, he wasn't happy about having to go back to living solo and no one in his bed at night. With Julian living across Lake Washington and the hideously tortured traffic-jammed route of the 520 bridge connecting them, how often would they see one another? Weekends? "Oh crap…"

"What?" Julian asked after a long silence had elapsed while they ran.

Wondering if he should broach the subject or not, Brodie kept quiet.

"You okay? Get a stitch?"

"Huh?" Brodie glimpsed at him as they passed senior citizen power-walkers with earmuffs on.

"I thought you said, 'Oh crap'."

"Never mind." Brodie knew Julian wouldn't know the answer to his question. And after less than a week, how could they consider cohabitating? It didn't seem sensible. It would sound like they were rushing, being rash. Brodie went over a scenario in his head that deeply disturbed him. What if when they went back to their busy lives they simply had no time to see each other? Almost letting out another, "oh crap" in disgust, Brodie checked his watch. He was growing tired and his legs ached.

"Sprint the last half, then we're done."

Julian agreed. They squeezed more energy into their spent bodies, racing to the front of the boat. Crossing the imaginary finish line, Brodie halted, bending over his knees, gasping.

"Shit." Julian leaned against the metal ship's wall. "I love the run but its killing me lately."

"I don't like running in this wind." Brodie wiped at his face. "Let's go inside before we freeze."

Nodding, Julian followed him to the staircase.

"Sauna?"

"No," Brodie replied, preoccupied and growing antsy.

"You okay? What's going on, Brodie?"

"Nothing." He trotted down the stairs, feeling the sweat pouring out of his skin as he cooled down. With a brisk stride, Brodie made the long walk to their cabin.

After he was in, taking the damp t-shirt off over his head, Julian confronted him. "I know what's going on."

"Do you?"

"We're getting closer to home."

Exhaling in a blast of air, Brodie wiped his dripping face with his shirt. "It's not what you think. It's not telling my family that's upsetting me."

"What then?" Julian leaned back on the desk, crossing his arms and legs.

Brodie placed his hands on his hips, looking into Julian's eyes. "I just feel that once we get back to our routine we'll never see each other. And that fucking bridge? 520? I hate that thing. It's always jammed."

"I know. What do you suggest?"

He knew what he wanted to say, but he thought it would sound as if he were pushing them, desperate.

As he waited for a reply, Julian wiped at the drops rolling down his temple. "Hello?"

"Never mind." Brodie threw his shirt on a chair and headed to the bathroom.

Julian stepped in behind him while Brodie relieved himself in the toilet. "We'll make time, Brodie. I want to see you."

"Make time," Brodie scoffed, flushing the toilet and slipping out of his running shorts. "Whoopee."

"Are you implying we should live together?"

Brodie spun around to face him.

Julian gestured with his hands as if he were egging him on to reply. "Well?"

Biting his lip, Brodie didn't want to admit that was what he was thinking. It was rash! It was too soon!

"Why the hell are you ignoring me?"

"I'm not." Brodie started to feel chilly as his sweat-soaked skin cooled off.

"You're sure as hell not answering my question."

Wanting to shower and get dressed, Brodie reached into the stall and turned on the water.

"Jesus, Brodie!"

Giving up, confronting Julian, Brodie said, "Yes, all right?"

It was Julian's turn to go silent.

Knowing that would happen, Brodie climbed into the heat and sighed as it washed the sweat and cold off his body.

~

Julian slowly took off his damp clothing. Live together? Was he ready for that? And who would move in with whom? Did he want to sell his condominium downtown? Make a long jammed-packed commute over the lake in rush hour traffic to live in Bellevue?

Watching Brodie shampooing his hair through the glass doors, Julian felt an ache inside. He did want Brodie with him. He did realize if they lived apart, they would never get to see one another. Back to sleeping alone, eating alone, and missing that man lying next to him in his bed. Sliding the door open, seeing Brodie's massive muscular body shimmering in the running water made Julian feel anxious, as if he had to make some kind of decision now.

Stepping in behind him, Julian rolled the door closed and waited his turn. When Brodie relinquished the shower head to him, Julian asked, "Would you move my way?"

Brodie blinked in surprise. "You...you want me to move in with you?"

Shrugging, squeezing shampoo into his palm, Julian asked, "I assumed that was what you meant."

"You don't think we're being too irrational? I know if I knew a woman for only a week, I'd never ask her to live with me."

"I'm not a woman."

Brodie's eyes flashed down to Julian's cock.

Scrubbing his hair, staring at Brodie's expression, Julian added, "I just don't know which one of us is willing to relocate to make that crappy commute." Julian closed his eyes as he rinsed the soap out of his hair. Opening his eyes, wiping them off, he found Brodie's lost expression. "I guess it's more complicated than we first thought."

"I don't know. I'm not sure it has to be."

Julian ran the soap over his chest, down his abdomen to his crotch, washing himself. "I've dealt with the commute to that city in the past, Brodie. I'm not eager to do it again. My bank is downtown. I walk there."

"Where do you live?"

"Fifth and Madison."

"You have a place in that new tower?"

"Yes."

"View of the Sound?"

"Yes…" Julian smiled.

"Two bedroom?"

Chuckling, Julian replied, "Two bed, two and a half bath. I assume you won't be in the guest bedroom." Setting down the soap, Julian faced the showerhead and rinsed off. "You done?"

"Yes."

Julian turned off the water. Dripping as the steam swirled around them, Julian asked, "Does this mean you can move in with me? That you'll deal with the commute eastbound?"

"I may not have to commute."

"Oh?"

As if snapping out of a dream, Brodie opened the shower door and handed Julian a towel. "Thanks," Julian said, rubbing it over his hair and face.

Brodie stepped out, drying off, wrapping the towel around his hips.

"I didn't know Microsoft had an office downtown."

"No," Brodie answered, finding his shaving cream and razor. "I may be able to work from home."

"Really?" Julian felt a spark of hope. Standing beside Brodie at the second basin, Julian wiped the steam off the mirror so he could see his reflection to shave.

"I'm not sure. It's something I'll have to discuss with my supervisor."

"Of course." Julian took the can and sprayed cream on his hand to smear on his jaw. "Well, if you can swing that, then our problem is solved."

"You really want to live with me?"

Peeking over at him, seeing his foamy face, Julian smiled sweetly at him. "I think I can stand you."

Appearing pleased with the reply, Brodie continued to shave. "You ever live with anyone before?"

"No. Just Mom and Dad. I've been living on my own for the last six years, since I graduated from the U-Dub."

"You went to the University of Washington?"

"Yeah. Why?"

"So did I."

"Huh." Julian plowed the sharp razor through the thick foam efficiently.

"But you're a year younger than me, so I graduated a year ahead of you."

"Yes. Sounds right." Julian checked for missed spots on his chin and lip, rinsing the razor under the running water, splashing his face.

"We have a lot in common."

"We do." Julian dried his face on a towel, turning to watch Brodie finish his shaving at the same time.

"So…" Brodie shrugged, "That's it? I'm moving in with you?"

Dabbing moisturizer on his skin, rubbing it in, Julian thought it did sound impulsive. He wondered if his parents would think he was on drugs. "Uh, I guess."

"You guess?"

Holding up his hand as if to correct himself, Julian replied, "No. Yes. You can. If you want to."

"Crap," Brodie grumbled, pushing passed him to the cabin's main room.

Stepping out slowly, seeing Brodie getting dressed, Julian didn't know what to say. It was all happening too quickly.

"I'm starved. Get dressed or we'll miss breakfast."

Moving to the dresser to find clean briefs, Julian felt slightly ill. He didn't know what to do for the best. Never in his wildest dreams did he imagine Amelia and him parting on this cruise and meeting a man he'd fall in love with. He simply wasn't prepared.

~

Brodie brooded. Silent during breakfast, eating his waffles and sausages quietly, sipping his coffee, looking out of the window at the sight of the coast of Alaska, he was lost. It felt like rejection even though it had been an invitation. There was no enthusiastic welcome, no jumping up and down and high-fiving. Is that really what he expected? Julian to be ecstatic after knowing him less than a week? Well? Yes.

Brodie was convinced this was the nail in the coffin for them. They'd go back to their lives, get busy, and fade away.

"Julian Richards! You bastard!"

Cringing at Amelia's scream, Brodie figured this was all they needed for a perfect morning.

"You cut me off! We had a deal!"

"You were getting a little carried away, Amelia. Twelve hundred bucks? Come on. What the hell could you buy on this boat that costs so much? Give me a break."

"A deal's a deal, Julian." She knotted her arms tightly over her chest.

"I already spent a thousand on your fare. Okay? Can we draw the line at twenty-two hundred? How greedy can you get, Amelia?"

"Fine. Be that way."

As she stormed off, Julian jumped to stop her. "I know what you're going to do. Don't."

In a huff she replied, "I don't know what you're so afraid of. If you think you've found your Mr. Right, why are you so scared to tell Mommy?"

Brodie rubbed his face in agony. They did not need this right now.

"Amelia! I will tell her, face to face. I don't want her finding out something like that from a phone call."

"Tough." She jerked out of his grasp.

"Amelia!"

When Julian ran after her, out of the room, Brodie slumped in his seat. A busboy cleared the table efficiently. Brodie thanked him, trying to smile. As passengers passed by, Brodie gazed out at the clouds and choppy water. He was nuts to think it would work. Completely nuts.

~

"Amelia, stop." Julian blocked her path to the elevators.

"Get away from me, Julian."

"Let me tell her. It's not your place to do it."

"Screw you. You know how humiliating this is? First you shack up with a guy, then you take away my spending money on our first real trip together. You owe me."

"What happened to Harry? I thought you two were a pair now?"

She made a bland face. "I'm not so sure about that. He lives in California, and his family are fishermen. Blah."

"So? Because you and he aren't getting along, I have to pay the price?"

"Yes! Look, Julian, I'm stuck on this stupid boat with a gay ex-boyfriend and a guy who sells fish! Life in hell, take one."

"I'm sorry, okay? I didn't know it would end up like this either." Julian was an emotional wreck. Where the hell did it all go off track?

Amelia softened her tone. "Do you miss me?"

Julian jumped in surprise as Amelia caressed his chin. Right before he answered her question, Brodie appeared next to them, the picture of fury and betrayal.

"Brodie!" Julian shoved Amelia's hand away.

"Nice." Brodie's jaw twitched as he ground it.

"No, it's not that." Julian panicked as Amelia looked on smugly.

"Not what, Julian?" Brodie asked sarcastically. "Not what it looks like? Not what it seems?"

"No."

Giving him a disgusted sneer, Brodie walked away.

"Shit." Julian ran after him looking behind him to see Amelia's gloat.

~

Brodie's head was pounding he was so angry and confused. Storming back toward his cabin, for lack of another idea, he felt Julian grasping after him.

"Brodie, stop running away."

"Screw you."

"Brodie!" Julian grabbed him roughly and jerked him around to face him.

In reflex Brodie pulled back for a punch, his fist clenched, his teeth grinding. Julian looked shocked.

Lowering his arm slowly, Brodie asked, "What the hell do you want from me? Huh? Maybe all it was a stupid onboard fling after all."

"No. No, Brodie. You know that's bullshit."

"Bullshit?" Brodie spat out. "You want to go back with her."

"No way." Julian shook his head to emphasize it. "Not in a million years."

"She was touching you!"

Seeing Julian looking around as so many passengers were present and appeared to be listening, Brodie felt Julian's nudge to keep moving. As he encouraged him to go, Julian held Brodie's elbow, whispering to him as he walked, "She probably had an argument with big-head-Harry, Brodie. She's a moron. I don't want anything to do with her. I was just about to swat her nasty claw away when you showed up."

They descended the staircase winding down to the main level. Silent as they walked the long stretch to the cabin, Brodie tried to calm down, be rational. Julian wasn't lying to him. Brodie had to convince himself Julian wasn't. Faith. Julian had asked him to have faith in him. He wasn't used to that, giving people the benefit of the doubt. He'd been let down too many times.

Finally at their cabin, Brodie opened the door. The bed wasn't made yet. That meant the maid would be knocking soon.

"Sit down," Julian commanded.

Brody obeyed.

"It's my fault." Julian began, pacing in front of him. "I was vague when we talked about living together. I know in my heart it's what I want. No question. But I'm thinking about the reaction of my family to all this. It shouldn't be a priority, and it isn't, but it is a factor."

"I expected you to get excited. So much for expectations."

"I am." Julian knelt down in front of him, clasping Brodie's hands. "I want you with me, to be in my bed every night. Are you kidding me?"

"You sure?"

"Yes!" Julian lay across Brodie's lap. "Yes. Very sure. But, Brodie, at least admit that this is going to shock some people. That not only are we admitting to them we're gay, but we're going to live together as well. And it's not only the fact that we're two men. Even if I had met a woman on this trip, my parents would wonder about my decision making process."

"I know." Brodie expected the same.

"Good. I knew you'd understand."

"I do. Believe me. But I feel as if I have my own priorities straight finally. And the top dog on that list is you. Period."

Julian's blue eyes grew wider.

"Next on that list, and not to be underestimated," Brodie smiled, "is me. And with those two things as the ultimate guide in my own decision making process, the answer is clear."

A bright grin appeared on Julian's face. "Brodie, Brodie, Brodie…"

"Yes, dear?"

"I agree. What can I say?"

"Good. Kiss me."

Julian reached around Brodie's neck and pulled him close. When their lips met, Brodie knew it was magic.

~

It was pouring rain in Ketchikan. The men stayed onboard, swimming, taking in a sauna, the Jacuzzi, and relaxing by the indoor pool. By four the loud blasting horn sounded as the luxury cruise ship pushed back from the port, through the Inside Passage, headed south to Vancouver and finally Seattle.

Dressed for dinner, Brodie stood near the dresser, looking down at his mobile phone. Julian was finishing up in the bathroom. Brodie turned the phone on. No signal. Shutting it off, he pocketed it, getting a strange urge to call his parents to touch base with them.

"Ready?" Julian asked. "We need to swing by the gallery for that eight by ten I ordered."

"Yes. Right."

"You okay?"

"Yup." Brodie kissed him.

"Good. Gallery, then booze?"

"Sounds good." Brodie followed Julian out of the cabin. As they ascended deck levels, climbing the soft carpeted stairs, Brodie removed his phone to keep an eye on the LCD. As they passed the promenade deck, it displayed a signal. He dropped it into his pocket while Julian walked ahead of him to the wall of photos.

"Yes, I ordered an eight by ten..."

Brodie looked around at the rest of the snapshots. Ordinary people, happy smiles, cuddling couples. Who knew what really went on once they were home? Vacations were odd that way. They weren't reality.

With the bag in his hand, Julian said, "Let me drop it in the cabin so I'm not carrying it all over."

"Okay."

"Go get us a drink in that lounge off the dining room."

"What do you want?" Brodie asked as Julian began leaving.

"Ah, Irish coffee." He winked.

As Julian jogged away, Brodie found the exit to the outer deck. He took out his phone, keeping his back to the wind, dialing. Putting the tiny phone to his ear he heard it ringing.

"Hello?"

"Mom?"

"Brodie! Are you home already? I wasn't expecting you until Monday."

"No. I'm still on the ship. I just wanted to touch base with you."

"How is Melanie? Are you enjoying it?"

"Look, Mom, I know I should probably wait to talk to you when I get home, but I can't."

"What? What's wrong? Is it good news or bad news, and should

I get your father on the line?"

Brodie could hear his father's voice in the background asking what was going on. "I don't care if Dad hears."

"Get on the line, Keith," his mother shouted.

A moment later, Brodie heard his dad's voice. "What's going on, son?"

"Look, I just told Mom I know I should wait to talk to you when I get home, but I can't wait anymore."

"Are you and Melanie getting married?" his mother blurted.

Brodie died. "No. She ditched me."

"Ditched you?" his mother responded flatly.

"What do you mean?" his father added.

"Right before the boat took off, she ran away. She left me here on my own."

"Oh no." His mother gasped loudly. "I am so sorry, Brodie. How have you managed on your own? Did you meet any nice people?"

"Yes. I did."

"I'm glad to hear that."

"Mom, Dad…" Brodie braced himself. "I met a guy."

It was quiet until his mother asked, "A man? Was he on his own as well?"

"Brodie?" his father asked with more suspicion.

"Yes, Dad?"

"The way you said that, am I getting some other message here?"

"What, Keith?" his mother asked. "What message?"

"Yes, Dad."

As Brodie's mother questioned his father on the line, Brodie's dad said in an even tone, "He's telling us he's gay, Lucy."

"What?" she choked. "No. That can't be what he's saying."

"It is, Mom. I met a guy."

"And this couldn't wait for you to get home first?" his mom asked.

"No. I needed to tell you. I'm going crazy here wondering what you'll think."

"Is he local? Will you continue to see him?" his father questioned.

"Yes. He lives in downtown Seattle. He's a financial adviser at one of the big banks."

"How old is he?"

"Only twenty-seven. Look, I know this is completely insane, but when you meet him, you'll love him. He's the most incredible person I have ever met."

The line was silent.

"Hello?" Brodie wondered if they'd been disconnected.

"We're here, son."

"Dad? I know it's upsetting."

"Are you sure you'll feel this way once you're off the ship? Maybe it's just the loneliness."

"No. I'm sure. I have to go. I just wanted to tell you because it's been driving me crazy."

"As long as you're happy, Brodie," his mother whispered.

"I am. I can't wait for you to meet him."

"Okay, son."

"Let me go. I have to run."

"Goodbye. Call us when you get home."

"I will." He disconnected the line, felt slightly exhilarated, but not too much. It was as if a weight had been lifted from him. There had been some trepidation in their voices, but no anger. He hurried to the bar.

~

Julian walked into the dim lounge, looking for Brodie. Surprised he was just getting their drinks, expecting him to be sitting, finishing the first round, Julian met him at the table.

"Hey."

"Hiya." Brodie thanked the waitress.

"Is the service slow tonight?" Julian relaxed next to him, raising the cup to his lips.

"No. Why?"

"I'm just surprised you are only getting the drinks now. I assumed you'd be on your second scotch by the time I showed up."

"I called my parents."

Julian removed the coffee from his mouth. "What? Just now?"

"Yes. I couldn't stand it anymore."

"What did they do?"

Brodie shrugged. "I think they were okay. I know it was a lot to dump on them that way, but at least now they'll have some time to ruminate over it before I get home."

"Wow."

"Yeah, wow." Brodie took a gulp of his scotch.

"But how did they sound?"

"Good. Honest. Mom said something like as long as I'm happy. I don't think they'll be that bad."

"Did you tell them we're moving in together?"

"No. I didn't think I should go that far. I know how it would sound to them. Sometimes I wonder if they'll think I'm behaving like an impulsive child."

Julian smiled and was about to reply when Amelia showed up. "Great. Time for another showdown."

"Let me just tell her to fuck off." Brodie set his drink on the table.

"Don't worry." Julian reached to stop him from getting up.

"Hello, Julian," she sang.

"What now, Amelia? You want to go back to our vacant old room? Had a fight with big-head-Harry?"

"No. Why do you call him that? I don't get it. I like sleeping with him. He's good in bed, not like you."

Brodie made a sarcastic choking sound in reply.

"Is that all you came to tell me?" Julian asked. "That you're enjoying sex with the fisherman from California?"

"No. That's not all. I spoke to your mom."

Julian felt pale as Brodie jerked his head in his direction.

"You're bluffing."

"Am I?" she laughed.

"You wicked bitch!" Brodie growled. "If you weren't a girl, I'd beat the crap out of you."

"Save the macho act, fag." She flipped him off.

As Brodie prepared for the attack, Julian grabbed his arm again to stop him. "Did you really call my mother, Amelia?"

"Yes."

"Why?"

"To tell her, duh." She rolled her eyes.

"I can't believe you did that. I never pegged you as being that cruel."

"And I never pegged you as a fag. So we're even. Gotta go, just wanted to tell you." She spun around and left.

"Let me choke her." Brodie stood, clenching his fists.

"Forget it, Brodie." Julian finished his coffee. "See? Now both our families know."

Brodie dropped down on the chair again. "I'm so sorry, Julian."

"I should have listened to you and called her myself. My fault."

"No, it's my fault. If you hadn't cut off the credit card, Amelia wouldn't have done it."

Waving his hand to act as if it wasn't terrifying, Julian replied, "Forget it."

"Shit."

"Forget it, Brodie. It's done."

"Maybe they'll think she's full of shit."

"In a way, I hope not. At least the ice has been broken."

Brodie checked his watch. "It's after six. You want to eat?"

"Yes." Julian set his empty mug down.

Reaching out his hand, Brodie offered to haul Julian to his feet. Once they were both walking to the dining room, Julian had the urge to call home. He had to know what his family thought.

~

At dinner the three couples exchanged emails, promising to keep in touch. It was melancholy for all of them, getting closer to the end of the cruise and the last supper. With tomorrow being the last day, entirely at sea, Julian was glad it was ending. It felt controlled and artificial. They needed a dose of reality. One more day to go and they'd be there.

After dinner as they walked along the interior promenade deck, Julian removed his mobile phone from his pocket.

Brodie stopped his progress down the corridor, looking back at him. "Uh oh."

"How did you make a call? I'm not showing a signal here."

"Outside."

"Brr!"

"Yes, it was cold. You want to go out and try?"

"I feel obligated. But I don't want to know."

"I understand."

Julian stared at the tiny cell phone. "What should I do?"

Shrugging, Brodie replied, "You know what I'd do."

"Shit. Come with me."

Putting his arm around his waist, Brodie walked with Julian to the outer deck. The cold wind slapped him the moment they opened the heavy metal door. "Let's move to the back of the ship."

Brodie nodded, bracing himself against the constant gust.

Once they huddled against the side of the ship, Julian checked his phone.

"You getting a signal?"

"Yes."

"Want me to give you some privacy?"

"No. Stay here." Julian hit some buttons, putting the phone to his ear.

"Hello?"

"Karen?"

"Julian? Are you home?"

"No. I'll be home the day after tomorrow. Is Mom around?"

"Yes. You know Amelia called here?"

"I know." Julian frowned looking at Brodie's expression of concern. "How's Mom taking it?"

"You mean it's true?" Karen choked.

"Yes. Karen, put Mom or Dad on the phone." Julian rolled his eyes, whispering to Brodie, "My kid sister."

Brodie nodded.

"Hello?"

"Hi, Dad."

"Where are you, Julian?"

"I'm still on the boat. I'm standing outside freezing my nuts off, but it's the only way to use my damn cell phone."

"You know, Amelia called here."

"Yes, both she and Karen informed me."

"She made some allegations about you, Julian."

Cringing, Julian grabbed onto Brodie for strength. "I know. It's true, Dad."

"How can it be true? I don't understand? You and Amelia went on that trip as a couple. You've never shown an interest in men. What's going on?"

"Christ, I wish I was having this conversation with you in person. It sucks that she did this to me." Julian started to shiver from the cold. He pressed against Brodie tightly.

"I wish you were here as well. Your mother and I assumed it was some kind of prank."

"No. No, Dad. It isn't."

"I don't know what to say."

"Neither do I. Look, I just wanted to contact you after I heard what that witch did. When I get back to Seattle I'll call you and we can get together. Is that okay?"

"Yes."

"Good. I love you, Dad."

"I love you too, son. I just hope you know what the hell you're doing."

"Probably not, but that's life. See ya soon." He disconnected, jumped up and down and shouted, "I'm freezing!"

Brodie cuddled against him, running with him to the door. Once they were inside, Julian shivered and rubbed his arms.

"Come here." Brodie embraced him, wrapping around him tightly, rocking side to side. "So? Are you dead?"

"I don't think so."

"Good."

"I still can't believe she did that to me."

"Maybe she did us a favor. At least it's out of the bag."

Julian noticed some prying eyes passing them. Nudging Brodie slightly, he broke their hug. "I need another coffee. I'm frozen."

Clasping his hand, Brodie smiled, leading the way back to the lounge.

~

Waking up early the next morning, getting in their run, Julian led the way back to the cabin, feeling the sweat dripping from every pore. Brodie opened the lock, pushing back the door.

"Last full day on this stupid boat and we're home free." Julian took off his shirt to use to wipe his face.

"We're at sea all day as well. I'm getting really bored." Brodie began undressing. "There's nothing to do but sit around and eat."

"I'd go to the gym, but the run is enough. It's taking it out of me. I don't know if it's the rocking this boat is doing, or what. I feel light-headed all the time."

"Too much sex."

Julian caught Brodie's wicked smirk. "Seriously, Brodie, what the hell are we going to do all day?"

"I don't know. I don't really like the gambling, or hanging around by the lido pool."

Julian followed him into the bathroom. "This sucks."

"We could just get naked and lie in bed all day. I wouldn't mind a little time to snuggle, nap, lick you up and down."

"All day?" Julian stared at Brodie's ass as he leaned in to turn on the shower.

"You got a better suggestion?"

Stepping in behind him into the spraying water, Julian didn't. "What would you do at home?"

"I'd probably do something active. You know, take the bicycle out and ride the Burke Gilman Trail."

"Sounds nice."

"You own a bike?"

"Yes. I have a mountain bike, but I rarely use it." Julian changed places with Brodie so he could wash his hair.

"We should go one day."

"Yes. I'd like that."

Rinsing in silence, Julian indicated he was done, so Brodie shut the water. Rubbing towels through their hair, climbing out of the shower, Brodie sighed, "Still leaves the problem of killing the day."

"Forget it. Let's just laze around and eat. Everyone else does, and it is a vacation, right?"

"Okay." Brodie hung up the towel and leaned on the sink to shave.

Getting his razor out to do the same, Julian was ready to get on with his life. The waiting was becoming the hardest part.

~

The last night in the dining room was somber and uneventful. It was as if a feeling of melancholy had pervaded everyone's mood.

It wasn't until almost midnight that they wandered back to the cabin. They had bumped into Marlene and Glenda and chatted in the lounge together about keeping up an email correspondence.

Brodie yawned as he took of his shoes and trousers. "I'm beat."

"Me too. No run in the morning? I assume we need to pack."

"I don't think we have to be out early. We don't get to Vancouver until afternoon, and we still have to get to Seattle after that."

"Yes, you're right." Julian hung up his slacks in the closet. "But I still want to pass on the run."

"Okay." Brodie was about to hang up his shirt when he noticed Melanie's floral suitcase. Picking it up, he shook his head sadly. "I've been trying to get them to toss it. I even put the garbage pail in it. No use."

"Did you get rid of the newspapers?"

"Yes. They took those." Brodie threw it back where it was, against the wall near the door.

"Maybe I should donate it to Amelia. My guess is she bought so much shit, she'll need an extra bag."

Pausing, Brodie replied, "Leave it by her room."

"I don't want to give her anything. No way. I was just being sarcastic."

"What the fuck am I supposed to do with it?"

"Just leave it behind."

Brodie continued to undress, trying not to stare at the annoying thing. Once he had washed up, he waited for Julian to do the same, and joined him in bed. They cuddled warmly together. Brodie petted Julian's hair lazily. "So, both our folks know. I suppose that's a good thing."

"I suppose."

"And the housing market is still strong there, or it would take a while to sell my place."

"You have a house?" Julian leaned his chin on his fist as he rested on Brodie's chest.

"Yes."

"Oh."

"Oh what?"

"You're swapping a house for a condo."

"So?"

"You sure you want to do that?"

"Yeah, I'm sick of mowing the damn lawn."

"It is a neat place. The view is something special."

"I bet you paid the same for that condo as I did for my house."

"Maybe more."

"No!" Brodie cringed. "I don't want to know."

"Okay."

"What are your mortgage payments?"

"I thought you didn't want to know," Julian laughed.

"Well, I intend to pay half."

"Oh!" Julian leaned up on his elbows.

"What?"

"I didn't expect that. How much equity do you have in your house?"

"Good point. I could give you a lump sum to take a chunk out of your principle."

"Wait. Let's not talk about that now. We'll work something out. I just don't want you to lose in this transaction."

"If I get to keep you, I can't lose." Brodie wrapped around him.

"You're such a romantic!" Julian chuckled.

"Mm, you smell good." Brodie sniffed his hair.

"Get out the rubbers," Julian hissed seductively.

Sitting up, Brodie dug into the drawer by the bed, setting out the strip of condoms and the lube. "Good thing we're almost home. That tube isn't going to last much longer, and *you're* buying the next one!"

"Yeah, yeah. Shut up and get over here."

Lowering to Julian's level on the bed, Brodie closed his eyes and went for his lips. Whenever they touched sexually it reinforced his determination to keep them together. It was as if the contact reminded him of what he had. Yes, it was more than sex with Julian, but the uniting of their bodies communicated the strength of their bond.

Brodie loved that tongue as it spun around his own, licked at his teeth, and explored his mouth. As if it wasn't interested before they kissed, his cock went solid, poking Julian as it rose. Julian obviously felt it throbbing against his hip because he reached for it, smoothing his palm against it. Brodie whimpered at the caress as well as the thought of the coming sex. His body seemed to have a life of its own. His legs wrapped around Julian's, drawing him nearer. Beginning at Julian's dark hair, savoring its thickness and softness, he moved his hands down Julian's neck to his broad muscular back, narrow waist, and ultimately his ass cheeks. Gripping one in each hand, Brodie ground his cock against Julian, trapping Julian's hand between them. As if Julian needed the total cock on cock contact as well, he removed his hand, rolling on top of Brodie, in an effort to grind back.

Needing more air, his pulse rising, his chest expanding, Brodie knew he should break the kiss to gasp for breath. But the kissing was so hot he didn't want to. Easing up just enough to lap at Julian's lips, inhale a few long breaths to calm his demand, Brodie cupped the back of Julian's head and dug deeper into his wet mouth with his tongue. As he did his cock twitched and throbbed against Julian's pelvis. He wanted to fuck his mouth with his tongue. or with his dick. He needed to be inside this man, somehow. Now. Pulling back again, needing to breathe as the passion sizzled and sparked, Brodie stared down at Julian's face as he continued to pivot his hips, getting some hot, strong friction. Their eyes connected, unblinking, telling each other how incredible it was without words. Brodie knew his jaw was twitching just like Julian's. That cheek muscle contracting like a pulsing vein. Showing his teeth in a snarl as the grinding got rougher, Brodie gripped his fist into Julian's hair, growling deep and low, "I want to *fuck* you, *fuck* you," and with every repetition, Brodie jammed his hips upwards into Julian's body.

Julian spread his legs wide, smiling greedily.

With both hands pressed beside Julian on the bed, Brodie pushed himself up quickly so he was kneeling, straddling Julian's thighs. Tearing open a condom, Brodie slid it on. Julian watched the act. Smearing some lube on himself, Brodie backed off Julian's legs. "How do you want it?"

In reply Julian lay flat on his back, bending his knees. Moving between Julian's legs, Brodie raised one at a time to rest on his shoulders. "Want me to jerk you off?"

"No. I want to come in you."

Brodie smiled wickedly. "Good." Pushing inside Julian's body, Brodie hissed out a breath at the intensity of the tightness surrounding him. Moving slowly until he was completely enveloped, Brodie stilled himself, savoring the union. Julian began pushing up and down, as if it was too good not to. Opening his eyes, not realizing he had closed them, Brodie stared down at Julian's swollen cock, his tight ripped abdomen, and rounded chest. Gently Brodie began moving in and out. With each stroke his body covered with chills. Julian had splayed his arms out beside him, resting them on the bed, closing his eyes, his head tilted into the pillow.

With each thrust of Brodie's hips, Julian's cock elevated and bobbed. It was completely engorged and blushing in color. Brodie wished he could suck it at the same time as he screwed him, but that wasn't physically possible. As he arched his back and clung onto Julian's ankles, Brodie knew he couldn't even reach his hand down to stroke it at the moment. As the climax drew near, Brodie opened his lips to inhale deeply. "I want to *fuck* you, *fuck* you," he rumbled as he thrust, deeper, harder.

And to his delight, Julian responded in a low husky voice, "*Fuck me, fuck me…*"

It was the last push off the cliff. Brodie pressed as close to Julian's body as he could, feeling his cock pulse and throb like mad. "*Ah…*" Brodie grunted, clamping his eyes shut tight. His head drooping forward, Brodie caught his breath. Taking a moment to recover, he finally opened his eyes to that loving smile. Pulling out, kissing Julian's legs affectionately, Brodie allowed them to fall back to the bed.

~

Staring at Brodie, his proud posture, his dewy serious expression, Julian wondered if he had ever seen anything so beautiful in his life. Unable to prevent it, Julian grabbed his own dick and pulled on it several times, the craving gnawing at him.

Brodie seemed to wake from his dream. He tugged the rubber off

.A. Hauser

with some difficulty, because he was still fully erect.

Julian couldn't take his eyes off that engorged cock of his. "My turn," Julian hissed seductively, feeling like a predatory cat.

Still panting from the excitement, Brodie whispered, "Where do you want me?"

"On. Your. Knees." Julian ordered, pointing in front of him.

"Wow. Yes, sir!" Brodie's cock twitched as he assumed the position.

With Brodie watching him from over his shoulder, Julian ran his hand over Brodie's back and hips, savoring him, knowing they may be apart for a little while until things settled down in Seattle. Julian ran kisses over Brodie's skin. Tasting the slight depression of his muscle on the outside of his upper thigh, Julian ran his tongue along it. As he licked Brodie's tight left ass cheek, he teased Brodie's dangling balls with his fingers. Brodie arched his back, moaning.

Julian reached for the condoms. Meeting Brodie's eyes again as Brodie stretched his neck to watch, Julian made a show of smoothing lubrication on himself, running his hand up and down his own length. Brodie shivered visibly.

On his knees behind Brodie, Julian smoothed his hands over his waist and hips with a feather touch, as a cat torments its prey. He knew Brodie was waiting, wanting it. With slick hands, Julian pushed his index finger inside him. Brodie pushed back against his hand, getting it deeper. Gently moving in and out, Julian's finger glided effortlessly.

"Christ, Julian, stop teasing me!"

Julian chuckled in amusement. He was waiting for Brodie to recover enough to give him another orgasm. His wait appeared to be over. Removing his finger, Julian set his cock on target, leaning over Brodie's back, hugging him tight. With a tilt of his hips he slipped in. Brodie let out a low whimpering moan. As he penetrated to the root of his cock, Julian advanced both hands in the same direction, Brodie's genitals. Reaching underneath, smearing silky lubrication all over his balls and shaft, Julian felt Brodie's intake of air as his ribcage expanded under him. Once he had a good grip on Brodie's cock, both palms holding him, Julian began pumping his hips in time with his fingers. And in sync, Brodie matched that rhythm. Feeling Brodie's cock slide in his hands from the base to over the head of his penis, Julian lit on fire. The sweat building up between Julian's chest and Brodie's back, their gasping groans growing in intensity, Julian knew he was there. As his body jerked involuntarily deeper as he came, Julian felt Brodie's length quiver under him and his hand fill with sticky heat. Slowing down, resting on Brodie's back, Julian closed his eyes to savor the scent of sex, the warmth, the mingling of their perspiration. When he found the strength to sit back, pulling out, Brodie collapsed onto the bed.

Sitting on his heels, Julian slowed his breathing down, trying to recover from the intense bout. Managing to stand, rocking to gain his balance as the ship made him unsteady, Julian took Brodie's spent condom with him to the bathroom to dispose of. He got rid of them both, washed his hands and relieved himself. Making his way back to the bed, he found Brodie had crawled under the blanket. Joining him, he hit the light switch on the headboard, creating total darkness. Snuggling up behind him, sniffing his neck, Julian whispered, "I love you, Brodie."

"You too, babe."

Letting go of a deep exhale, Julian fell fast asleep.

Chapter Fourteen

They ate breakfast before they packed. The crowd seemed slightly more anxious than normal as the end was nigh and their trip coming to a close.

Brodie ate his food in silence. They were both preoccupied by what was ahead. It seemed strange to dread it since they had agreed to live together, but there were so many unknowns to the plan perhaps it was too early to be too calm as well.

"More coffee?" Brodie offered from the carafe.

"Sure. One more."

Pouring, Brodie smiled as he watched Julian shaking the packet of sugar into it. He'd remember how Julian liked it. One sugar, milky. That way when he woke up earlier than him, he could fix it for him and bring it to him in bed.

"Do you have to be at work tomorrow?" Julian asked as he stirred his cup.

"Yes. You?"

"Yes."

Brodie nodded. "I gave you all my home info, right?"

"Yes."

"Good." Brodie bit his lip. "Did you drive to the port?"

"No. We took a cab. What about you?"

"I parked near the terminal."

Julian nodded.

"I can give you a lift home."

"Okay. If you're not too tired."

"No. It's on the way. I have to pass through downtown to get to the highway anyway."

"All right."

It was awkward. Why the hell is it awkward after the sex they had last night? Brodie wanted to mention it, but thought it may just be him who's feeling that way.

"You okay?"

Instantly wondering if Julian was clairvoyant, Brodie met his eyes. "Uh."

Julian tilted his head, as if asking the same thing again silently.

"No. Since you ask. I'm a nervous wreck."

"Why? Both our parents know and have had time to digest it, and we've agreed to live together in my condo."

"I know."

"Are you having second thoughts?"

"No!" Brodie shouted, looking around in paranoia. "No," he said calmly. "I just don't want to wait."

Laughing at the compliment, Julian sipped his coffee, his eyes shining.

"I want to be with you now. Tonight. It sucks going back to my empty house, my empty bed."

"I get it. I do." Julian reached out his hand.

Brodie clasped it.

"But it'll be temporary, Brodie. And if you want, move in while you sell the place."

"Yeah?"

"Why not? I hate being around when realtors show it. And you have to keep it spotless. It's a pain in the ass."

"And not in a good way," Brodie giggled.

"No. Not in a good way."

"Okay. I feel better about that. That way it's weeks not months."

"What if you have to commute?"

Shrugging, Brodie replied, "So? I'll commute. Millions of people do it."

"I know. That's why the freeways are so impossible."

"Look, I consider it a small price to pay to come home to you at night."

"Wow, that's an amazing thing to say."

Brodie squeezed his hand. "I mean it."

"Good. Then there's nothing to worry about, is there?"

Smiling brightly, Brodie said, "No. There isn't."

~

They had packed, giving their luggage to the porter to stow until they departed. As the boat left Vancouver for its final destination in Seattle, Julian stood on the deck watching as people waved to friends they made while onboard.

"It was a good trip, all in all." Brodie's view was aimed at the Vancouver skyline.

"Memorable, I can say that with conviction."

Brodie gave Julian a sly look. "Yes, memorable."

"One to tell the grandkids about."

"Funny."

"Come on, let's get a drink."

"I have to drive."

"Non-alcoholic." Julian found a vacant seat in the lounge. Half the passengers had disembarked in Canada so the place seemed empty.

The waitress approached them.

"I'll have a cup of coffee," Brodie ordered.

"Me too."

When she left Brodie gave Julian a questioning tilt of the head. "You could have an Irish coffee."

"I felt bad. I didn't want to drink when you couldn't."

Brodie moved his leg to touch Julian's. "So considerate. I can get used to that."

"Hey, I'm a nice guy."

"I know."

The waitress brought them their coffee. "You have to pay cash, I'm sorry," she whispered.

"Oh!" Brodie remembered he had settled up the bill already. He took a five out of his wallet, handing it to her, telling her to keep the change. She thanked him, leaving them with a smile.

"I owe you some money." Julian shook a packet of sugar into his cup.

"You buy the first dinner out."

Exhaling in annoyance, Julian sat back, holding his coffee. "Why do I get the feeling the spoiling may run both ways."

"Enjoy it. I will."

"We meet again!" Marlene and Glenda approached their table.

"Hello, ladies. Care to join us?" Brodie asked.

"You mind? We're bored. Nothing's going on anymore with the trip almost over. We can't even nap in our rooms." Marlene sat down. The waitress came over immediately. "Coffee?" Marlene asked Glenda.

"Sure."

"Two coffee's please," Marlene requested. After the waitress had left, Marlene asked, "So? You guys ready for reality?"

"We were discussing that." Julian set his cup down. "No. Funny isn't it? I really feel the need to finally get off the boat, but I'm not too excited to get back into the routine."

Glenda said, "Me too. I actually have tomorrow off. I figured after the long drive down to Portland, I'd be too tired the next day."

Julian noticed Marlene staring at him. Before he asked her what was on her mind, the waitress returned with their coffees. Both Marlene and Glenda handed her some singles. The moment the waitress left, Julian caught Marlene's eye again. "Yes?"

"Hm?" She blinked as if she were surprised by his attention.

"I thought maybe you were going to ask me something."

"I was. I'm just trying to decide if it's tasteless or not."

Julian looked over at Brodie to see his expression. He just shrugged. "Go for it," Julian replied. "It's the last chance you'll get before we hit Seattle."

After taking a sip of her coffee, Marlene paused for a moment. "I get the feeling since you just met on this trip, and you, Julian, were with a woman, that your families don't know about you two."

"They do," Brodie answered. "We called and told them."

"Whoa." Glenda's eyes widened.

"So? Things going to be okay?" Marlene asked.

"I think so." Julian reached out for Brodie's hand.

"Well, if you ever get down my way, I can show you some nice places to stay on the Oregon coast." Marlene smiled.

"Thanks. I appreciate that." Julian caught Brodie's grin, squeezing his hand.

"It was really great getting to know you guys," Marlene whispered, slightly teary eyed.

"You too, Marlene." Brodie leaned over and kissed her cheek.
She touched the spot and gave him an adoring smile.

~

Standing outside on the promenade deck, Brodie watched the
port of Seattle coming closer as the massive ship docked. Inhaling
the sea air, thankful it wasn't raining, Brodie looked up at the
skyline, glad he was home again. The Space Needle, the Columbia
Tower, the Aurora Viaduct, all looking welcoming and familiar
compared to the sparse Alaskan towns they had visited.

Julian leaned against him warmly. "Home sweet home."

"Yes. Can you see your condo from here?"

Leaning around the railing, Julian pointed, "Just a little bit of it.
You can see the top peeking out."

"I know the one. They just finished it. It's a great location."

"Beats Bellevue," Julian winked.

"I'm sure it does."

"We're here. Let's go." Julian led the way to the gangplank as it
was secured and a line formed. Their luggage was waiting for them.
Each man picked up a suitcase and waved at the crew who thanked
them and bid them a goodbye.

"My car's over here." Brodie took the key out of his pocket.
They walked to a parking lot jammed with cars. Chirping his key
fob, Brodie unlocked the door on his gold Porsche.

"Nice!" Julian gushed over it.

"Thanks." Brodie opened the trunk and loaded their bags.

Once they were inside the car, Brodie started the ignition,
fastening his seatbelt. "Okay. Here we go."

Julian read the clock on the dash. "It's only four. Uh, you want
to come up and have a look around?"

"Yes. I'd like that."

Backing out, Brodie tried to get going before the rest of the
passengers did the same thing. Heading uphill to Fifth Avenue,
Brodie listened as Julian pointed the easiest route in the downtown
tangle.

"I've got a garage and a parking space. I just don't have my
opener with me."

"Should I park and wait?"

"You mind?"

"No." Brodie pulled the car up to the garage gate.

"I'll be quick."

"Okay." Julian climbed out, sprinting to the front door. As Brodie waited he looked around the area wondering how it would feel to live here, and live with a man.

Within a few minutes, the gate began opening. Brodie inched the car in as the path was made clear. Julian was waving to him from the inside. A garage door elevated showing off a Mercedes and an open space beside it. *Two-car garage, nice.*

Brodie pulled in, shutting off the motor. He met Julian at the trunk and took his case out for him. Once they had cleared the garage, Julian clicked a remote, closing the door again.

"This way."

Following him to the door to the elevator and lobby, Brodie kept quiet as they ascended to the top of the thirty-one floors. As Julian turned a key, Brodie knew what to expect, it was going to be unbelievable. He wasn't disappointed. His focus immediately went to the wall of windows overlooking the Sound. He had to pull his attention back from the Olympic Mountain Range to actually inspect the contents of the penthouse condominium. A steel and dark marble kitchen with an island, open-plan space connecting the dining area to the living room, a plasma screen television imbedded into the wall, a leather sectional sofa surrounding it, recessed lighting, slick polished wood flooring. Brodie walked to a doorway of a bedroom, inspecting the clean lines and immaculate designing. The king-size bed seemed dwarfed by the dimensions of the master bedroom. The connecting bath had a whirlpool jet bathtub, a shower stall with two heads protruding from either wall and a marble and chrome cabinet with double basin. He didn't even care what the guest bathroom looked like.

"Jesus, Julian."

"You like it?"

"Yes!"

"Good." Julian connected to his back, hugging him close. "I don't want you to leave."

"I don't want to leave." Brodie trapped Julian's hands against his chest.

"I want you and me to make love in my bed."

Brodie smiled as he stared at it. "Better than trying to roll around on two twins, always sinking into the crack between."

"You have to get home right away?" Julian smoothed his hands down to Brodie's jeans.

Brodie checked his watch. It was nearing five. "No. I have some time. Want to christen the bed?"

Without a verbal answer, Julian was already turning down the spread.

"Where's the lube? Did I pack it or did you?" Brodie asked, getting undressed.

"Shit. I don't remember. Wait here."

After he left the room, Brodie stripped naked, moving to look out of the curtain of the covered window. They had a view across the entire downtown skyline, unobstructed because of the height of the tower. He had a decent house in Bellevue, but it was almost ten years old. It didn't compare to penthouse life in the newly renovated area of hip downtown Seattle. When Julian returned, condoms and lube in hand, Brodie couldn't help but ask. "Over a million, right?"

"No. Just under. I bought it off plan. I think the other two attached to this are a million and a half."

"Jesus Christ. How many square feet?"

"Nineteen hundred and fifty."

"It's as big as my house!"

"What did you pay for yours in Bellevue?"

"Four hundred thousand. I don't want to sound nosy, Julian, but how the hell did you afford this place?"

Smiling, setting the items in his hand onto the nightstand, Julian undressed. "Dad pitched in a little."

"Is that a fact?"

"And I don't do half bad. I make a decent living."

"No kidding. You share trade? The market's been so crappy."

"You, ah, wanna talk stocks or cocks?"

Watching Julian pump his a few times, Brodie laughed, "Definitely cocks."

"Good." Julian climbed onto the bed, reaching out for him.

Joining him on the huge, springy mattress, Brodie met him in the middle, lying on his side next to him. He cupped his face gently, moving in for a kiss. It was gentle at first, no tongues, just lips, soft, like petals brushing together. Brodie instantly felt his demand rising. It always seemed to bring him to the point of frenzied yearning at first kiss. He'd never felt anything quite like the connection he had with Julian. And truthfully he doubted he ever would again.

Julian opened his mouth, licking Brodie's top lip, moving to the bottom, only to push in-between quickly after. As Julian made his way inside him, Brodie felt his cock throb, knocking against Julian's as they faced each other.

Reaching down, going for that luscious, hard dick of Julian's, Brodie ran his thumb under the head and over it, smearing the drop that oozed out over the tip. As he did, Julian opened his lips wider, moaning, sucking Brodie's tongue into his mouth. Tongue-fucking Julian as they mashed lips, Brodie wrapped his hand around both their cocks, pressing them together. Julian's hips came alive, pumping through Brodie's palm, rubbing against the silky skin of Brodie's dick.

Parting from him, looking at his blue eyes, Brodie stared at him for a moment, relishing in his beauty. "You hot mother fucker."

Julian laughed softly, flattered.

After pecking his lips once more, Brodie lowered down on the bed. Just as he was getting ready to suck him, Julian tapped him, saying, "Bring it here."

Shifting his position so he was straddling Julian's head, Brodie leaned down to take him into his mouth, just as Julian reached up to do the same to him. Closing his eyes, enveloping Julian's cock to the base, Brodie felt Julian doing the exact same to him and it sent him reeling. Julian copied every movement. Getting the idea, Brodie went for Julian's balls, massaging them. His balls were massaged. Moving his finger to Julian's scrotum, Brodie fingered it firmly, feeling Julian's cock shiver and more pre-come juice slipped out of the tip. It was too much. Brodie wanted to come, and taste Julian's come simultaneously. He quickened his pace, pushed his finger inside Julian, and Julian reciprocated. Brodie came, almost choking as Julian did as well and he needed to gasp at the intensity. He had to remember to swallow as his eyes almost rolled back into his head from the strength of the climax. Gulping him down, backing away so he could pant for breath, Brodie wanted to continue licking Julian's cock, but the climax left him swooning for a moment. "Holy shit."

"How about that!" Julian breathed heavily. "It was like sucking on my own dick!"

Brodie choked with laughter, rolling to his side on the bed, holding his stomach. It struck him as the funniest thing he'd ever heard. As if the laughter was contagious, Julian was hysterical as well, coughing, holding his stomach.

Finally settling down, Brodie peeked up at Julian as he dabbed at his eyes. "Wow. I've never done sixty-nine before."

"We'll have to do that again." Julian let out another laugh. "Get over here."

Spinning around on the bed, Brodie crawled across the length of the mattress to drop down by Julian's side and snuggle. "Didn't even need the lube."

"No. Not this time." Julian kissed Brodie's cheek. "I don't want you to go!"

"I don't want to go!" Brodie whined back. "But I have to work tomorrow. I really wanted to do a load of wash, see my parents, you know."

"Yes." Julian brushed his hair back from his forehead.

"I'm calling a real estate agent tomorrow," Brodie said like a warning.

"You know a good one?"

"I do. She's great. She'll do it right."

"If you don't mind the commute, move here this week."

Brodie backed up, making good, strong eye contact. "It is right, isn't it? It isn't impulsive. We really do need to do this."

"Yes."

"Good. Yes." Brodie nodded, like it was now a formal agreement. "Let me go, get home, and get started."

"Okay. Last hug."

He wrapped around Julian, rolling side to side with him. "I love you, babe. A lot."

"You too, Brodie, you too."

~

On his drive over the 520 floating bridge, Brodie felt lonesome. Instead of going straight home, he detoured to his parents' house. Pulling in behind his father's SUV, Brodie shut off the engine of his Porsche and looked up at the house. Giving out a deep sigh, he climbed out to assess what time had done to their opinion. It didn't change anything, but it would be nice to know. He knocked, opening the screen door and trying the knob. His mother opened it.

"Brodie!"

"Hi, Mom." He kissed her cheek. "Is Dad here?"

"Yes, we're just finishing dinner. Did you eat?"

"No. Sorry to bother you."

"It's no bother. Come in and I'll make up a plate for you." She shouted, "Keith, Brodie's here!"

Brodie turned the corner of the hall and found his father sitting at the table. "Hi, Dad."

"Brodie. Come in, have a seat. Lucy, give him some food."

"I am." She hurried to fill a plate, setting it on the table for him.

"So?" His father chewed the food, staring at him.

"Why is your face all red?" His mother held Brodie's jaw to inspect it.

"Windburn." He nudged her hand away and began eating hungrily.

"Was it a nice trip?" his dad asked.

"Yes. It was. I recommend it. I'd rather have gone someplace warm though. It was very cold on deck. You couldn't swim in the outside pool."

"What's Alaska like?" his mother inquired.

As he answered he felt as if they were avoiding the elephant in the room. Maybe they were pretending he hadn't met a man. Perhaps they wondered if the end of the trip meant the end of the affair.

Once they had finished and the dishes were done, Brodie said, "Look, I need to talk to you. Can we sit in the living room for a minute?"

His parents exchanged pensive looks. He knew they knew what it was about.

Once they had made themselves comfortable, Brodie took something out of his shirt pocket. "This is Julian." He handed them a photo.

His father took it as his mother leaned over to see it. "Nice looking man," his mother whispered.

Not commenting, his father handed it back.

Taking it, putting it back into his shirt pocket, Brodie laced his hands as he leaned over his lap to speak more seriously. "I know it's unorthodox and completely coming from left field—"

"Yes." His father's expression was stern. "It's what we're both having a hard time coming to grips with, Brodie. You've dated women your whole life. Are you sure this isn't some weird curiosity on your part?"

"I'm sure. I didn't want to say anything about it to you before."

"What does that mean?" His mother glanced at his father.

"It means," Brodie stared straight at his dad, "I knew I was gay for a long time, but I tried to block it out."

"What do you mean, you knew?" his father asked.

"I can only get off when I think about guys, Dad. Even if I'm with a woman."

"You're sure?" His mother seemed to be hoping he wasn't.

"Yes. Very sure. I spent ten years dating women, maybe more, since I was in junior high. To be brutally honest, I don't like them. They turn me off."

"Maybe you haven't met the right one."

"Mom, it's not that. I know it isn't. You have any idea how many women I have dated?" He knew they did. "Twenty? More? I meet one guy. One. Julian. I fell head over heels in love with him. I can't even imagine not being with him. Tonight, I'll be on the phone to him for hours just to tell him I miss him."

His father sat up in surprise. "You feel that deeply about him this soon?"

"Yes. I'm in love. Madly in love. And it's not some experiment, some faze. I know myself enough to realize the real thing when I feel it."

"Does he feel the same?" his mother asked in concern.

"Yes. One hundred percent."

They exchanged looks between them again.

Brodie announced, "I'm not asking you for permission. I'm not even looking for approval, well, maybe I am, but I love you two. A lot. I want you to know how I feel first hand."

"Okay, son." His father nodded.

Brodie wanted to mention he was selling his house and moving in with Julian, but he couldn't do it. It sounded so damn irrational. "I want you to meet him. Soon."

"He can come over for dinner this weekend," his mother offered. "Can he come by?"

"Yes. Most likely." Brodie stood. "I still haven't been home. I need to do a few things. I have work in the morning."

They stood up, walking him to the door.

"Thanks for listening." Brodie kissed his mother's cheek.

"It's okay, Brodie. I understand. I'm not judging you."

Hugging her, he whispered, "I love you, Mom." When he parted from her hug, he looked at his father. Even though he was a police lieutenant, he still had kind eyes. "Dad." Brodie held out his hand.

His father brought him into an embrace. "It took guts to tell us, Brodie. I know it did."

Feeling like he was growing emotional, Brodie patted his dad's back and stood apart from him. "It did. But not as much as you think. Two things made me strong. Your love and Julian's. With that, I can do anything." He threw them a kiss. "See ya."

"Goodbye, son. Drive safely."

He waved at them, getting into his car, trying not to allow that hot tear to roll down his cheek. As he made the drive to his home, he used his mobile phone to call Paden.

"Hey, Brodie!"

"Hey, handsome."

"So?"

"I'm madly in love."

"Shut up!"

"No. I'm not joking."

"Son of a bitch, Brodie!"

"I just told my parents. Paden, you have to meet him. He's unbelievable."

"You sound really happy, Brodie. I've never heard you talk about a woman this way."

"I suppose that was our first clue. Let me go. I just got off the boat, had dinner with my parents, and now I need to get home."

"Okay, cutie. Call me when you get a chance. Or better yet, set up a date for us."

"I will. I can't wait for you and Tim to meet him."

"Me neither, Brodie. I'm very proud of you."

"Thanks. Talk to you later." Hanging up, Brodie couldn't wipe the smile from his face.

~

Julian found a frame for the eight by ten photo he had purchased of he and Brodie. Setting it on his dresser in his bedroom, he smiled as he admired Brodie's handsome face. Sitting on his bed, he picked up the cordless phone. "Hello, Mom? I'm home."

"Hello, dear. How was your trip?"

"Good. Very good." He kept his eye on the picture. "Anything you need to ask me? About what we talked about on the phone?"

"No. Your father and I had a long chat about it. Look, Julian, you're a big boy. You can do as you like. You don't need us to tell you what you can and can't do."

"I've invited him to live with me."

"All right. It's your life, your choice."

"Thank you, Mom. I can't believe you're not angry."

"Angry? Julian, we trust you. You've always been sensible, successful, and honest with us to a fault. Why would we suddenly judge you now because you fell in love? You want to know the truth? I'm glad. The women you bring by are horrible."

Julian laughed. "You'll like Brodie, Mom. He's fantastic."

"I can't wait to meet him. Karen is jealous."

Julian smiled warmly, brushing some lint off his slacks. "What are you guys doing Friday night? You want to come out to dinner downtown with us?"

"Yes. That would be lovely. Make reservations for us and we'll meet you at your place. How does seven sound?"

"Perfect. Thanks, Mom."

"My pleasure, sweetie. See you then."

He hung up and called Brodie.

"Hello?"

"Hey."

"Hi, good looking! Miss me?"

"Yes. I'm going through sex withdrawal." He waited as Brodie laughed. "Listen, what are you doing this Friday night?"

"Sleeping over your place for the weekend. Why?"

"Good. Because we'll have dinner with my mom and dad Friday night."

"Cool. Saturday night at my parents' house."

"Deal. So? Did we do it?"

"We did it."

"Baby, I cannot wait until you are here full time."

"Me neither, lover. I can be there very soon. I promise you."

Julian stared at the photo on his dresser. "I'm looking at you now."

"Me too. I have your picture in my hand. I'll be jerking off to it in another minute."

Chuckling, Julian whispered, "I love you, Brodie."

"I love you too, Julian."

"You buy the lube."

"No, you! I bought it last time!"

"No way. You do it!"

They both started laughing in a riot, then at the same time they announced, "Okay, we'll get it together."

The End

About the Author

Award-winning author G.A. Hauser was born in Fair Lawn,
New Jersey, USA and attended university in New York City.
She moved to Seattle, Washington where she worked as a
patrol officer with the Seattle Police Department. In early 2000
G.A. moved to Hertfordshire, England where she began her
writing in earnest and published her first book, In the Shadow
of Alexander. Now a full-time writer, G.A. has written over
fifty novels, including several best-sellers of gay fiction and is
an Honorary Board Member of Gay American Heroes for her
support of the foundation. For more information on other
books by G.A., visit the author at her official website.
www.authorgahauser.com

Email: ga@authorgahauser.com
Website: http://www.authorgahauser.com
MySpace: http://www.myspace.com/gahauserauthor
FaceBook: www.facebook.com/people/**Ga-**
Hauser/1486624188
GA Hauser's Blog; http://gahausersblog.blogspot.com

Please help my battle against ebook piracy and join my
Facebook fan page for taking down pirate sites
http://www.facebook.com/home.php?#/pages/Close-down-
Astalavista-pirate-site/226369672766?ref=mf

Awards:
All Romance eBook- Best Author 2009, 2008 and 2007

All Romance eBook- Best novel 2007 *Secrets and
Misdemeanors*

All Romance eBook- Best novel 2008 *Mile High*

Other works by G.A. Hauser:

Capital Games

Let the games begin...

Former Los Angeles Police officer Steve Miller has gone from walking a beat in the City of Angels to joining the rat race as an advertising executive. He knows how cut-throat the industry can be, so when his boss tells him that he's in direct competition with a newcomer from across the pond for a coveted account he's not surprised...then he meets Mark Richfield.

Born with a silver spoon in his mouth and fashion-model good looks, Mark is used to getting what he wants. About to be married, Mark has just nailed the job of his dreams. If the determined Brit could just steal the firm's biggest account right out from under Steve Miller, his life would be perfect.

When their boss sends them together to the Arizona desert for a team-building retreat the tension between the two dynamic men escalates until in the heat of the moment their uncontrollable passion leads them to a sexual experience that neither can forget.

Will Mark deny his feelings and follow through with marriage to a women he no longer wants, or will he realize in time that in the game of love, sometimes you have to let go and lose yourself in order to *really* win.

Secrets and Misdemeanors

When having to hide your love is a crime...

After losing his wife to his best friend and former law partner,

David Thornton couldn't imagine finding love again. With his divorce behind him, he wanted only to focus on his job and two children. But then something happened, making David realize that despite believing he had everything he needed, there was someone he desperately wanted—Lyle Wilson.

Young and determined, Lyle arrived in Los Angeles without a penny in his pocket. Before long, however, the sexy construction worker nailed a job remodeling the old office building that held the prestigious Thornton Law Firm. Little did Lyle realize when he gazed upon the handsome and successful David Thornton for the first time that a door would be opened that neither man could close.

Will the two men succumb to the tangled web of societal pressures placed before them, hiding who they are and whom they love? Or will they reveal the truth and set themselves free?

Naked Dragon

Police Officer Dave Harris has just been assigned to one of the worst serial murder cases in Seattle history: The Dragon is hunting young Asian men. In order to solve the crime it's going to take a bit more than good old-fashioned police work. It's going to take handsome FBI Agent Robbie Taylor.

Robbie is an experienced Federal Agent with psychic abilities that allow him to enter the minds of others. You can't hide your secrets and desires from someone that knows your every thought. Some think what Robbie has is a gift, others a skill, but when the mind you have to enter is that of a madman it can also be a curse.

As the corpses pile up and the tension mounts, so does the sexual attraction between the two men. Then a moment of passion leads to a secret affair. Will their love be the distraction that costs them the case and possibly even their lives? Or will the bond forged between them be the key to their survival?

The Kiss

Twenty-five year old actor Scott Epstein is no stranger to the modeling industry. He's done it himself between acting jobs. So when his sister, Claire, casts him in a chewing-gum commercial with the famous British model, Ian Sullivan, he doesn't ask any questions. He's a professional. He'll show up, hit his mark, say his lines, and collect his paycheck. Right?

Ian Sullivan is used to making heads turn. Stunningly handsome, he's accustomed to provocative photo shoots where sex sells everything from perfume to laundry soap. Ian was thrilled when Claire Epstein cast him in the new Minty gum commercial. He has to kiss his co-star on screen? No problem. Until he finds out Scott is the one he has to kiss!

Never before has a commercial featured two men, kissing on screen. Claire knows that the advertisement will be groundbreaking, and Scott knows that his sister needs his performance to be perfect. As the filming progresses and the media circus begins around the controversial advertisement, the chemistry between Ian and Scott heats up and the two men quite simply burn up the screen. Is it all an act? Or, have Ian and Scott entered into a clandestine affair that will lead them to love?

For Love and Money

Handsome Dr. Jason Philips, the heir to a vast fortune, had followed his heart and pursued his dream of becoming a physician. Ewan P. Gallagher had a different dream. Acting in local theater, the talented twenty-year-old was determined to be a famous success.

As fate would have it, Jason happened to be working in casualty one night when Ewan was admitted as a patient. Jason was more than flattered and surprisingly aroused by the younger man's obvious attraction to him. The two men entered into a steamy affair finding love, until their ambitions pulled them apart.

Now, one year later and stuck in a sham of a marriage that he entered into only to preserve his inheritance, Jason is filled with regret. Caught between obligation and freedom, duty and desire, Jason finds that he can no longer deny his passion. He plans to win Ewan, Hollywood's newest rising star, back!

The G.A. Hauser Collection

Unnecessary Roughness
Got Men?
Heart of Steele
All Man
Hot Rod
London, Bloody, London
Julian
Black Leather Phoenix
*In The Dark and What Should Never Be, Erotic Short
Stories*
Mark and Sharon (formally titled A Question of Sex)
A Man's Best Friend
It Takes a Man
The Physician and the Actor
For Love and Money
The Kiss
Naked Dragon
Secrets and Misdemeanors
Capital Games
Giving Up the Ghost
To Have and To Hostage
Love you, Loveday
The Boy Next Door
When Adam Met Jack
Exposure
The Vampire and the Man-eater
Murphy's Hero
Mark Antonious deMontford
Prince of Servitude
Calling Dr Love
The Rape of St. Peter
The Wedding Planner
Going Deep
Double Trouble
Pirates
Miller's Tale

Vampire Nights
Teacher's Pet
In the Shadow of Alexander
The Rise and Fall of the Sacred Band of Thebes

The Action Series
Acting Naughty
Playing Dirty
Getting it in the End
Behaving Badly
Dripping Hot
Packing Heat
Being Screwed

Men in Motion Series
Mile High
Cruising
Driving Hard
Leather Boys

Heroes Series
Man to Man
Two In Two Out
Top Men

G.A. Hauser
Writing as Amanda Winters
Sister Moonshine
Nothing Like Romance
Silent Reign
Butterfly Suicide
Mutley's Crew

11017646R0

Made in the USA
Lexington, KY
19 September 2011